GREEN⊙LANTERN
LEGACY

writer
JOE KELLY

penciller
BRENT ANDERSON

inker
BILL SIENKIEWICZ

letterer
SEAN M. KONOT

colorists and separators
RO & BLEYAERT

special thanks to
PHIL BOYLE

GREEN ⊡ LANTERN
LEGACY
THE LAST WILL & TESTAMENT OF HAL JORDAN

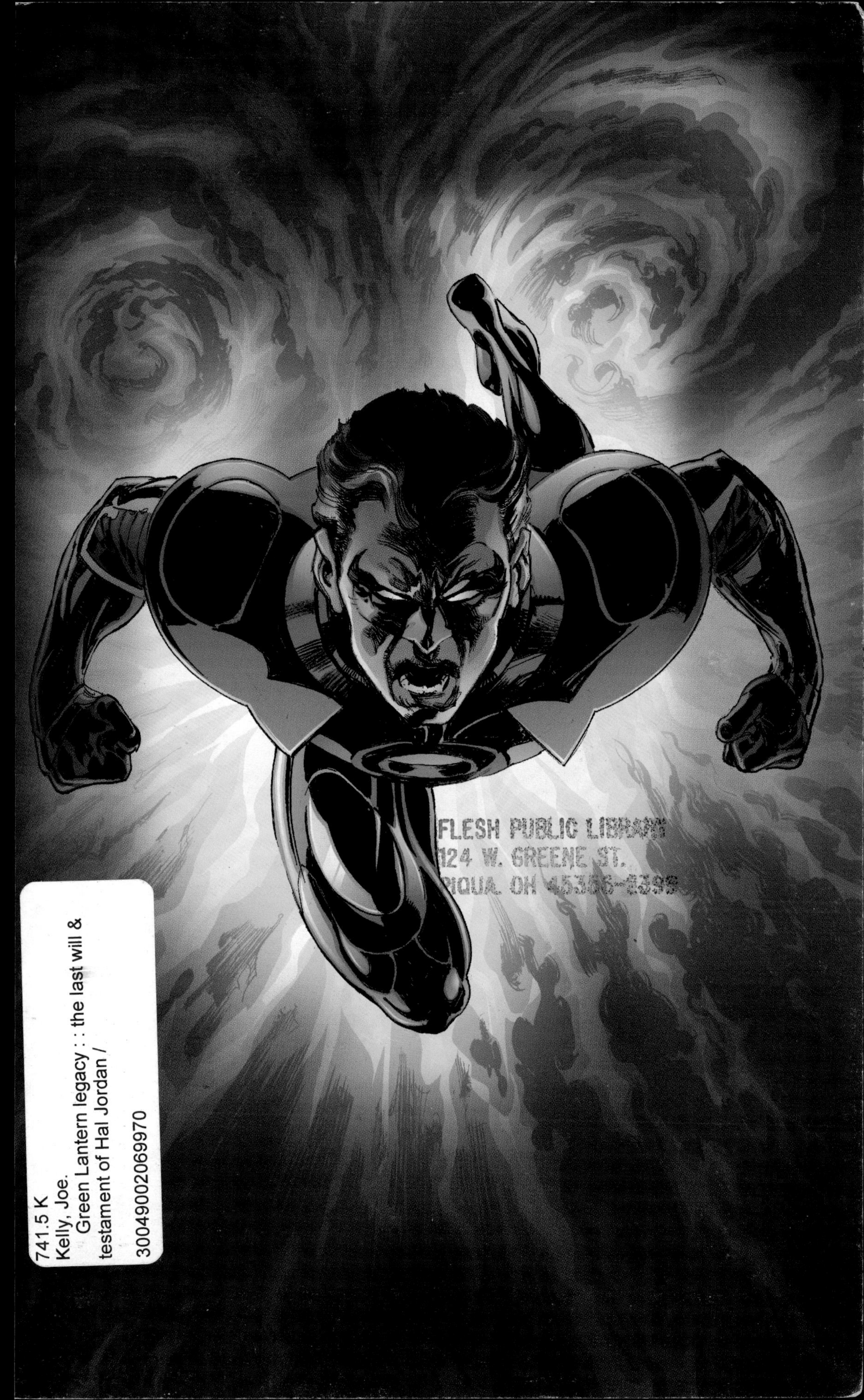

DC COMICS Jenette Kahn, President & Editor-in-Chief • Paul Levitz, Executive Vice President & Publisher
Mike Carlin, VP-Executive Editor • Bob Schreck, Editor • Nachie Castro, Assistant Editor • Amie Brockway-Metcalf, Art Director
Georg Brewer, VP-Design & Retail Product Development • Richard Bruning, VP-Creative Director
Patrick Caldon, Senior VP-Finance & Operations • Terri Cunningham, VP-Managing Editor
Dan DiDio, VP-Editorial • Joel Ehrlich, Senior VP-Advertising & Promotions
Alison Gill, VP-Manufacturing • Lillian Laserson, VP & General Counsel
Jim Lee, Editorial Director-WildStorm • David McKillips, VP-Advertising
John Nee, VP-Business Development • Cheryl Rubin, VP-Licensing &
Merchandising • Bob Wayne, VP-Sales & Marketing

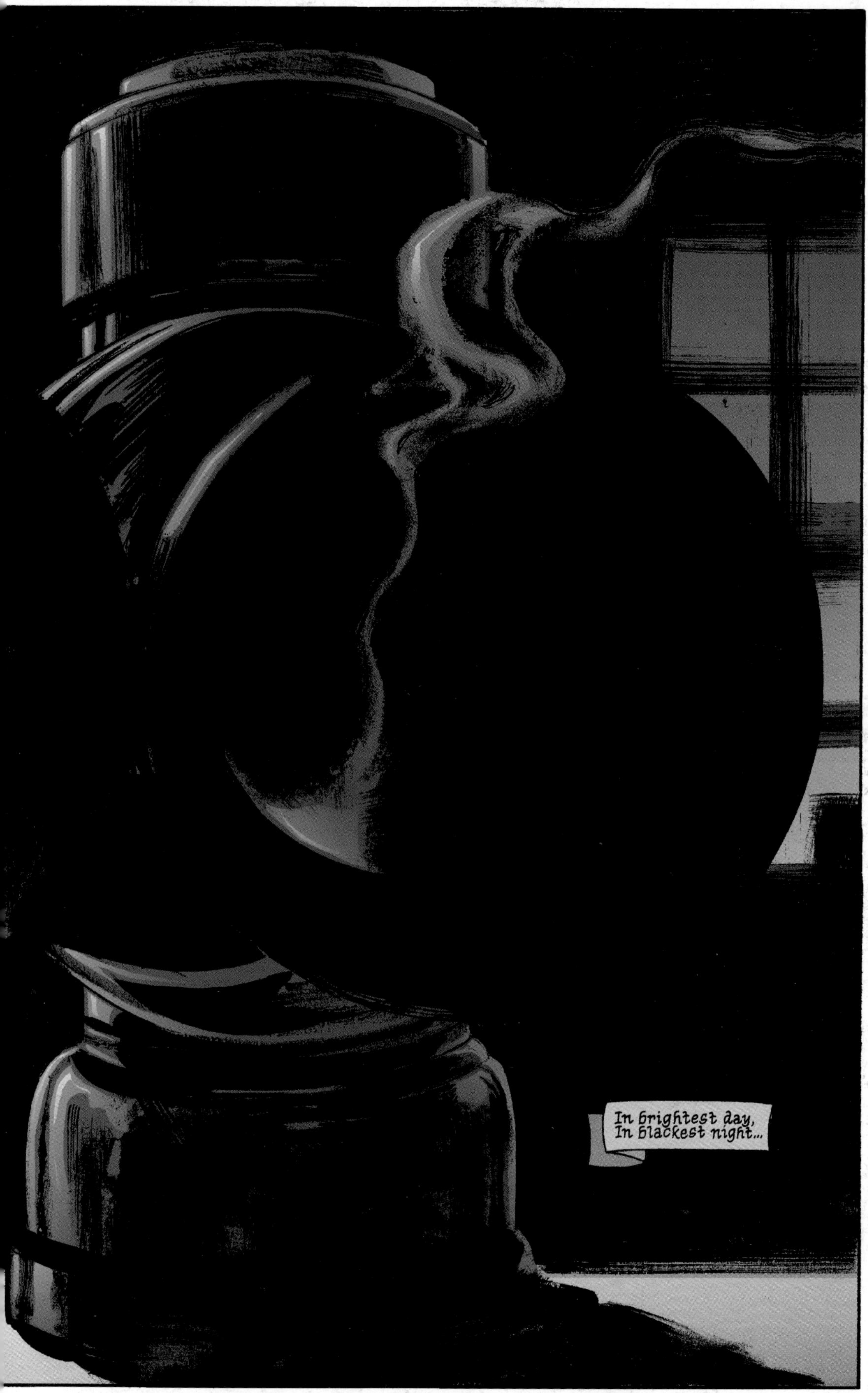
In brightest day,
In blackest night...

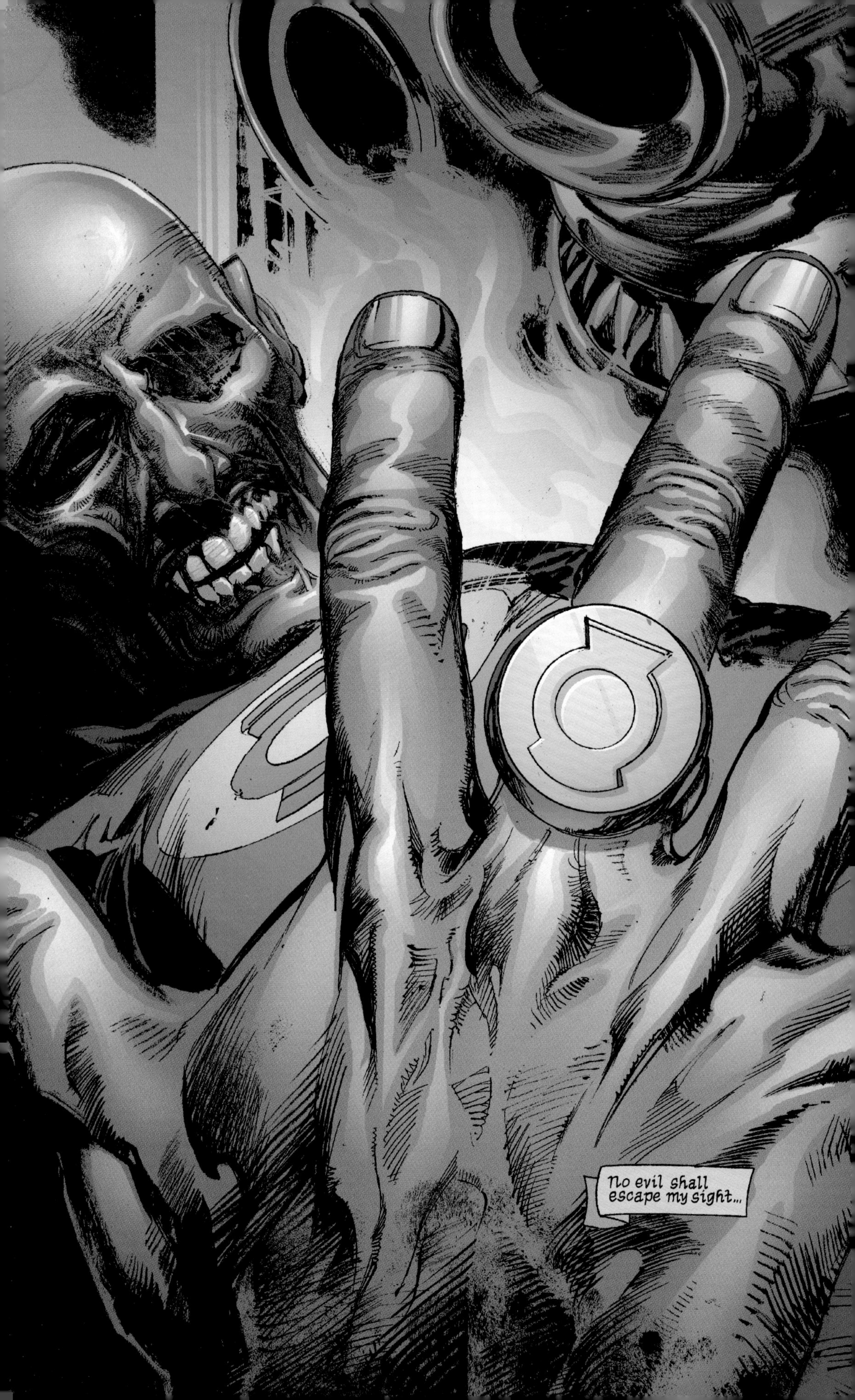
No evil shall escape my sight...

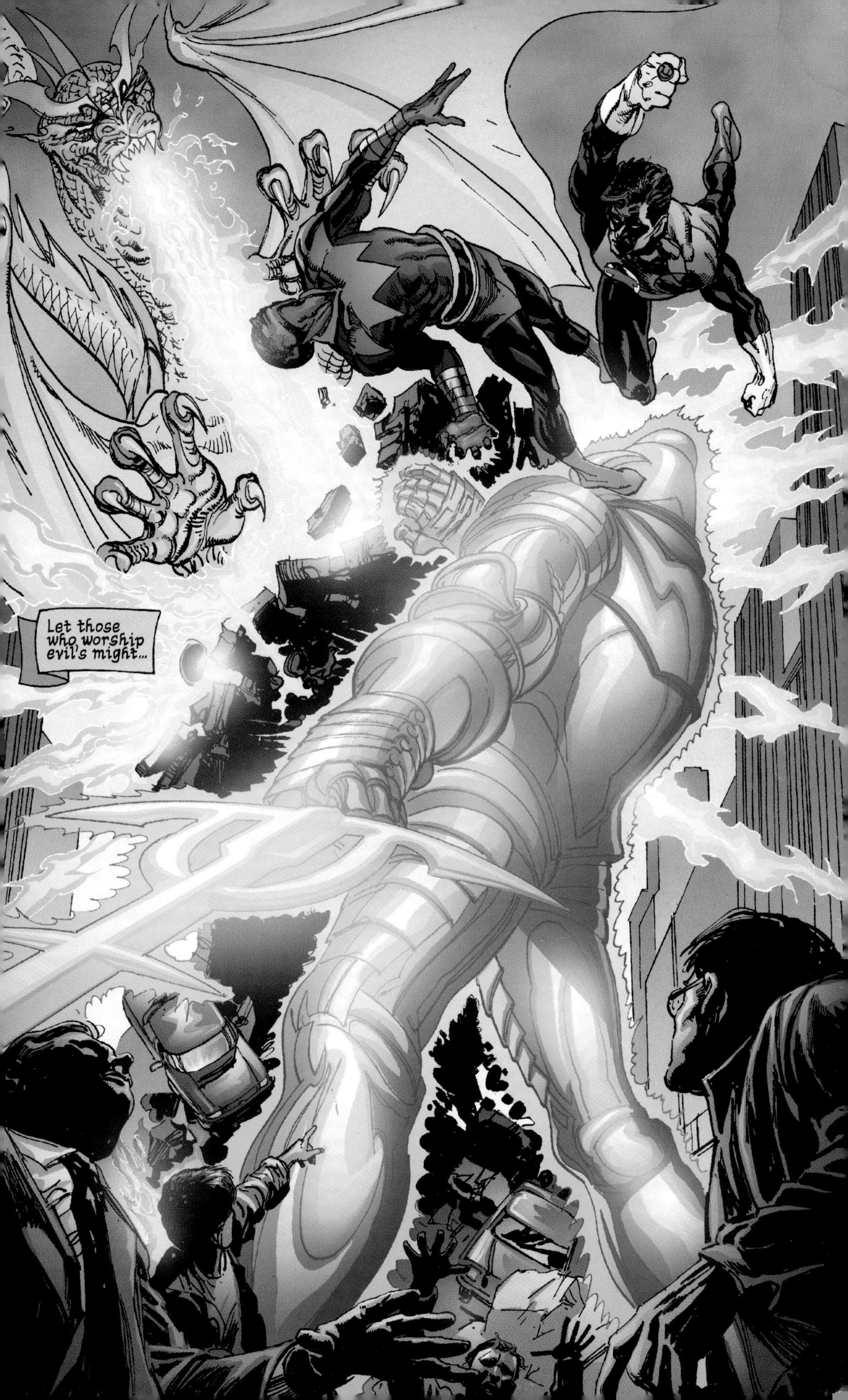
Let those who worship evil's might...

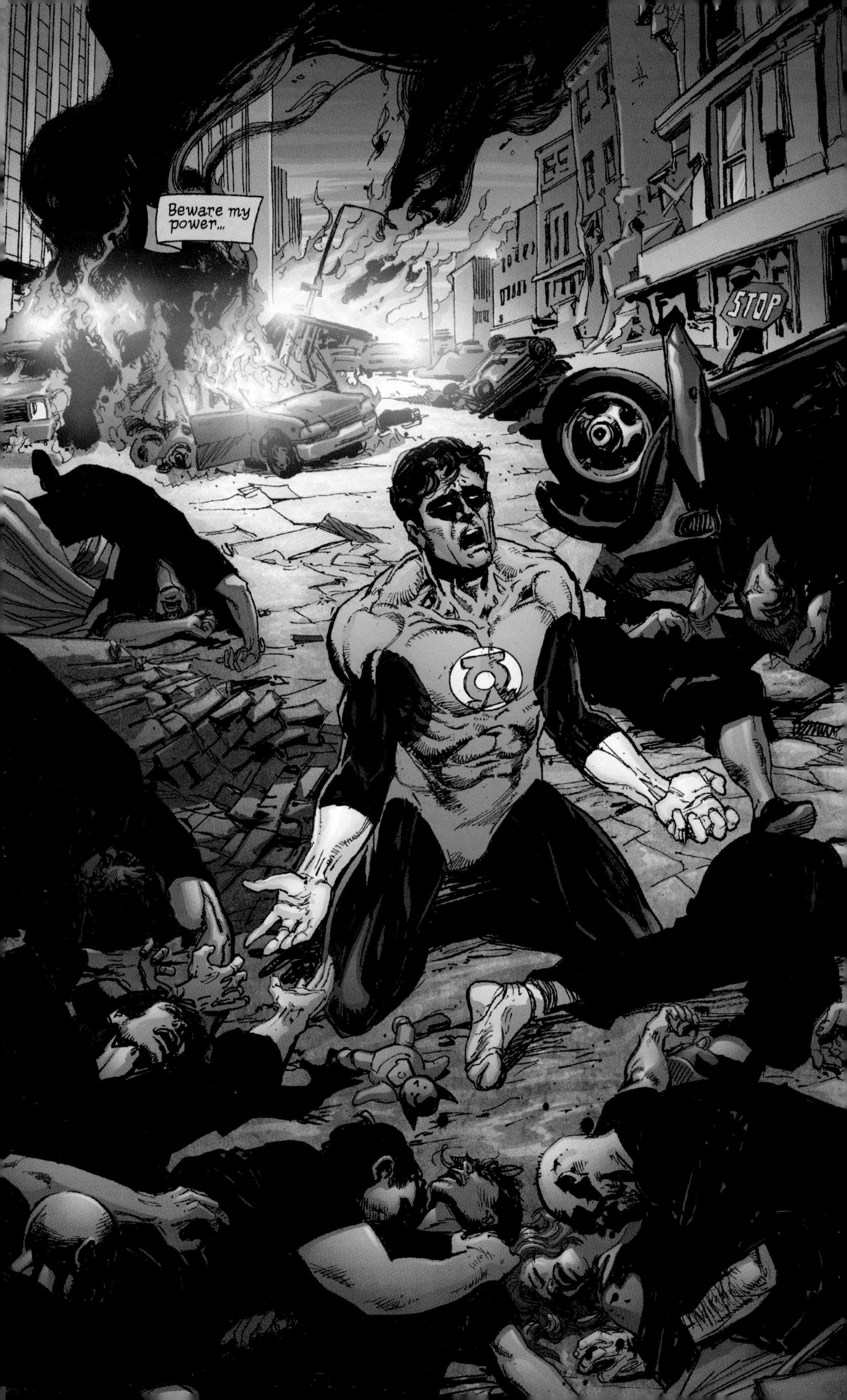
Beware my power...
STOP

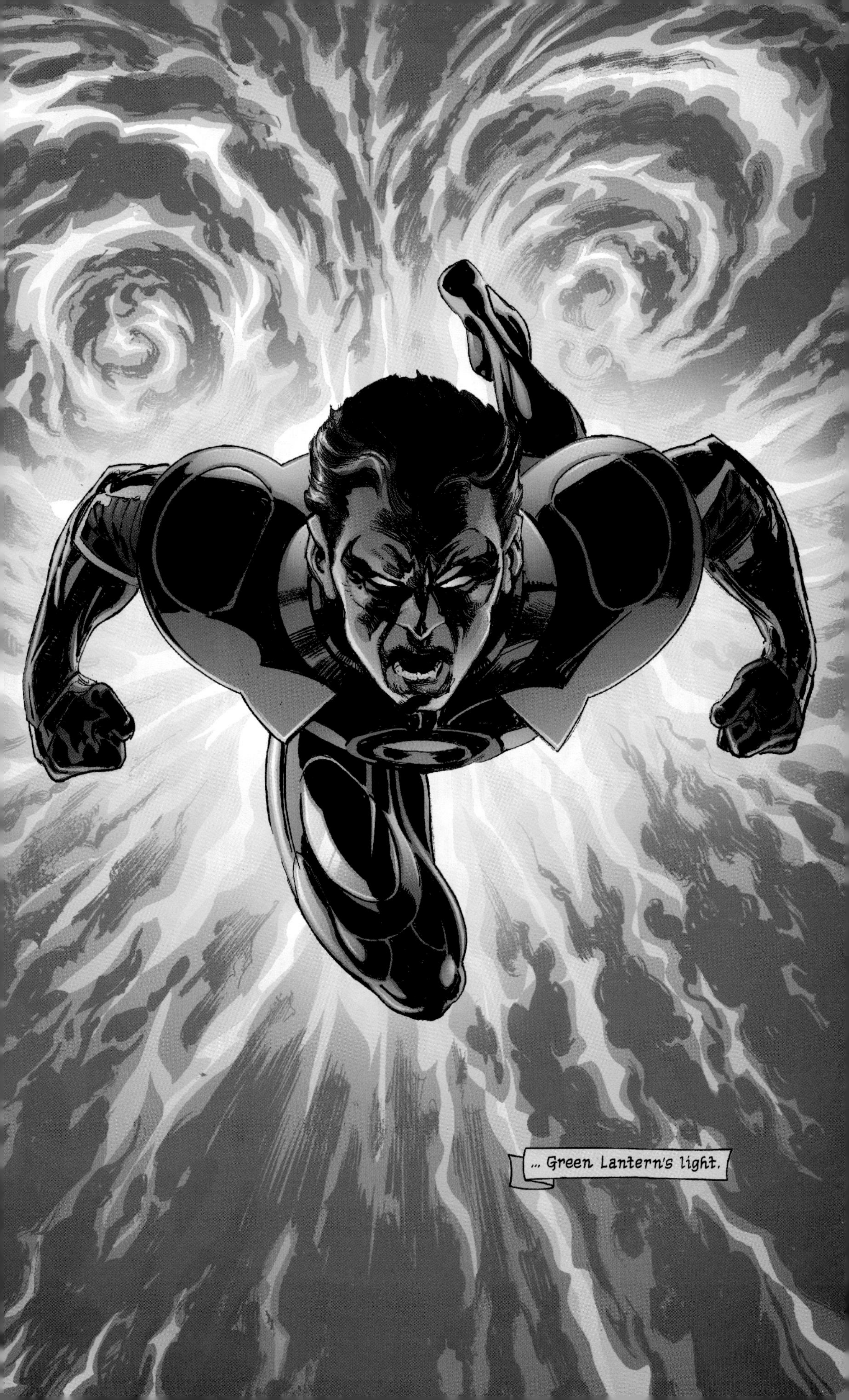
... Green Lantern's light.

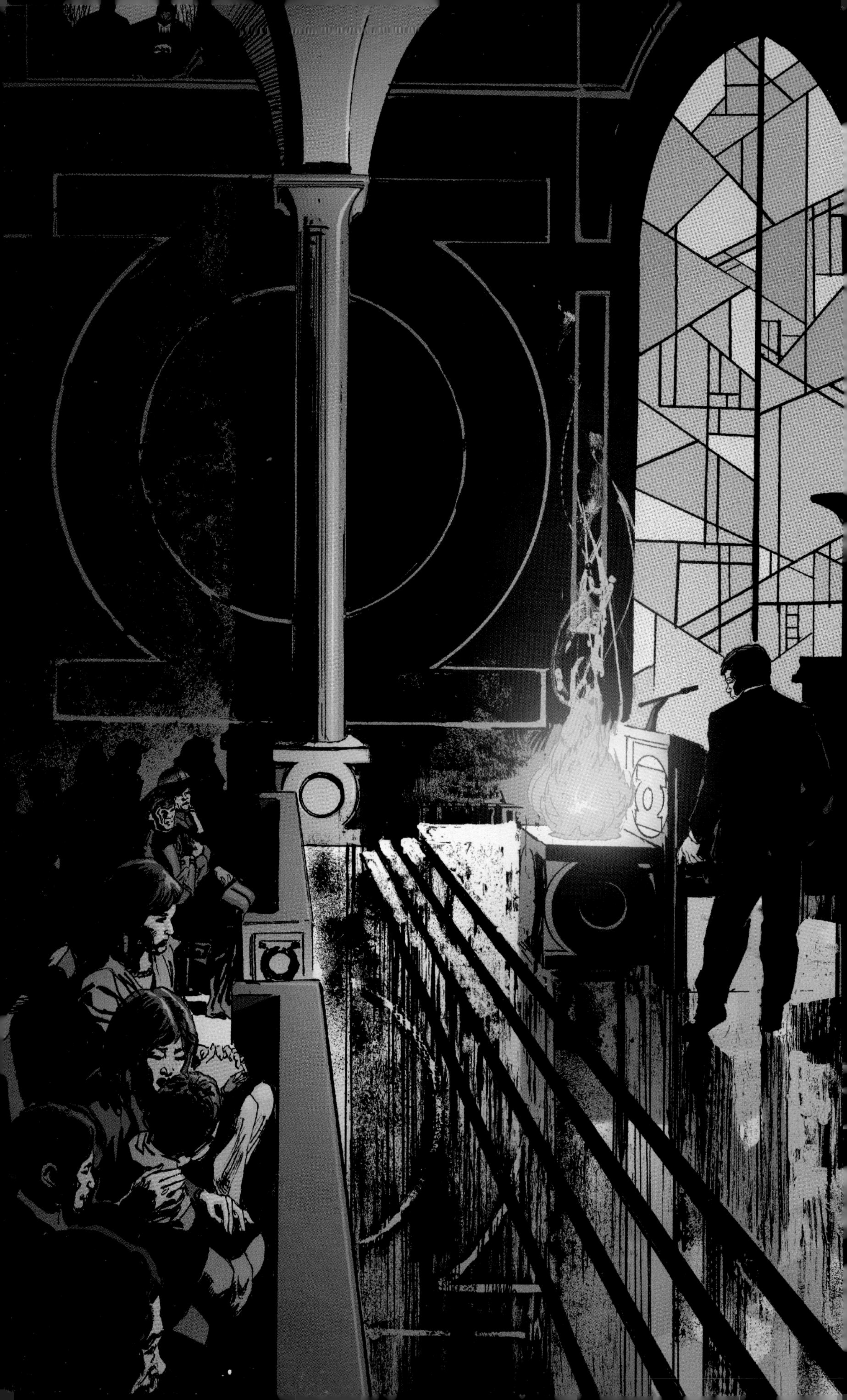

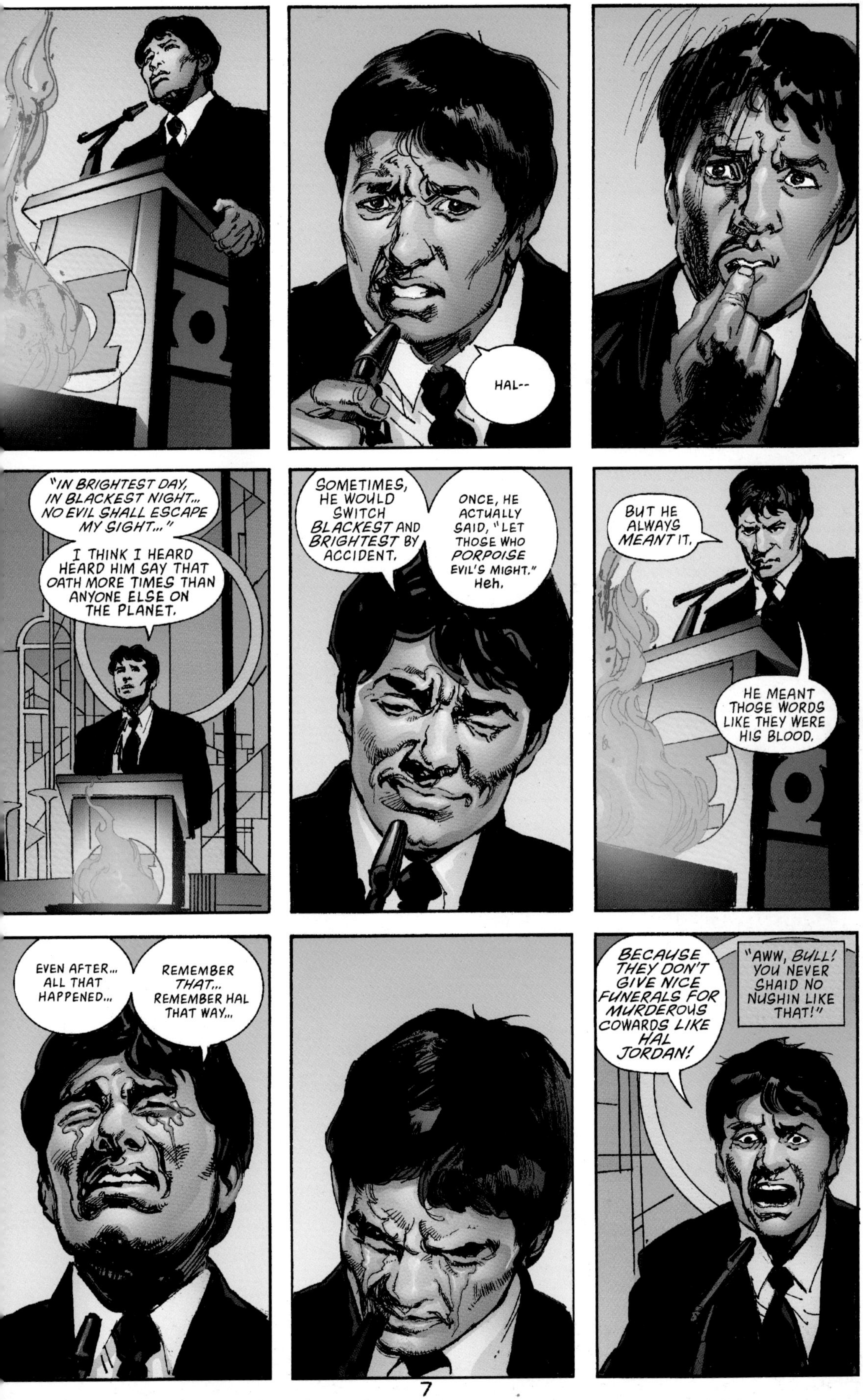
HAL--
"IN BRIGHTEST DAY, IN BLACKEST NIGHT... NO EVIL SHALL ESCAPE MY SIGHT..."
I THINK I HEARD HEARD HIM SAY THAT OATH MORE TIMES THAN ANYONE ELSE ON THE PLANET.
SOMETIMES, HE WOULD SWITCH BLACKEST AND BRIGHTEST BY ACCIDENT.
ONCE, HE ACTUALLY SAID, "LET THOSE WHO PORPOISE EVIL'S MIGHT." Heh.
BUT HE ALWAYS MEANT IT.
HE MEANT THOSE WORDS LIKE THEY WERE HIS BLOOD.
EVEN AFTER... ALL THAT HAPPENED...
REMEMBER THAT... REMEMBER HAL THAT WAY...
BECAUSE THEY DON'T GIVE NICE FUNERALS FOR MURDEROUS COWARDS LIKE HAL JORDAN!
"AWW, BULL! YOU NEVER SHAID NO NUSHIN LIKE THAT!"

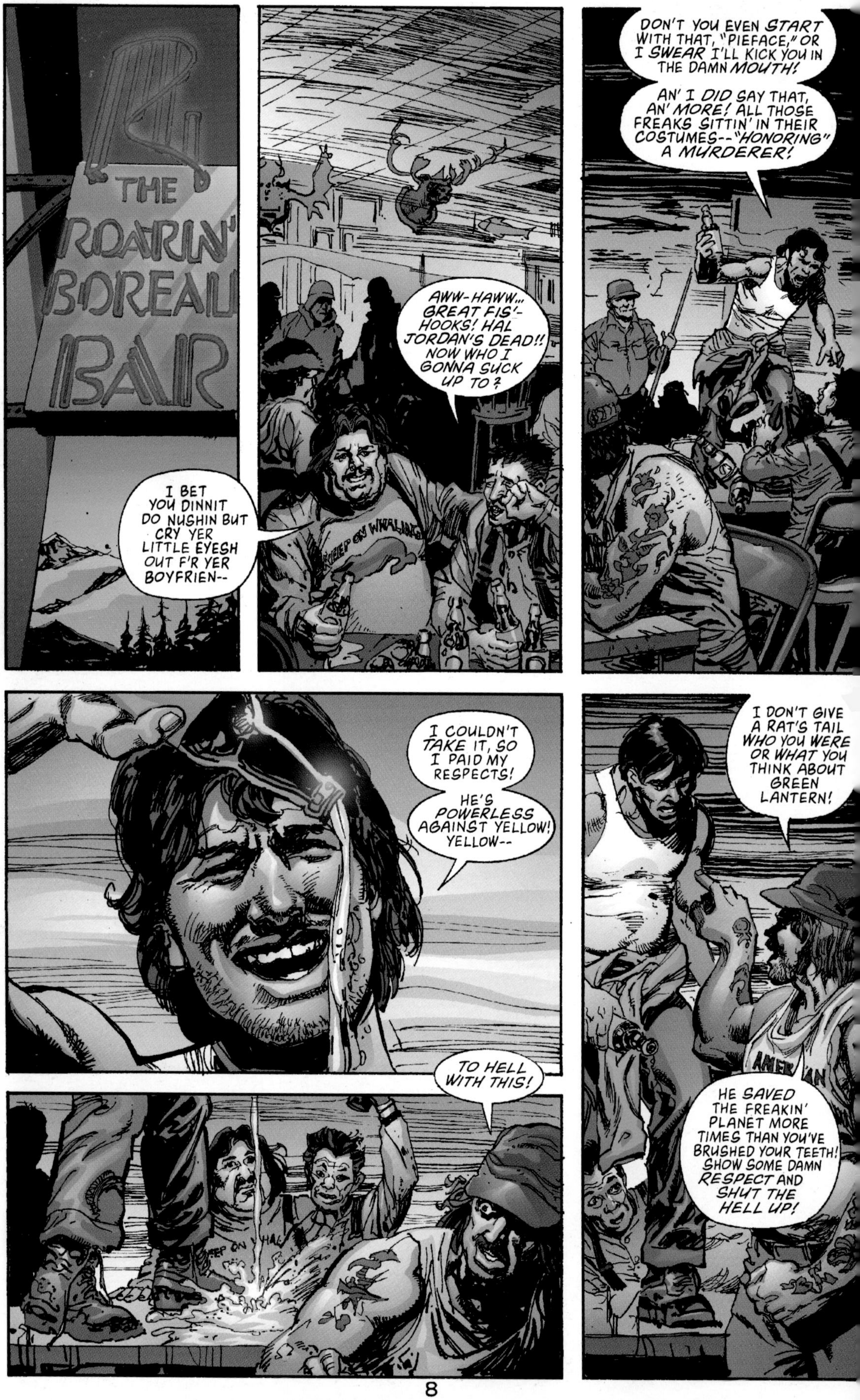
THE ROARIN' BOREALIS BAR
I BET YOU DINNIT DO NUSHIN BUT CRY YER LITTLE EYESH OUT F'R YER BOYFRIEN--
AWW-HAWW... GREAT FIS'-HOOKS! HAL JORDAN'S DEAD!! NOW WHO I GONNA SUCK UP TO?
KEEP ON WHALING
DON'T YOU EVEN START WITH THAT, "PIEFACE," OR I SWEAR I'LL KICK YOU IN THE DAMN MOUTH!
AN' I DID SAY THAT, AN' MORE! ALL THOSE FREAKS SITTIN' IN THEIR COSTUMES--"HONORING" A MURDERER!
I COULDN'T TAKE IT, SO I PAID MY RESPECTS!
HE'S POWERLESS AGAINST YELLOW! YELLOW--
TO HELL WITH THIS!
I DON'T GIVE A RAT'S TAIL WHO YOU WERE OR WHAT YOU THINK ABOUT GREEN LANTERN!
HE SAVED THE FREAKIN' PLANET MORE TIMES THAN YOU'VE BRUSHED YOUR TEETH! SHOW SOME DAMN RESPECT AND SHUT THE HELL UP!

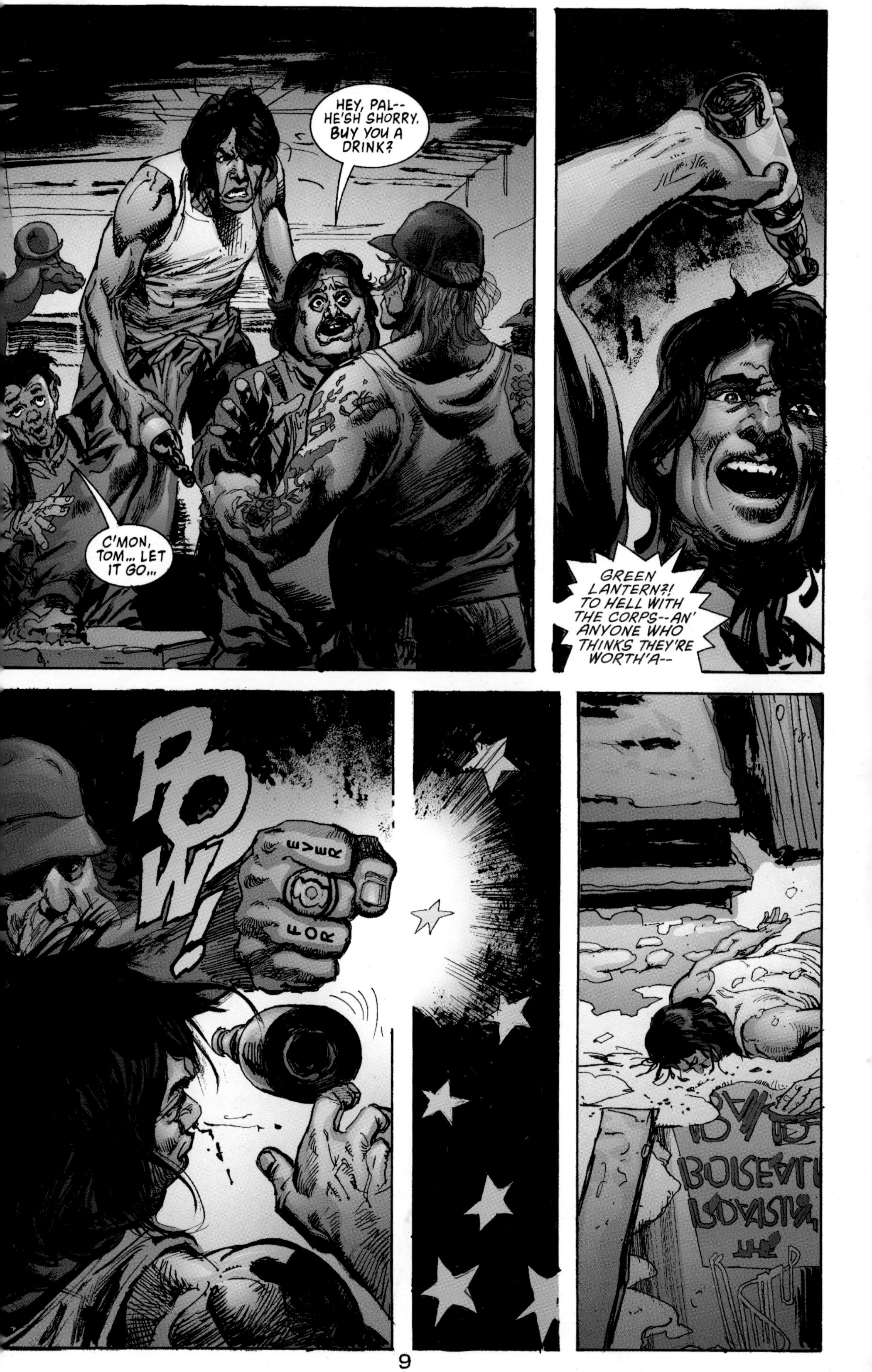
HEY, PAL--
HE'SH SHORRY.
BUY YOU A
DRINK?
C'MON,
TOM... LET
IT GO...
GREEN
LANTERN?!
TO HELL WITH
THE CORPS--AN'
ANYONE WHO
THINKS THEY'RE
WORTH'A--
POW!
FOR
EVER

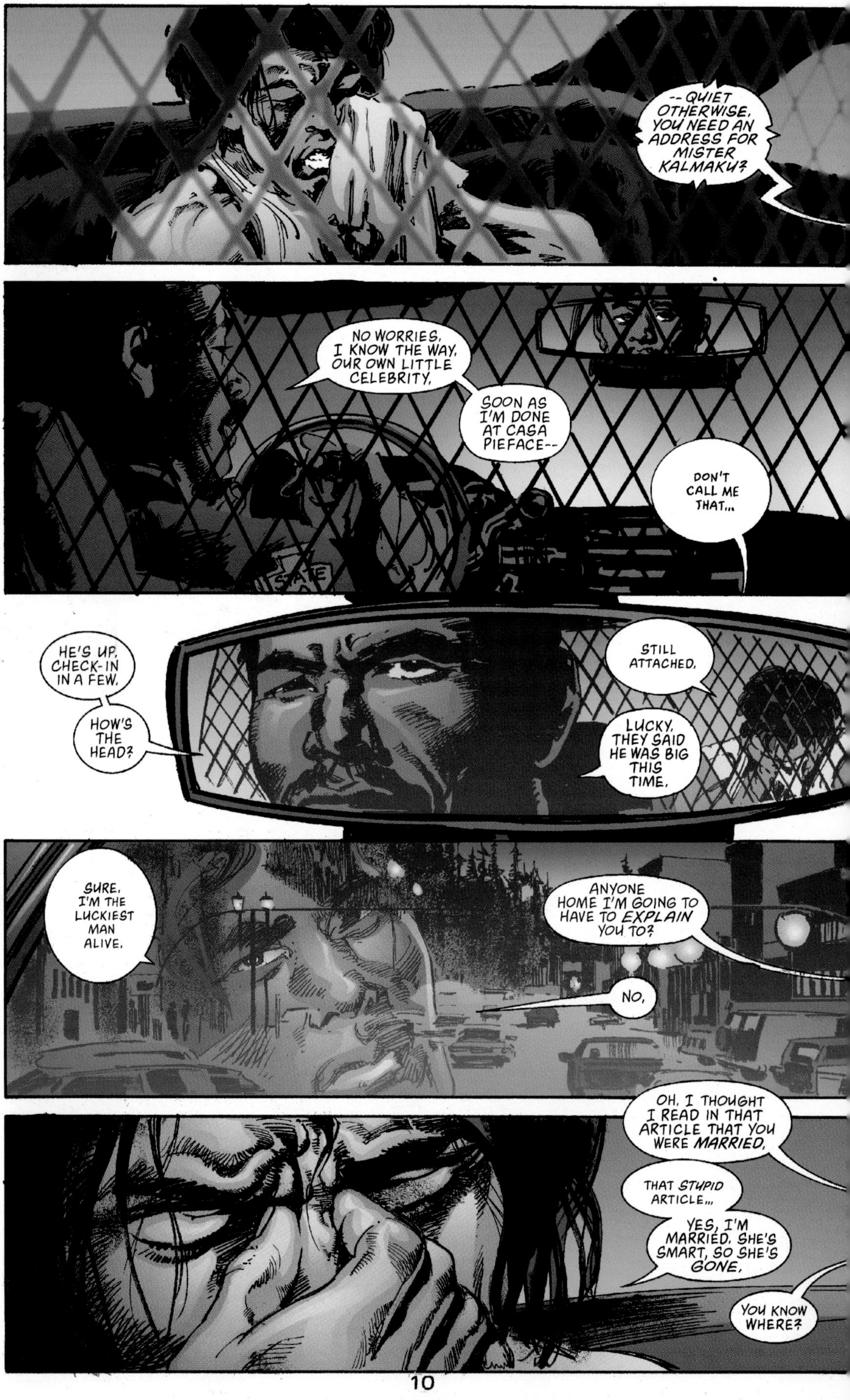
-- QUIET OTHERWISE. YOU NEED AN ADDRESS FOR MISTER KALMAKU?
NO WORRIES. I KNOW THE WAY. OUR OWN LITTLE CELEBRITY.
SOON AS I'M DONE AT CASA PIEFACE--
DON'T CALL ME THAT...
STATE
HE'S UP. CHECK-IN IN A FEW.
HOW'S THE HEAD?
STILL ATTACHED.
LUCKY. THEY SAID HE WAS BIG THIS TIME.
SURE. I'M THE LUCKIEST MAN ALIVE.
ANYONE HOME I'M GOING TO HAVE TO EXPLAIN YOU TO?
NO.
OH. I THOUGHT I READ IN THAT ARTICLE THAT YOU WERE MARRIED.
THAT STUPID ARTICLE...
YES, I'M MARRIED. SHE'S SMART, SO SHE'S GONE.
YOU KNOW WHERE?

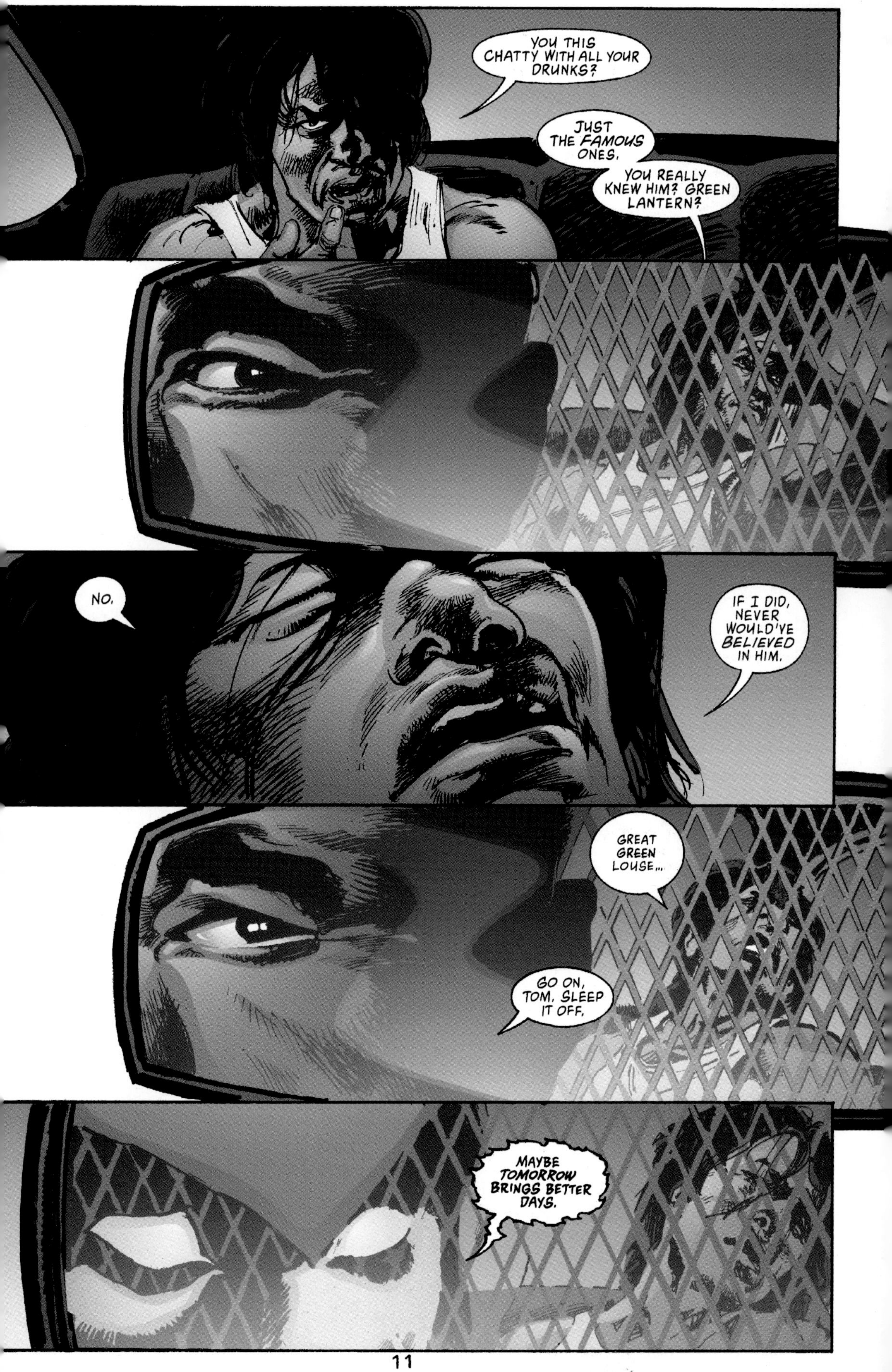
YOU THIS CHATTY WITH ALL YOUR DRUNKS?
JUST THE *FAMOUS* ONES.
YOU REALLY KNEW HIM? GREEN LANTERN?
NO.
IF I DID, NEVER WOULD'VE *BELIEVED* IN HIM.
GREAT GREEN LOUSE...
GO ON, TOM. SLEEP IT OFF.
MAYBE *TOMORROW* BRINGS BETTER DAYS.

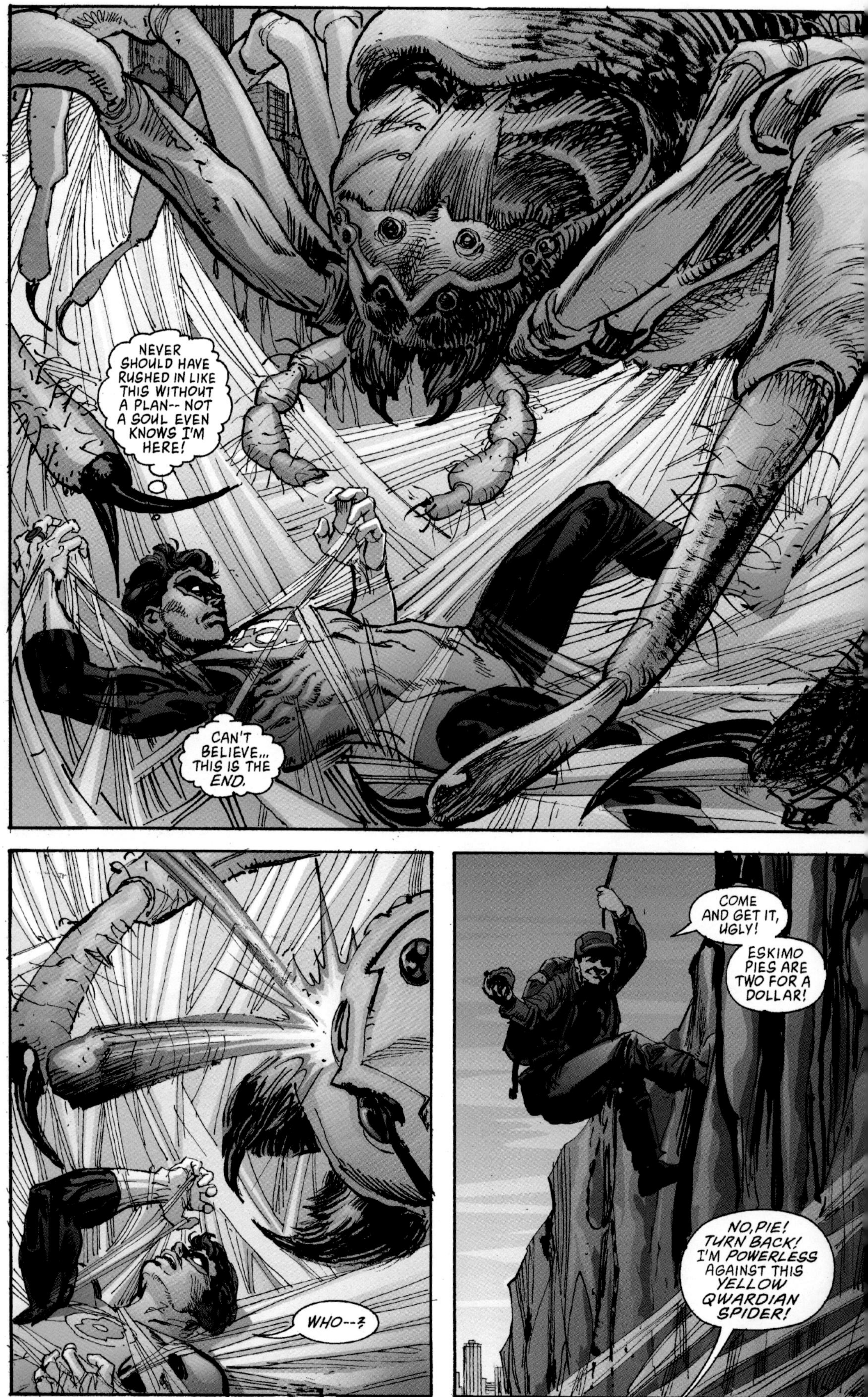

NEVER SHOULD HAVE RUSHED IN LIKE THIS WITHOUT A PLAN-- NOT A SOUL EVEN KNOWS I'M HERE!
CAN'T BELIEVE... THIS IS THE END.
WHO--?
COME AND GET IT, UGLY!
ESKIMO PIES ARE TWO FOR A DOLLAR!
NO, PIE! TURN BACK! I'M POWERLESS AGAINST THIS YELLOW QWARDIAN SPIDER!

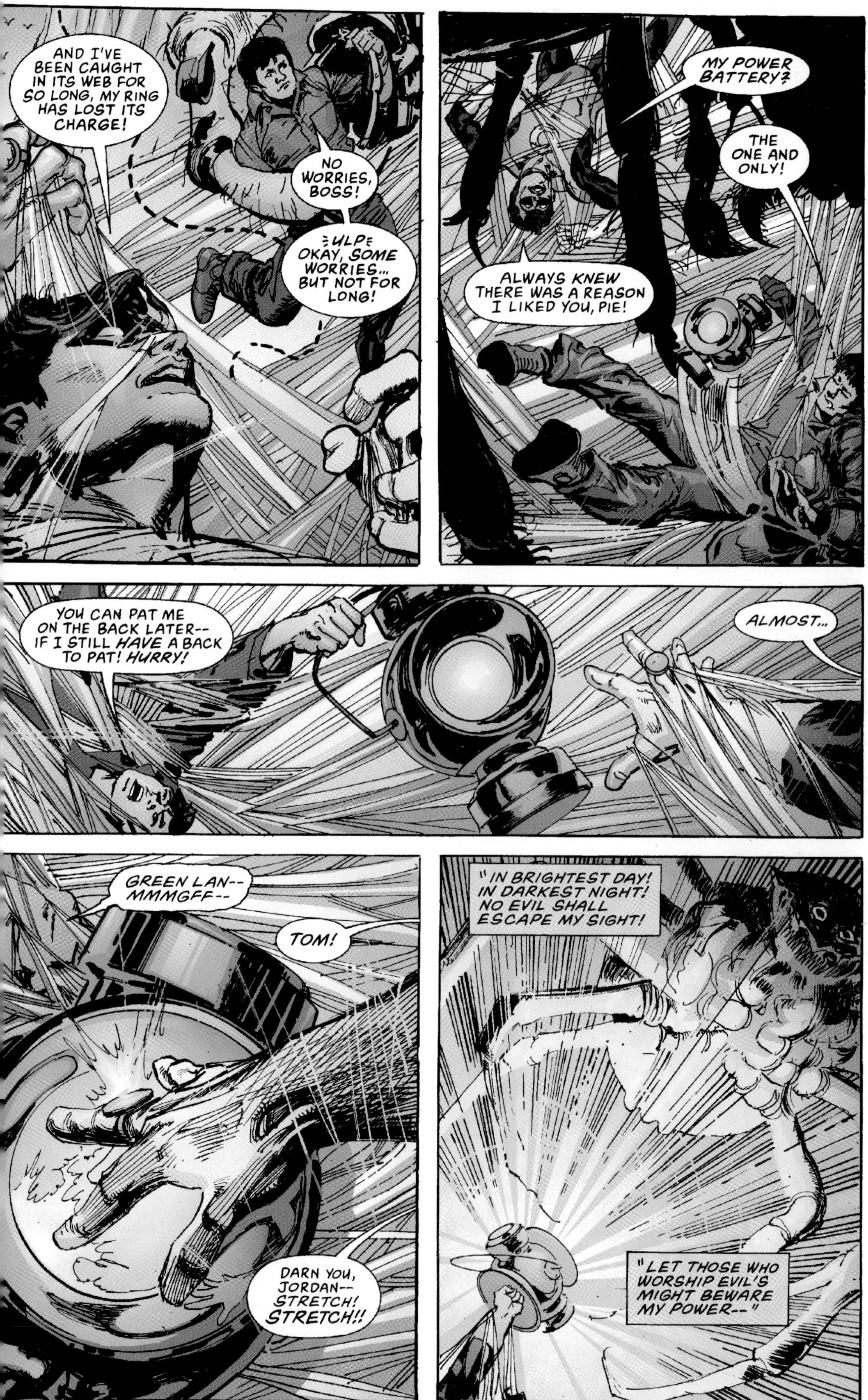
AND I'VE BEEN CAUGHT IN ITS WEB FOR SO LONG, MY RING HAS LOST ITS CHARGE!
NO WORRIES, BOSS!
ULP OKAY, SOME WORRIES... BUT NOT FOR LONG!
MY POWER BATTERY?
THE ONE AND ONLY!
ALWAYS KNEW THERE WAS A REASON I LIKED YOU, PIE!
YOU CAN PAT ME ON THE BACK LATER-- IF I STILL HAVE A BACK TO PAT! HURRY!
ALMOST...
GREEN LAN-- MMMGFF--
TOM!
DARN YOU, JORDAN-- STRETCH! STRETCH!!
"IN BRIGHTEST DAY! IN DARKEST NIGHT! NO EVIL SHALL ESCAPE MY SIGHT!
"LET THOSE WHO WORSHIP EVIL'S MIGHT BEWARE MY POWER--"

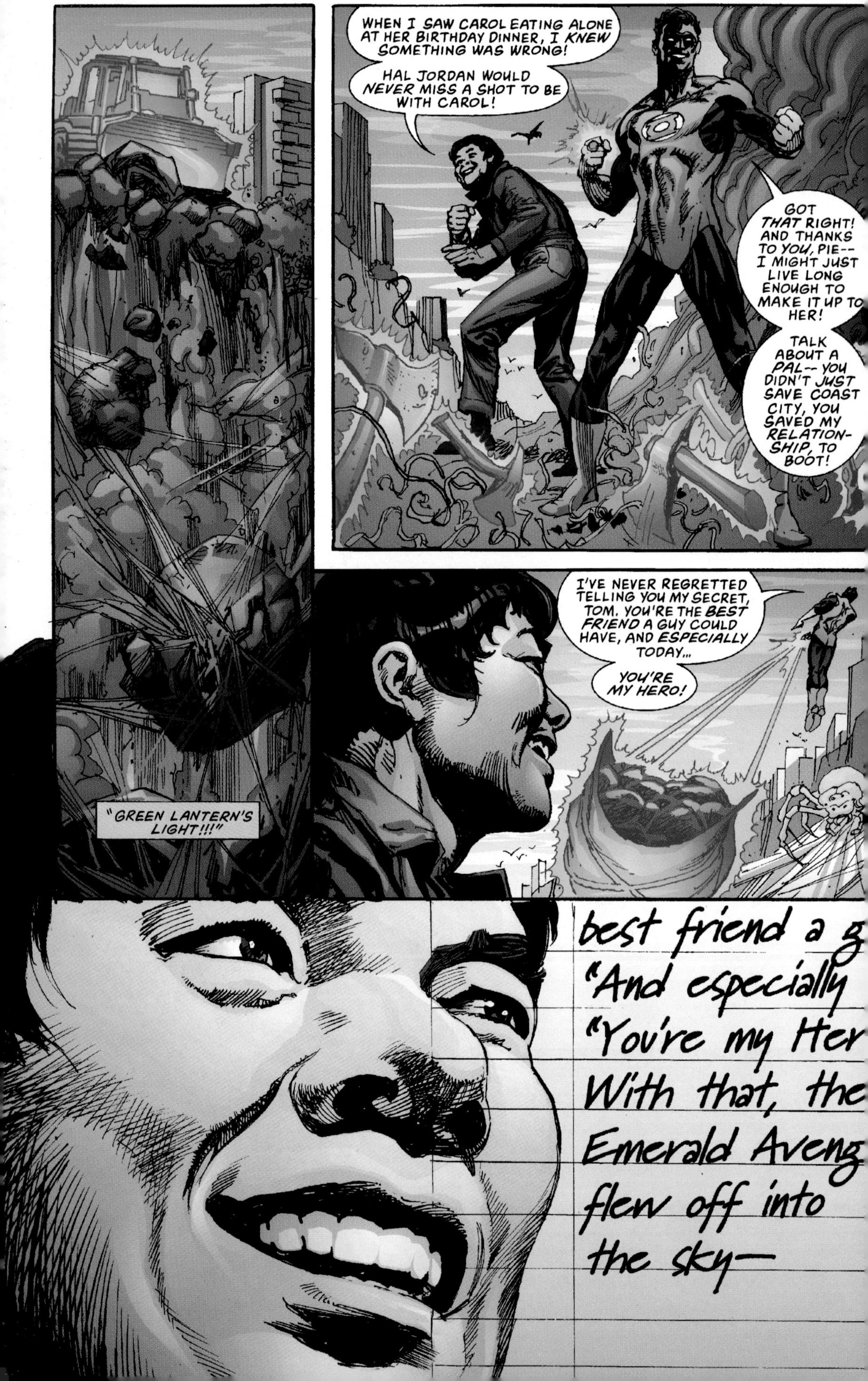

WHEN I SAW CAROL EATING ALONE AT HER BIRTHDAY DINNER, I KNEW SOMETHING WAS WRONG!
HAL JORDAN WOULD NEVER MISS A SHOT TO BE WITH CAROL!
GOT THAT RIGHT! AND THANKS TO YOU, PIE-- I MIGHT JUST LIVE LONG ENOUGH TO MAKE IT UP TO HER!
TALK ABOUT A PAL-- YOU DIDN'T JUST SAVE COAST CITY, YOU SAVED MY RELATIONSHIP, TO BOOT!
"GREEN LANTERN'S LIGHT!!!"
I'VE NEVER REGRETTED TELLING YOU MY SECRET, TOM. YOU'RE THE BEST FRIEND A GUY COULD HAVE, AND ESPECIALLY TODAY...
YOU'RE MY HERO!
best friend a g
"And especially
"You're my Her
With that, the
Emerald Aveng
flew off into
the sky—

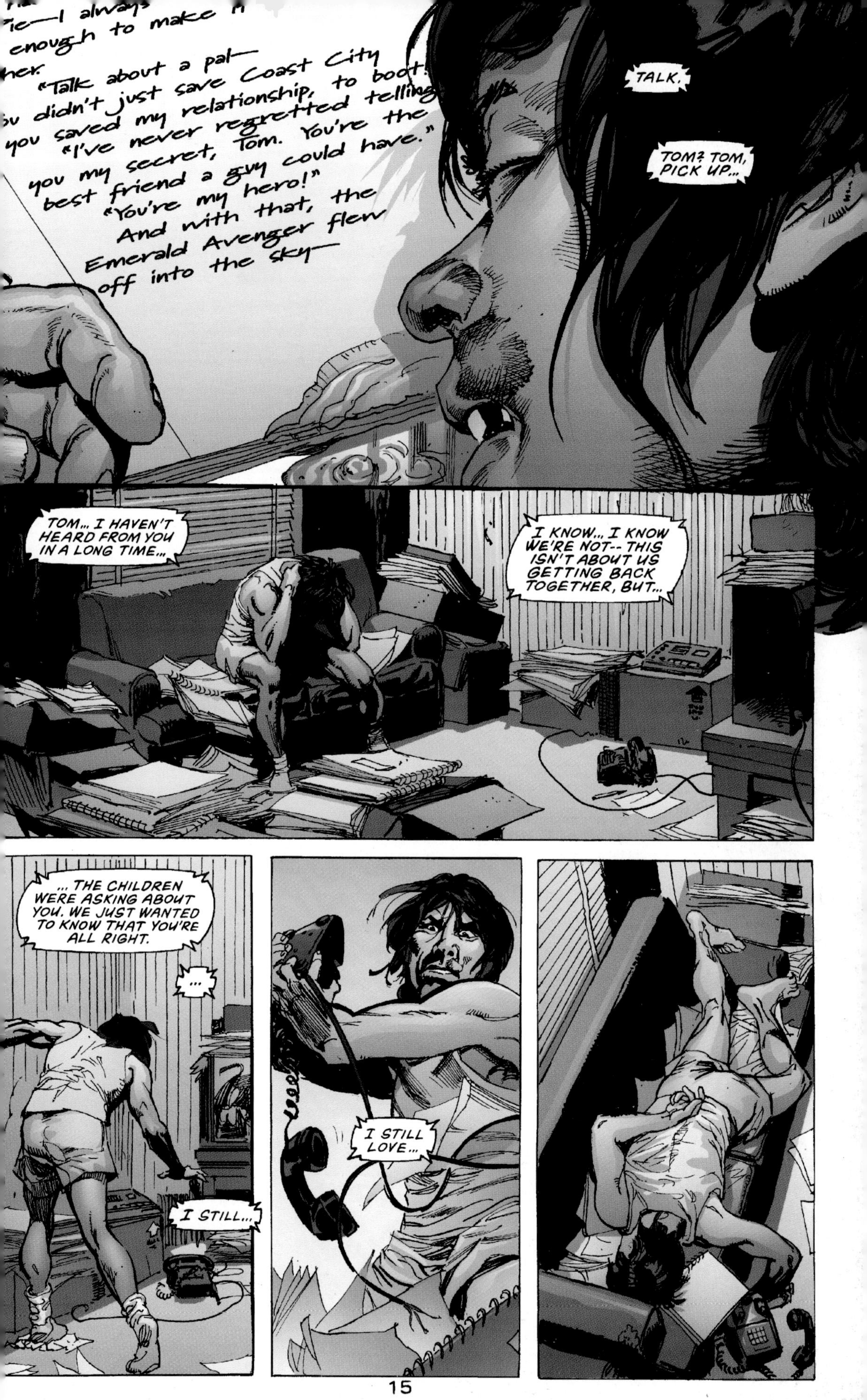

—I always
enough to make
her.
“Talk about a pal—
didn't just save Coast City
you saved my relationship, to boot!
“I've never regretted telling
you my secret, Tom. You're the
best friend a guy could have.”
“You're my hero!”
And with that, the
Emerald Avenger flew
off into the sky—
TALK.
TOM? TOM, PICK UP...
TOM... I HAVEN'T HEARD FROM YOU IN A LONG TIME...
I KNOW... I KNOW WE'RE NOT-- THIS ISN'T ABOUT US GETTING BACK TOGETHER, BUT...
... THE CHILDREN WERE ASKING ABOUT YOU. WE JUST WANTED TO KNOW THAT YOU'RE ALL RIGHT.
...
I STILL...
I STILL LOVE...

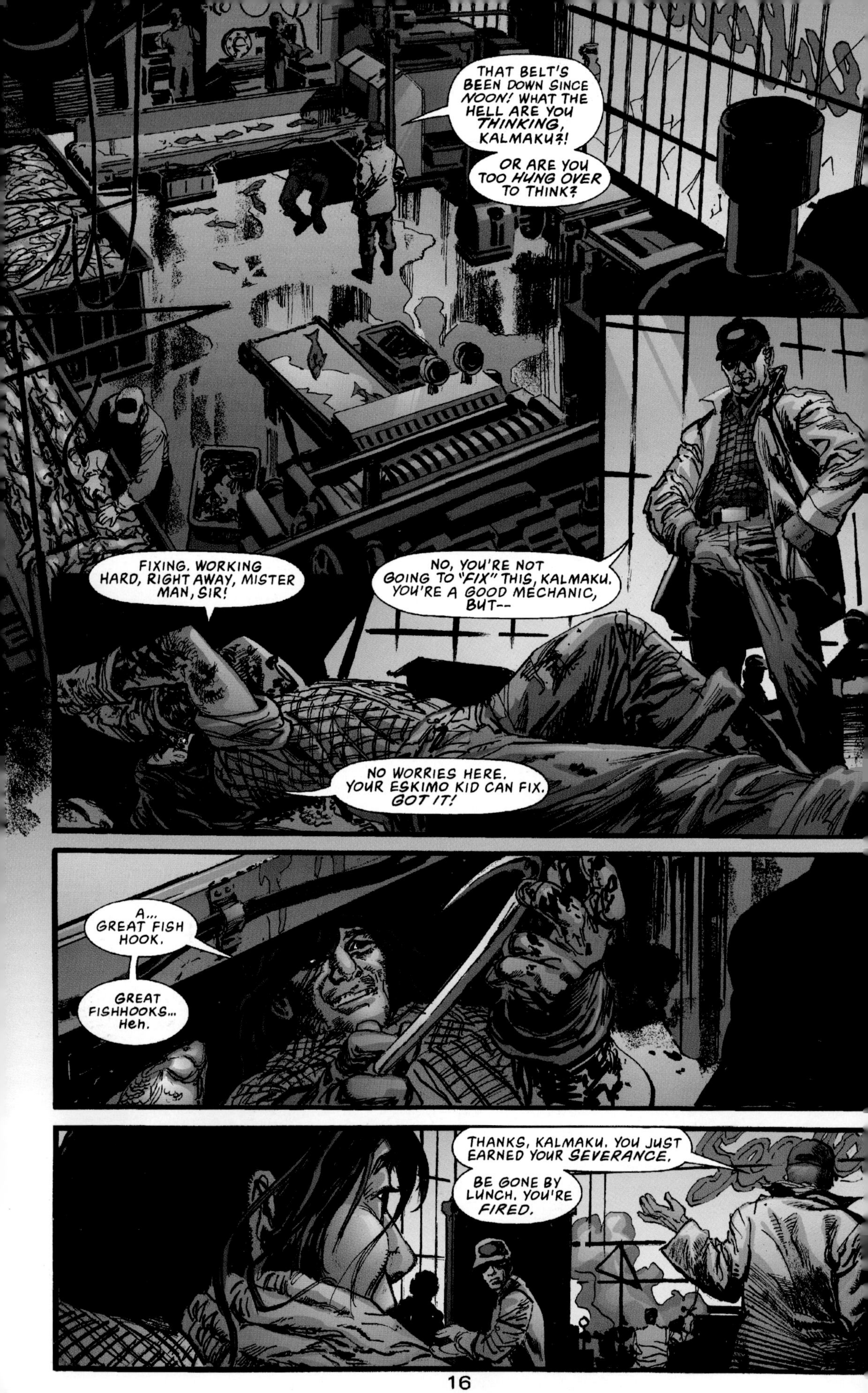
THAT BELT'S BEEN DOWN SINCE NOON! WHAT THE HELL ARE YOU THINKING, KALMAKU?!
OR ARE YOU TOO HUNG OVER TO THINK?
FIXING. WORKING HARD, RIGHT AWAY, MISTER MAN, SIR!
NO, YOU'RE NOT GOING TO "FIX" THIS, KALMAKU. YOU'RE A GOOD MECHANIC, BUT--
NO WORRIES HERE. YOUR ESKIMO KID CAN FIX. GOT IT!
A... GREAT FISH HOOK.
GREAT FISHHOOKS... Heh.
THANKS, KALMAKU. YOU JUST EARNED YOUR SEVERANCE.
BE GONE BY LUNCH. YOU'RE FIRED.

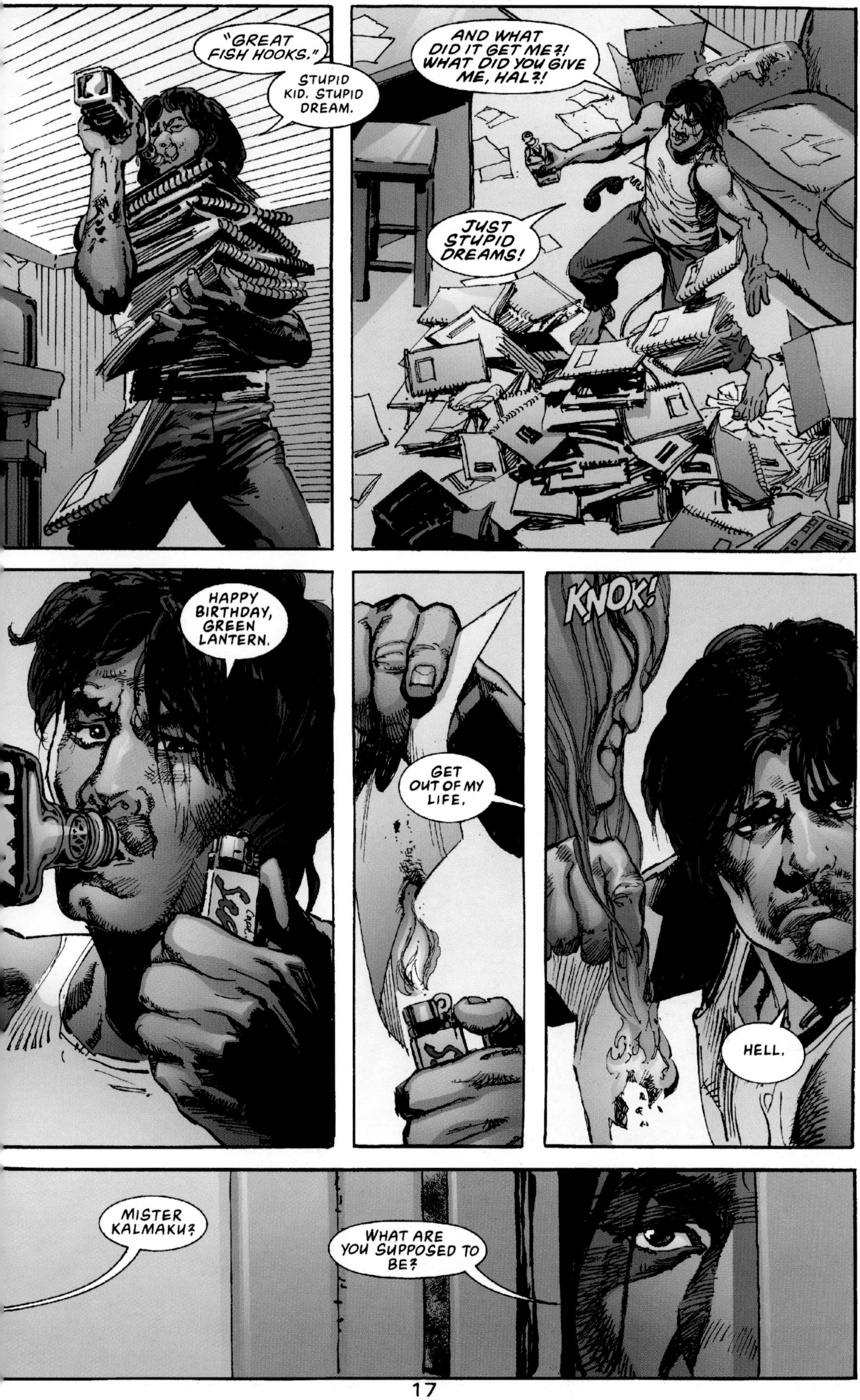
"GREAT FISH HOOKS."
STUPID KID. STUPID DREAM.
AND WHAT DID IT GET ME?! WHAT DID YOU GIVE ME, HAL?!
JUST STUPID DREAMS!
HAPPY BIRTHDAY, GREEN LANTERN.
GET OUT OF MY LIFE.
KNOK!
HELL.
MISTER KALMAKU?
WHAT ARE YOU SUPPOSED TO BE?

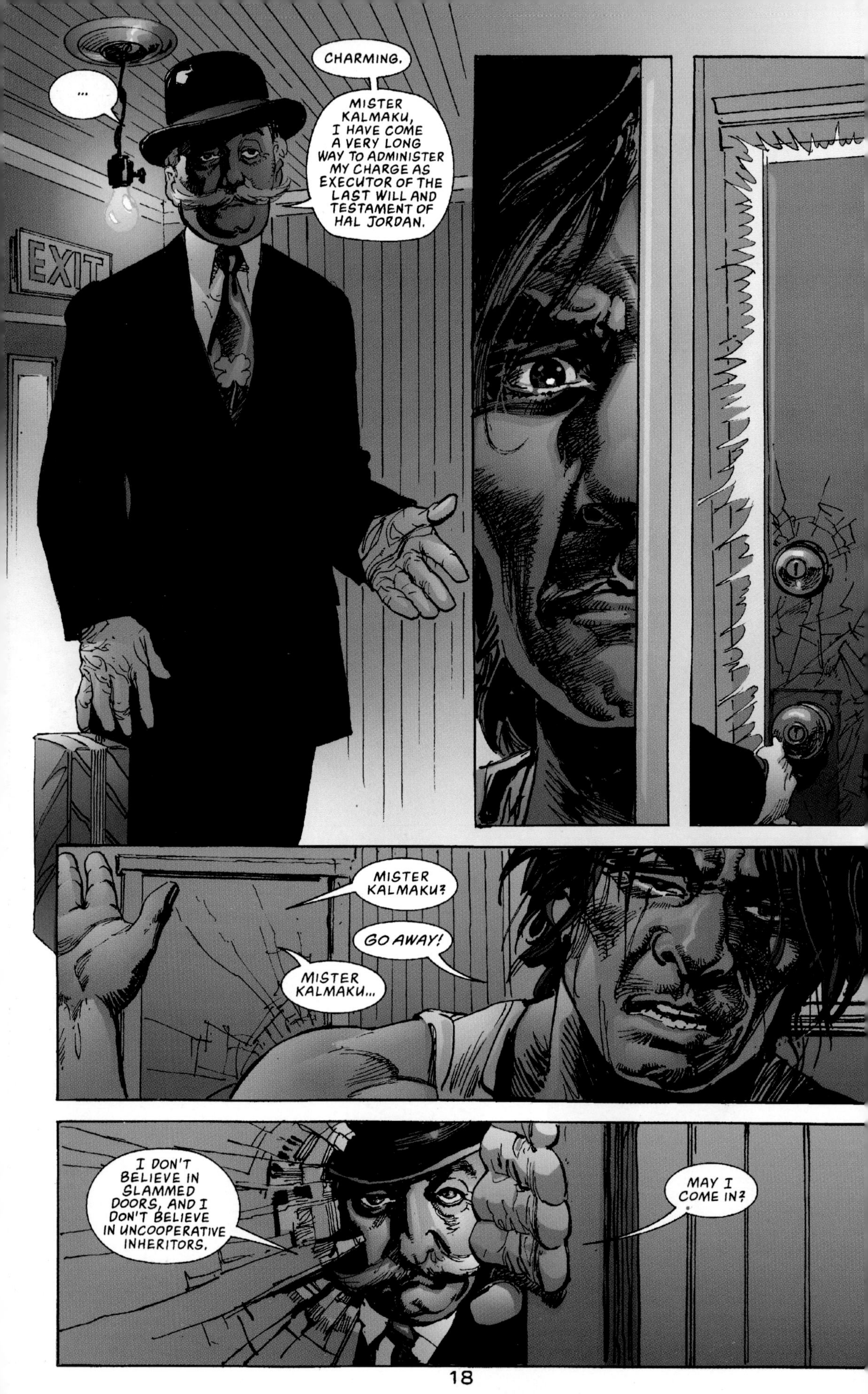
...
CHARMING.
MISTER KALMAKU, I HAVE COME A VERY LONG WAY TO ADMINISTER MY CHARGE AS EXECUTOR OF THE LAST WILL AND TESTAMENT OF HAL JORDAN.
MISTER KALMAKU?
GO AWAY!
MISTER KALMAKU...
I DON'T BELIEVE IN SLAMMED DOORS, AND I DON'T BELIEVE IN UNCOOPERATIVE INHERITORS.
MAY I COME IN?

AS I WAS SAYING, YOU HAVE BEEN NAMED IN THE LAST WILL AND TESTAMENT OF HAL JORDAN.

N-NO I WASN'T. I WAS THERE. I WASN'T EVEN MENTIONED...

WHO ARE YOU?

YOU WERE AT ONE READING OF A WILL, MISTER KALMAKU, THE WILL OF PUBLIC RECORD.

A MAN AS COMPLEX AS THE GREEN LANTERN OFTEN HAS... UNIQUE NEEDS THAT MUST BE ADMINISTERED TO AFTER HIS DEATH.

DISCRETION AND EFFICIENCY ARE THE HALL-MARKS OF MY TRADE.

I WOULD HAVE DELIVERED THIS SOONER... BUT FOR A MAN OF NO EXTRANORMAL TALENTS--

-- YOU'VE DONE A REMARKABLE JOB OF TURNING INVISIBLE.

I DON'T WANT IT.

AND NEITHER DO I. TAKE IT.

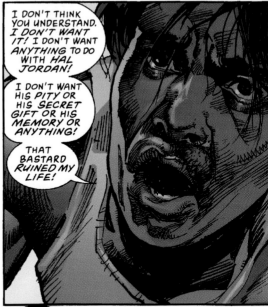

I DON'T THINK YOU UNDERSTAND. I DON'T WANT IT! I DON'T WANT ANYTHING TO DO WITH HAL JORDAN!

I DON'T WANT HIS PITY OR HIS SECRET GIFT OR HIS MEMORY OR ANYTHING!

THAT BASTARD RUINED MY LIFE!

EXCUSE ME, MISTER 'ECUTOR?

CAN I COME IN NOW?

WHAT THE HELL IS THAT?

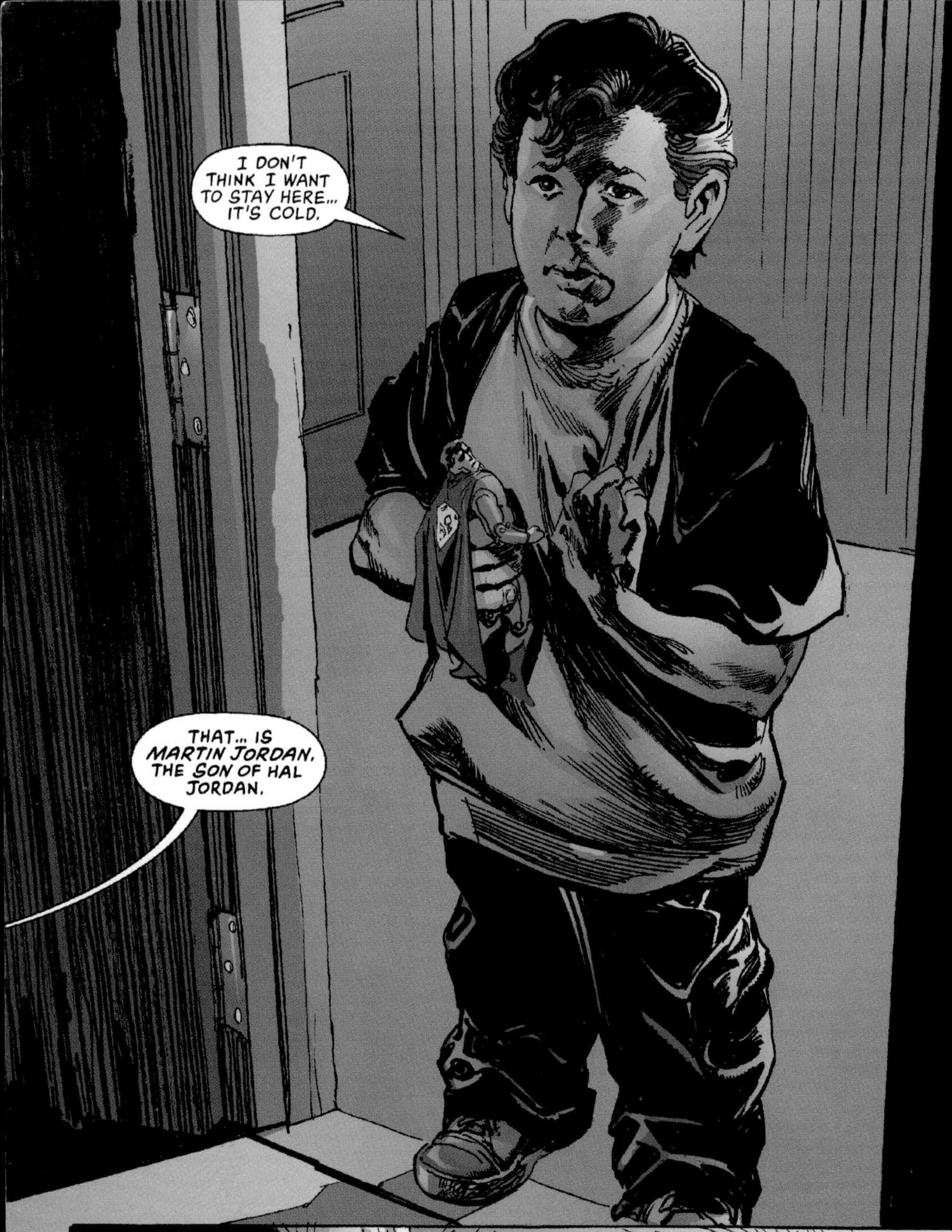
I DON'T THINK I WANT TO STAY HERE... IT'S COLD.
THAT... IS MARTIN JORDAN, THE SON OF HAL JORDAN.

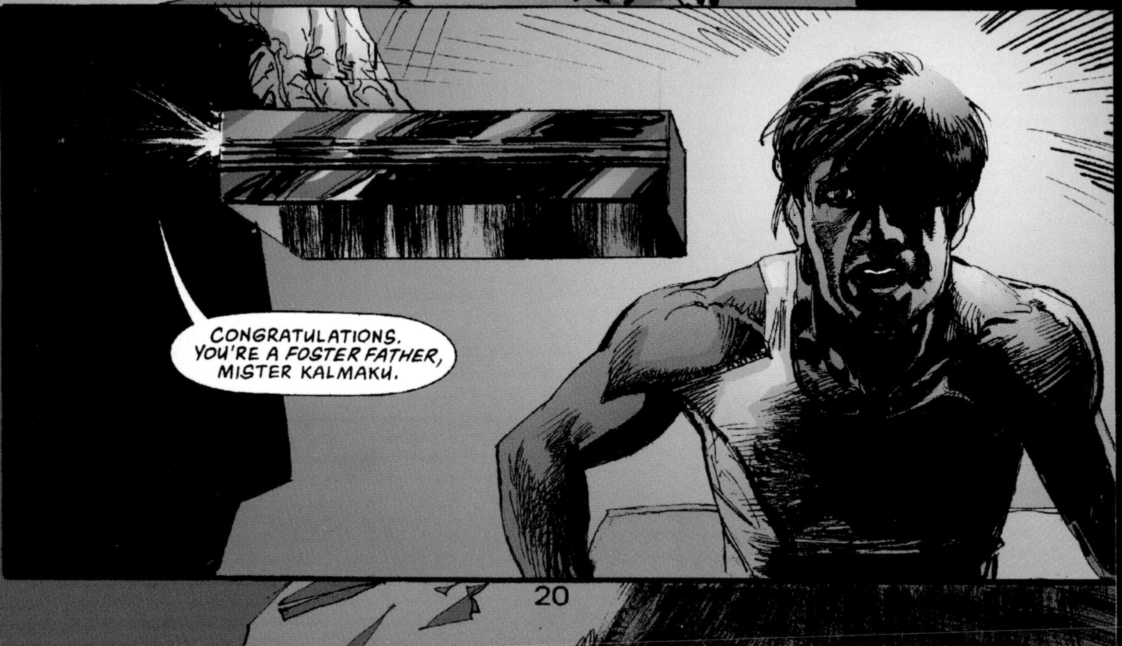
CONGRATULATIONS. YOU'RE A FOSTER FATHER, MISTER KALMAKU.

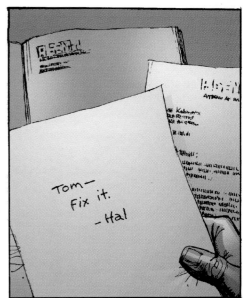

Tom—
Fix it.
—Hal

DO I CALL YOU "PIEFACE" OR "UNCLE TOM"?

"UNCLE PIEFACE"?

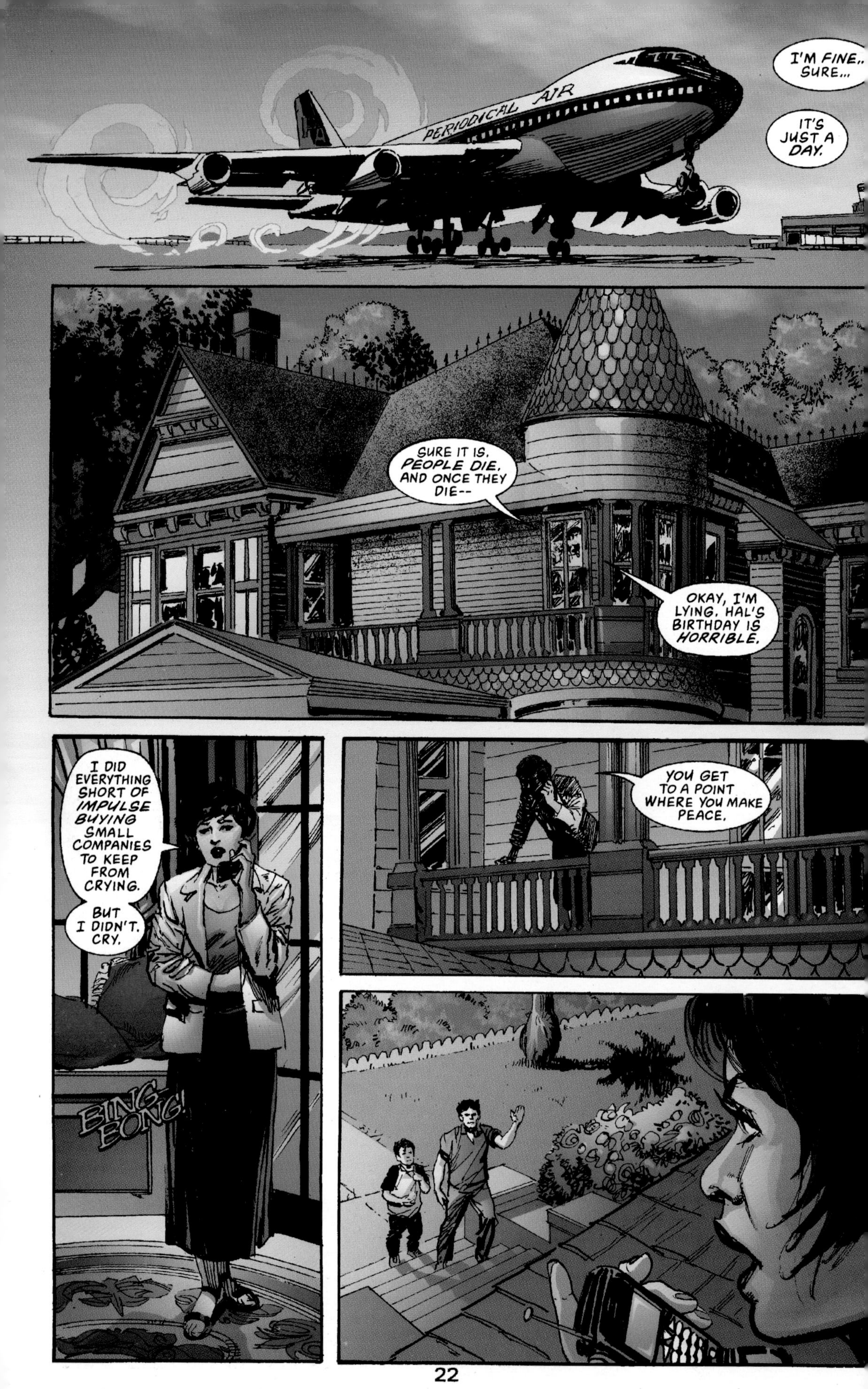
PERIODICAL AIR
I'M FINE.. SURE...
IT'S JUST A DAY.
SURE IT IS. PEOPLE DIE. AND ONCE THEY DIE--
OKAY, I'M LYING. HAL'S BIRTHDAY IS HORRIBLE.
I DID EVERYTHING SHORT OF IMPULSE BUYING SMALL COMPANIES TO KEEP FROM CRYING.
BUT I DIDN'T. CRY.
YOU GET TO A POINT WHERE YOU MAKE PEACE.
BING BONG!

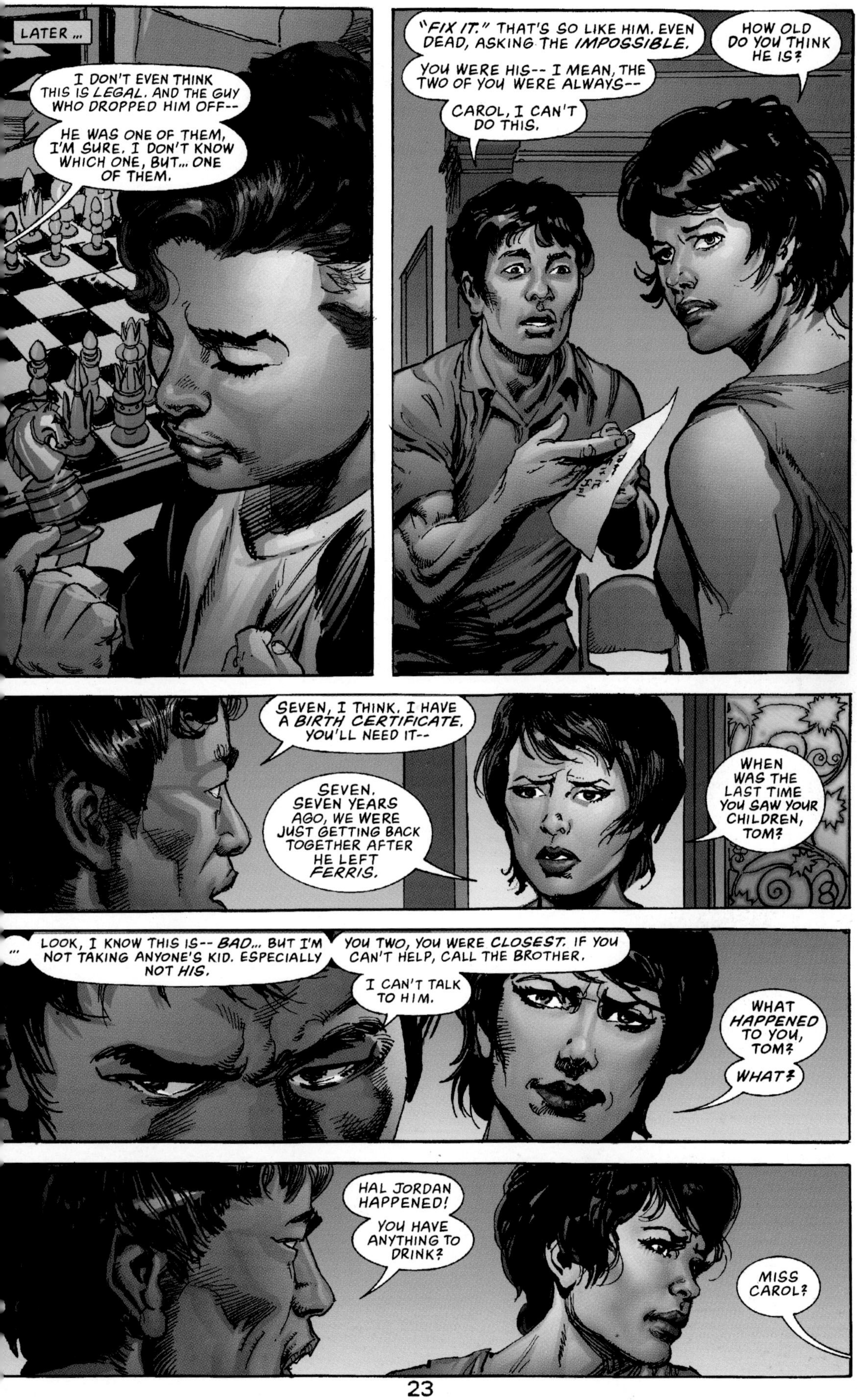
LATER...
I DON'T EVEN THINK THIS IS LEGAL. AND THE GUY WHO DROPPED HIM OFF--
HE WAS ONE OF THEM, I'M SURE. I DON'T KNOW WHICH ONE, BUT... ONE OF THEM.
"FIX IT." THAT'S SO LIKE HIM. EVEN DEAD, ASKING THE IMPOSSIBLE.
YOU WERE HIS-- I MEAN, THE TWO OF YOU WERE ALWAYS--
CAROL, I CAN'T DO THIS.
HOW OLD DO YOU THINK HE IS?
SEVEN, I THINK. I HAVE A BIRTH CERTIFICATE. YOU'LL NEED IT--
SEVEN. SEVEN YEARS AGO, WE WERE JUST GETTING BACK TOGETHER AFTER HE LEFT FERRIS.
WHEN WAS THE LAST TIME YOU SAW YOUR CHILDREN, TOM?
...
LOOK, I KNOW THIS IS-- BAD... BUT I'M NOT TAKING ANYONE'S KID. ESPECIALLY NOT HIS.
YOU TWO, YOU WERE CLOSEST. IF YOU CAN'T HELP, CALL THE BROTHER.
I CAN'T TALK TO HIM.
WHAT HAPPENED TO YOU, TOM?
WHAT?
HAL JORDAN HAPPENED!
YOU HAVE ANYTHING TO DRINK?
MISS CAROL?

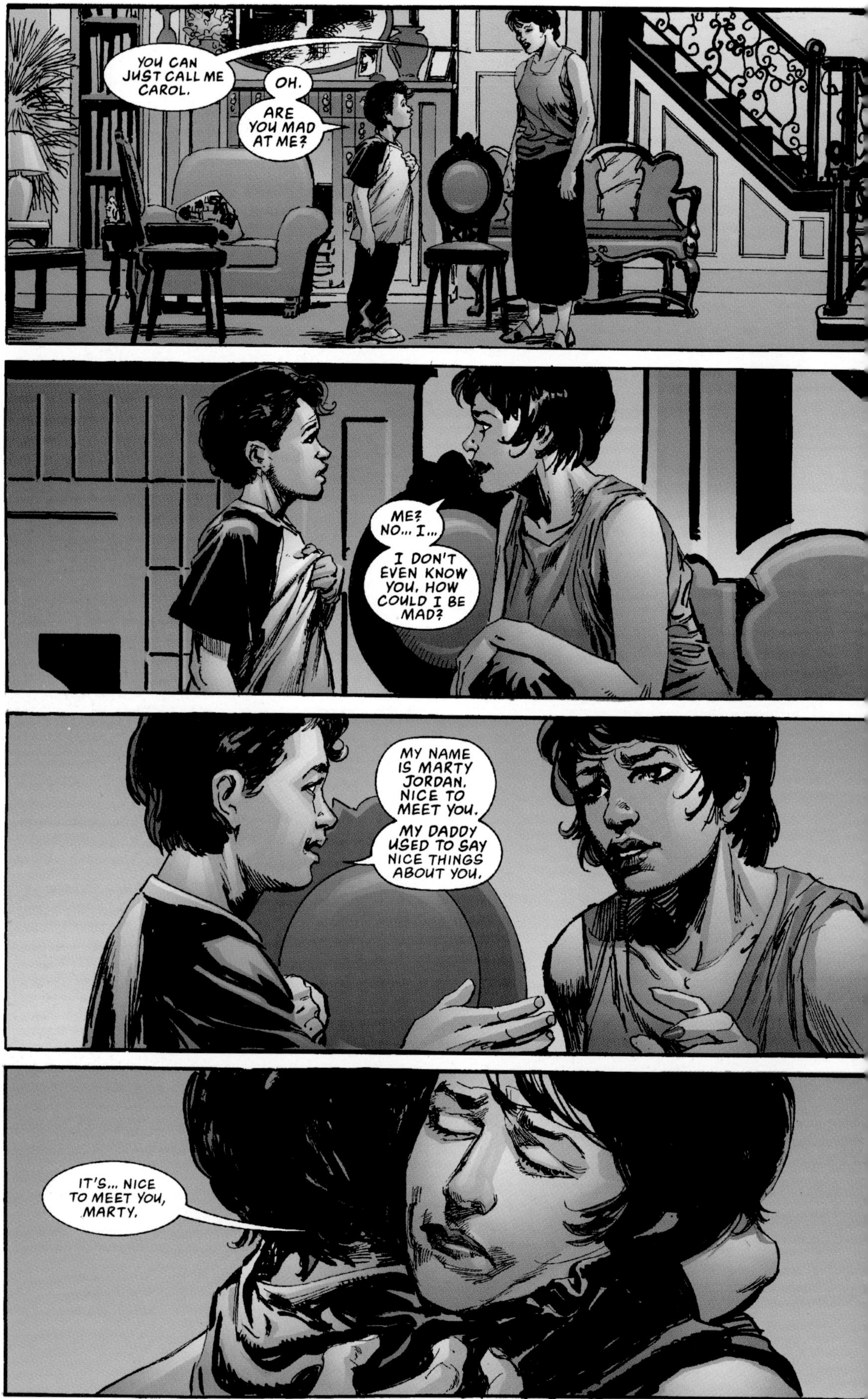
YOU CAN JUST CALL ME CAROL.
OH.
ARE YOU MAD AT ME?
ME? NO... I...
I DON'T EVEN KNOW YOU. HOW COULD I BE MAD?
MY NAME IS MARTY JORDAN. NICE TO MEET YOU.
MY DADDY USED TO SAY NICE THINGS ABOUT YOU.
IT'S... NICE TO MEET YOU, MARTY.

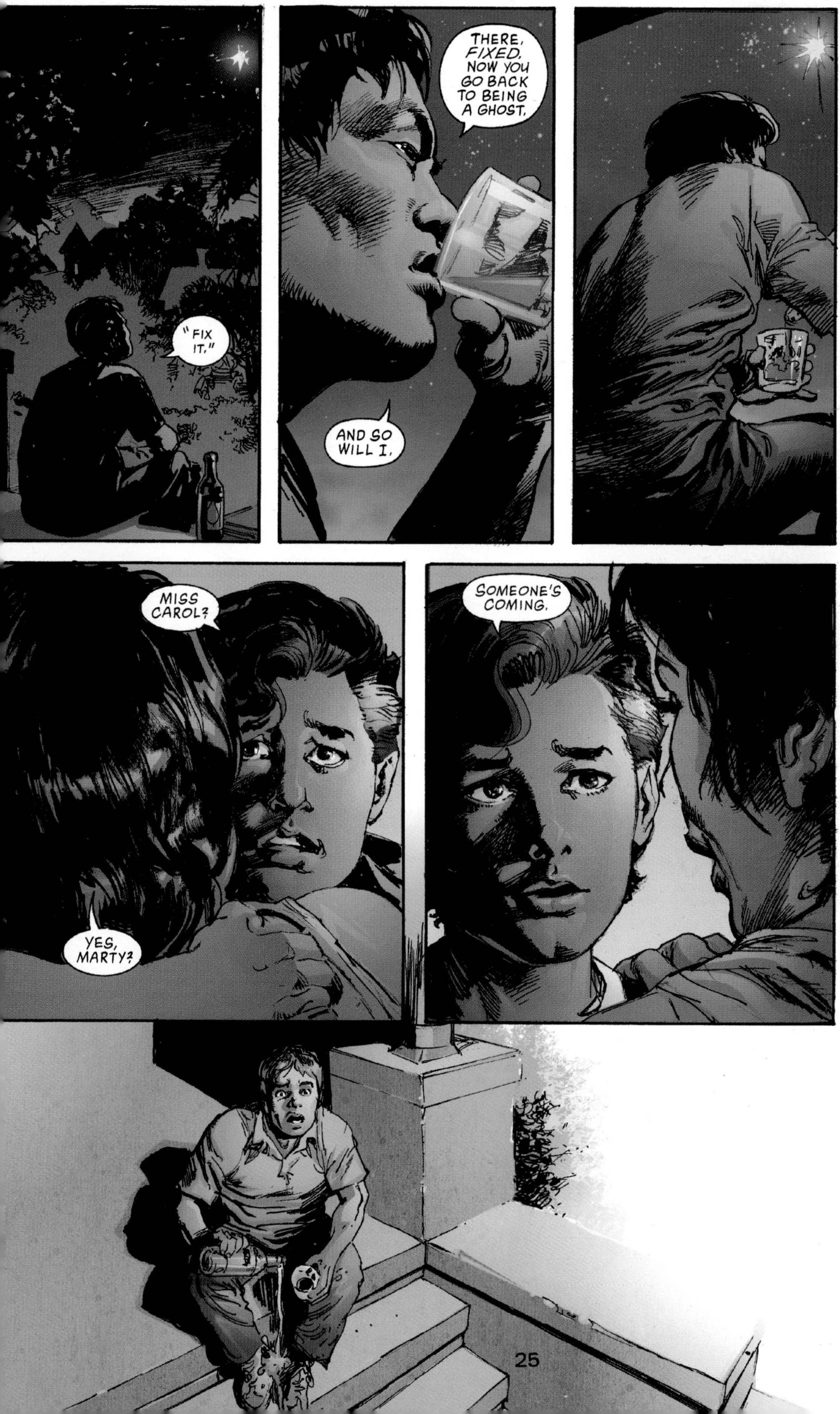
"FIX IT."
THERE, FIXED. NOW YOU GO BACK TO BEING A GHOST.
AND SO WILL I.
MISS CAROL?
YES, MARTY?
SOMEONE'S COMING.

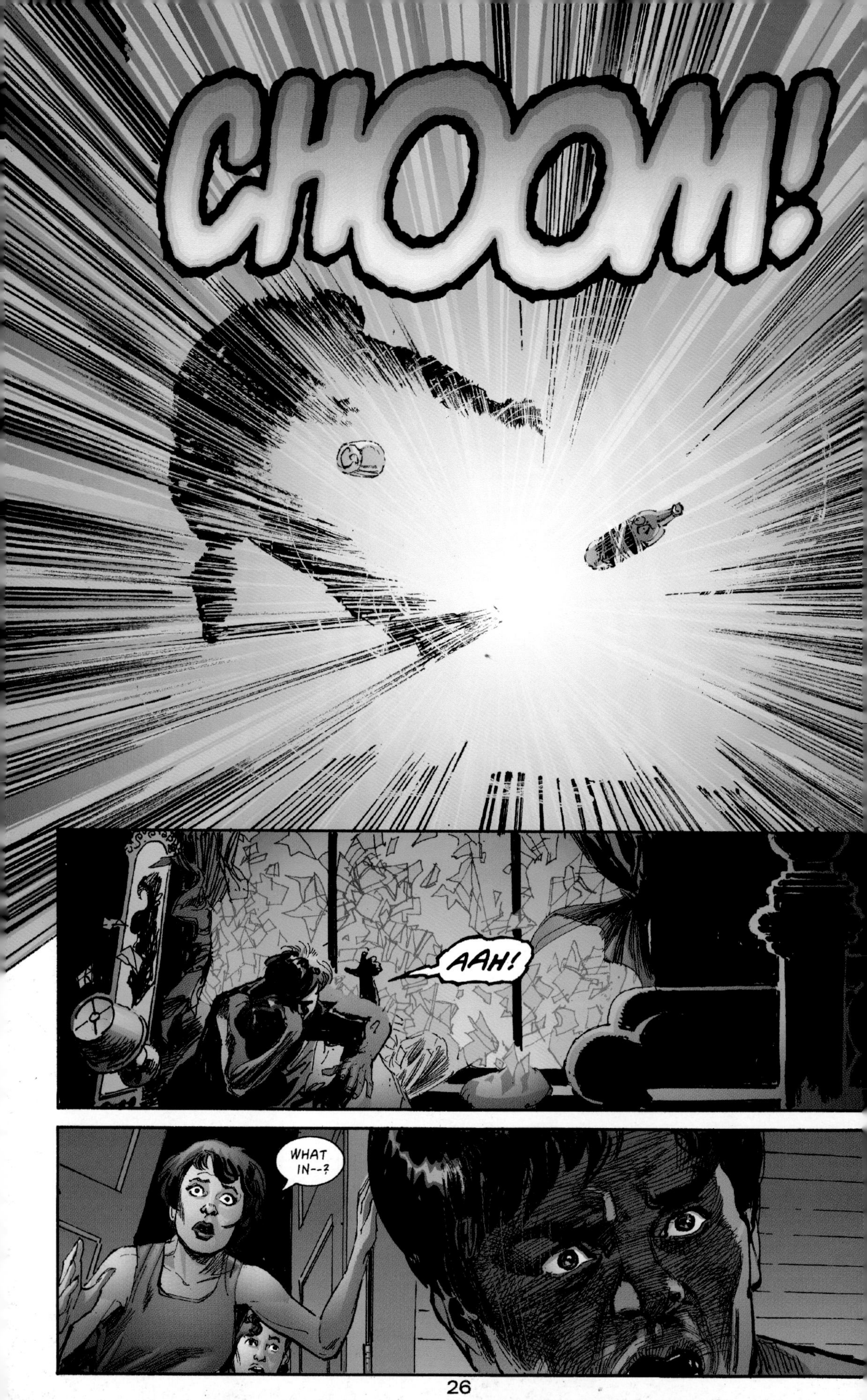
CHOOM!
AAH!
WHAT IN--?

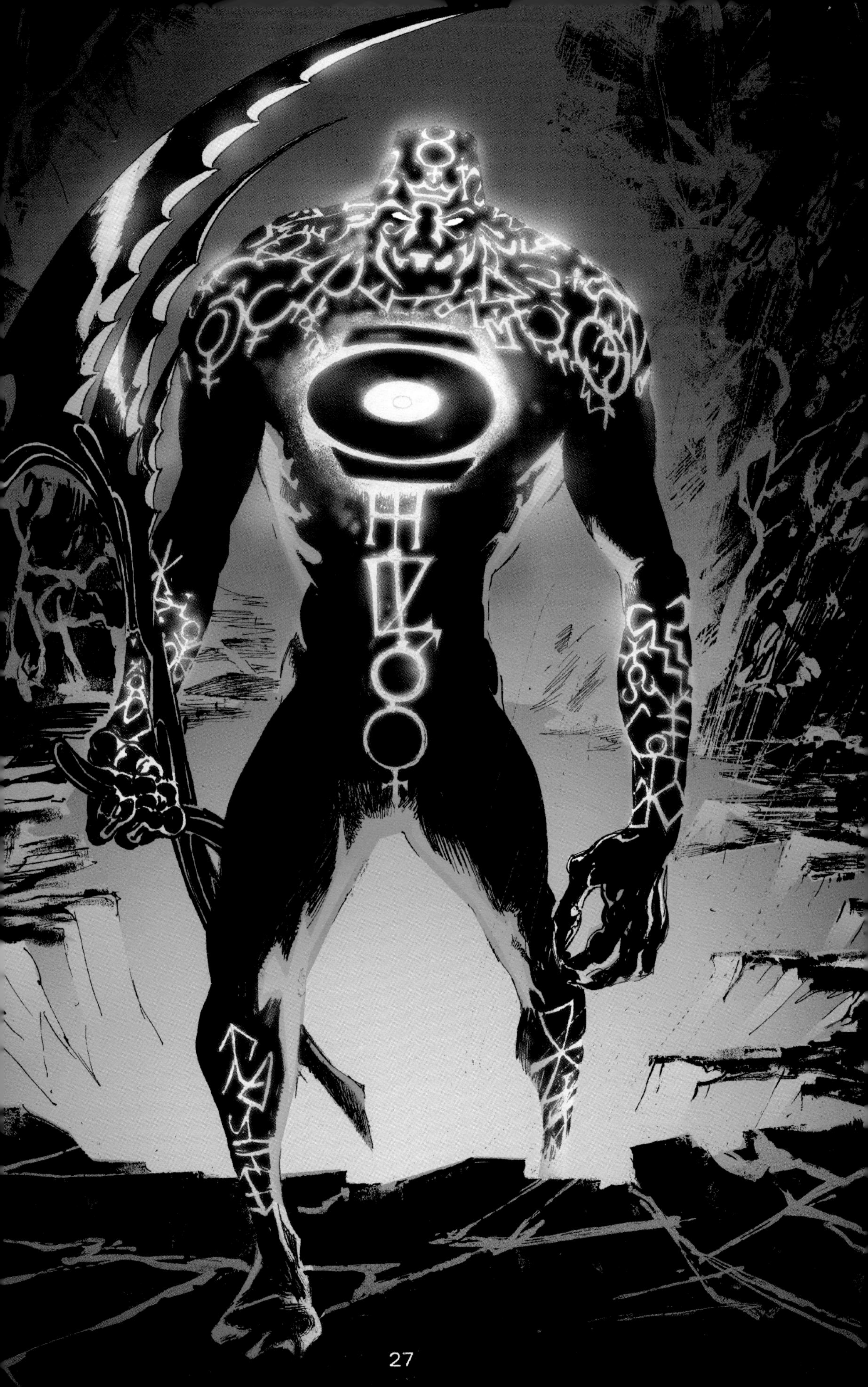

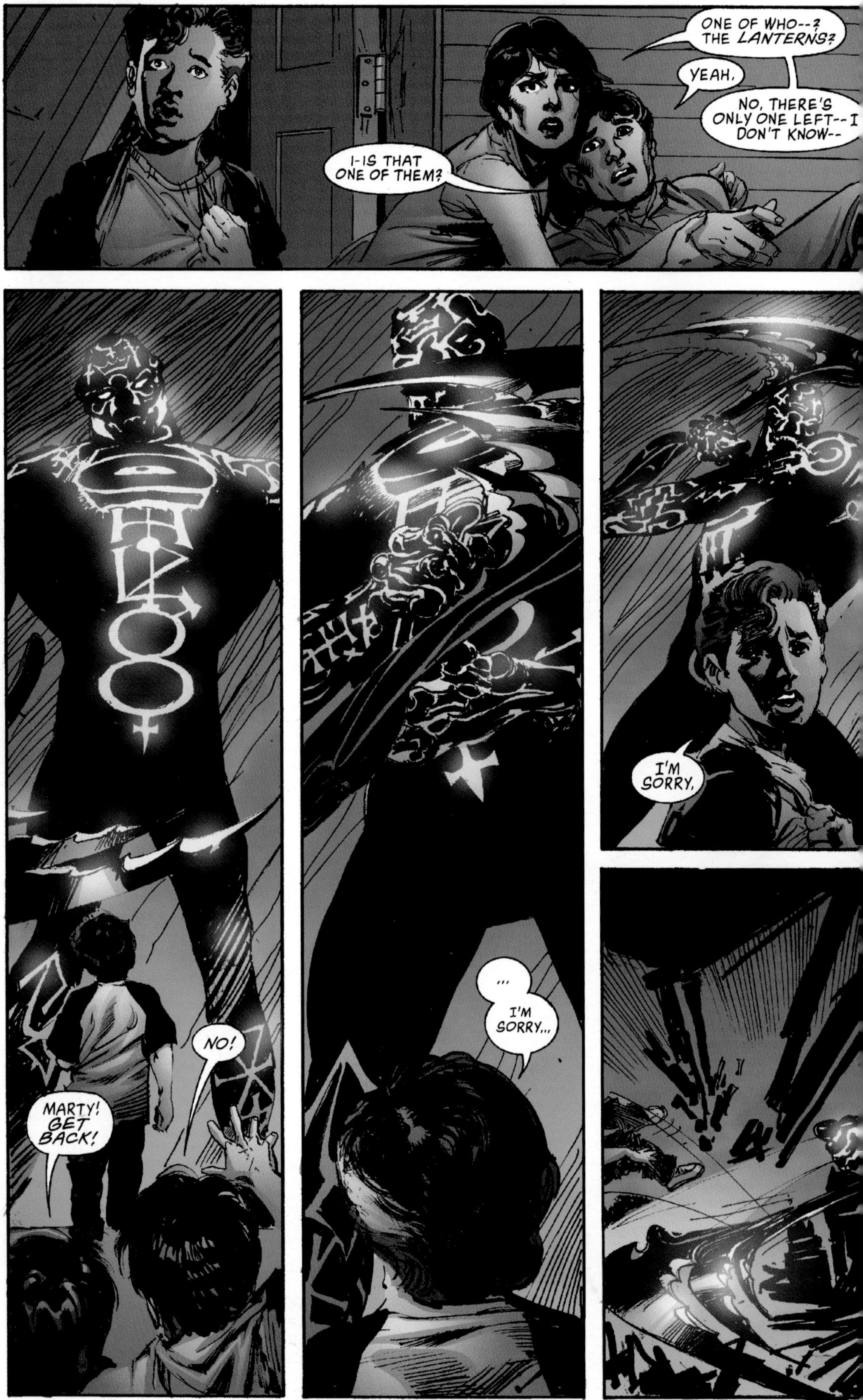
ONE OF WHO--? THE *LANTERNS*?
YEAH.
NO, THERE'S ONLY ONE LEFT-- I DON'T KNOW--
I-IS THAT ONE OF THEM?
NO!
MARTY! GET BACK!
...
I'M SORRY...
I'M SORRY.

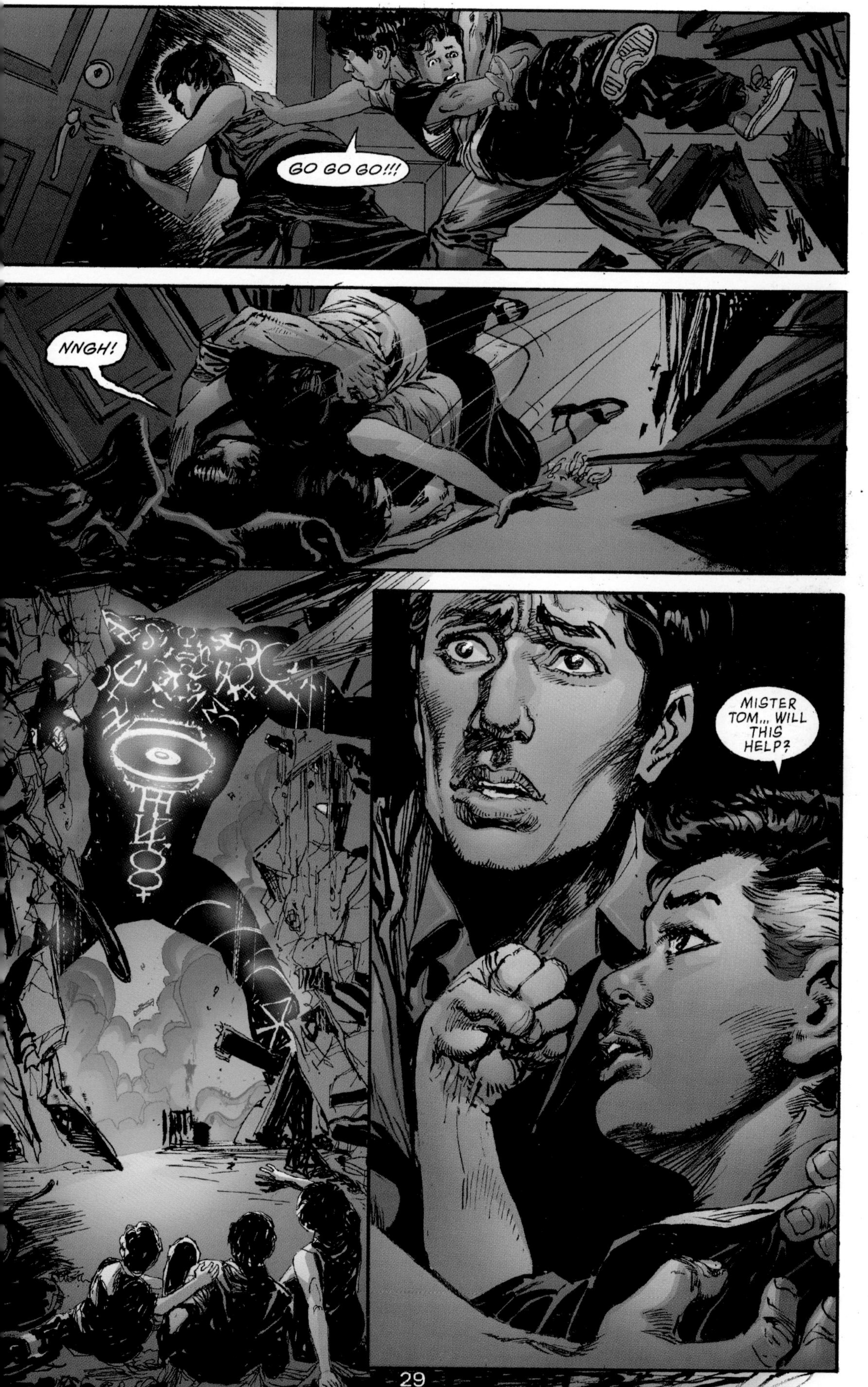
GO GO GO!!!
NNGH!
MISTER TOM... WILL THIS HELP?

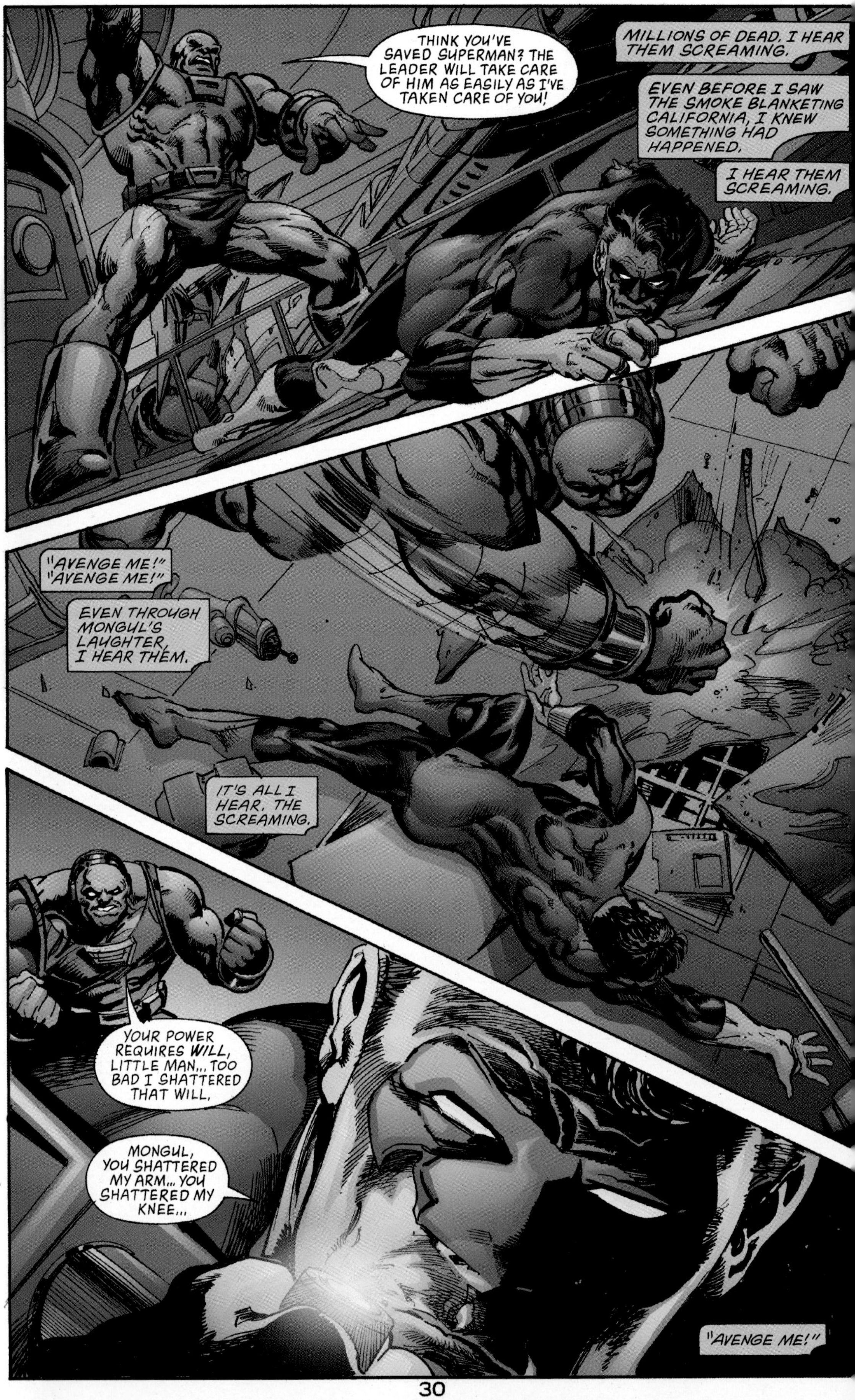
THINK YOU'VE SAVED SUPERMAN? THE LEADER WILL TAKE CARE OF HIM AS EASILY AS I'VE TAKEN CARE OF YOU!
MILLIONS OF DEAD. I HEAR THEM SCREAMING.
EVEN BEFORE I SAW THE SMOKE BLANKETING CALIFORNIA, I KNEW SOMETHING HAD HAPPENED.
I HEAR THEM SCREAMING.
"AVENGE ME!" "AVENGE ME!"
EVEN THROUGH MONGUL'S LAUGHTER, I HEAR THEM.
IT'S ALL I HEAR. THE SCREAMING.
YOUR POWER REQUIRES WILL, LITTLE MAN... TOO BAD I SHATTERED THAT WILL.
MONGUL, YOU SHATTERED MY ARM... YOU SHATTERED MY KNEE...
"AVENGE ME!"

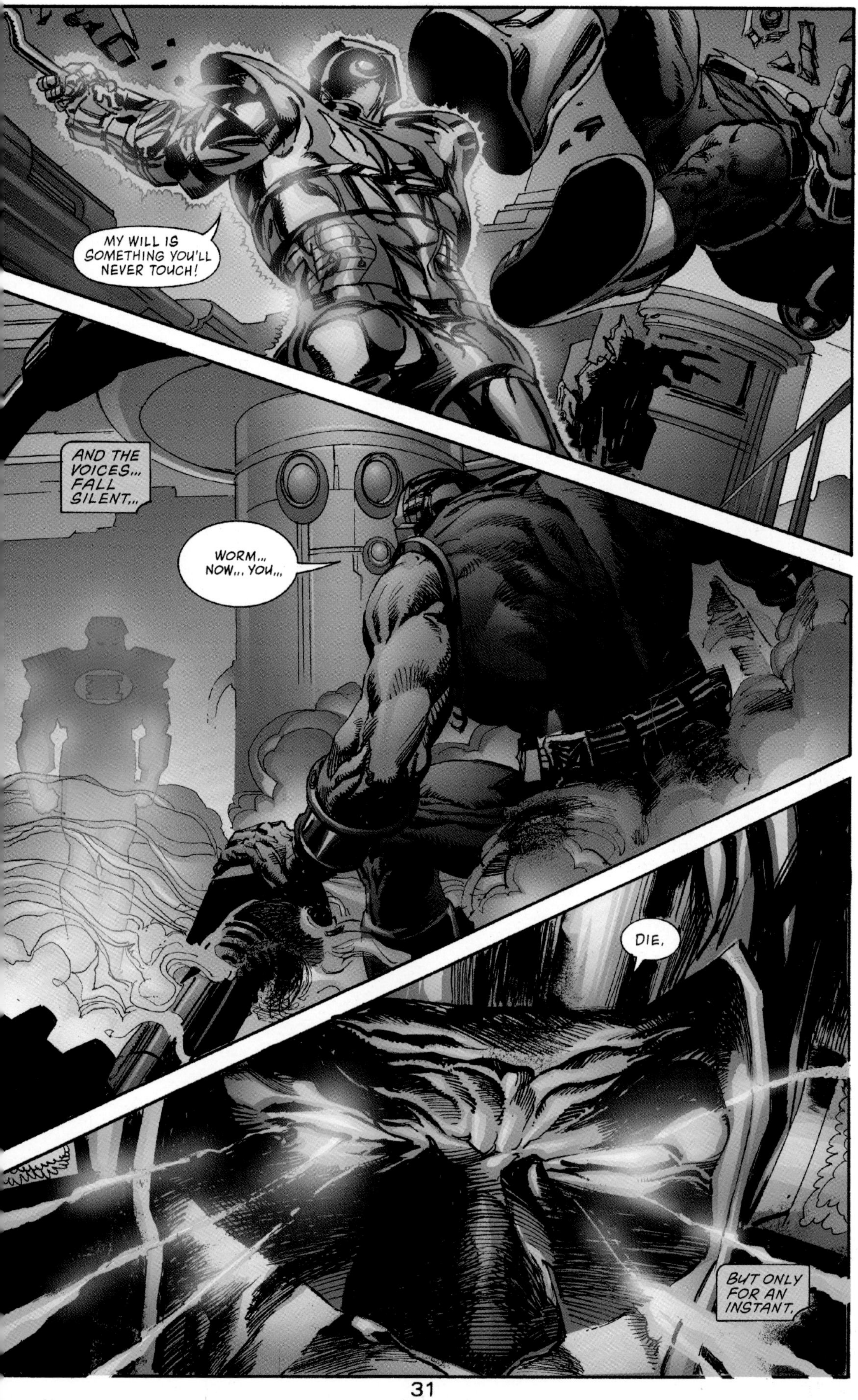
MY WILL IS SOMETHING YOU'LL NEVER TOUCH!
AND THE VOICES... FALL SILENT...
WORM... NOW... YOU...
DIE.
BUT ONLY FOR AN INSTANT.

SEVEN MILLION VOICES CRY OUT FOR VENGEANCE.

THEY WILL NOT BE SATISFIED WITHOUT REAL BLOOD.

THEY

WILL

NOT

BE

SILENCED.

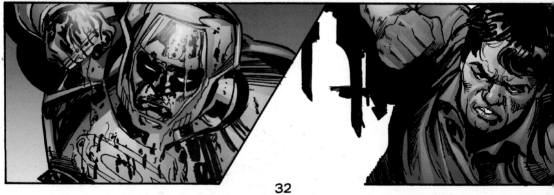

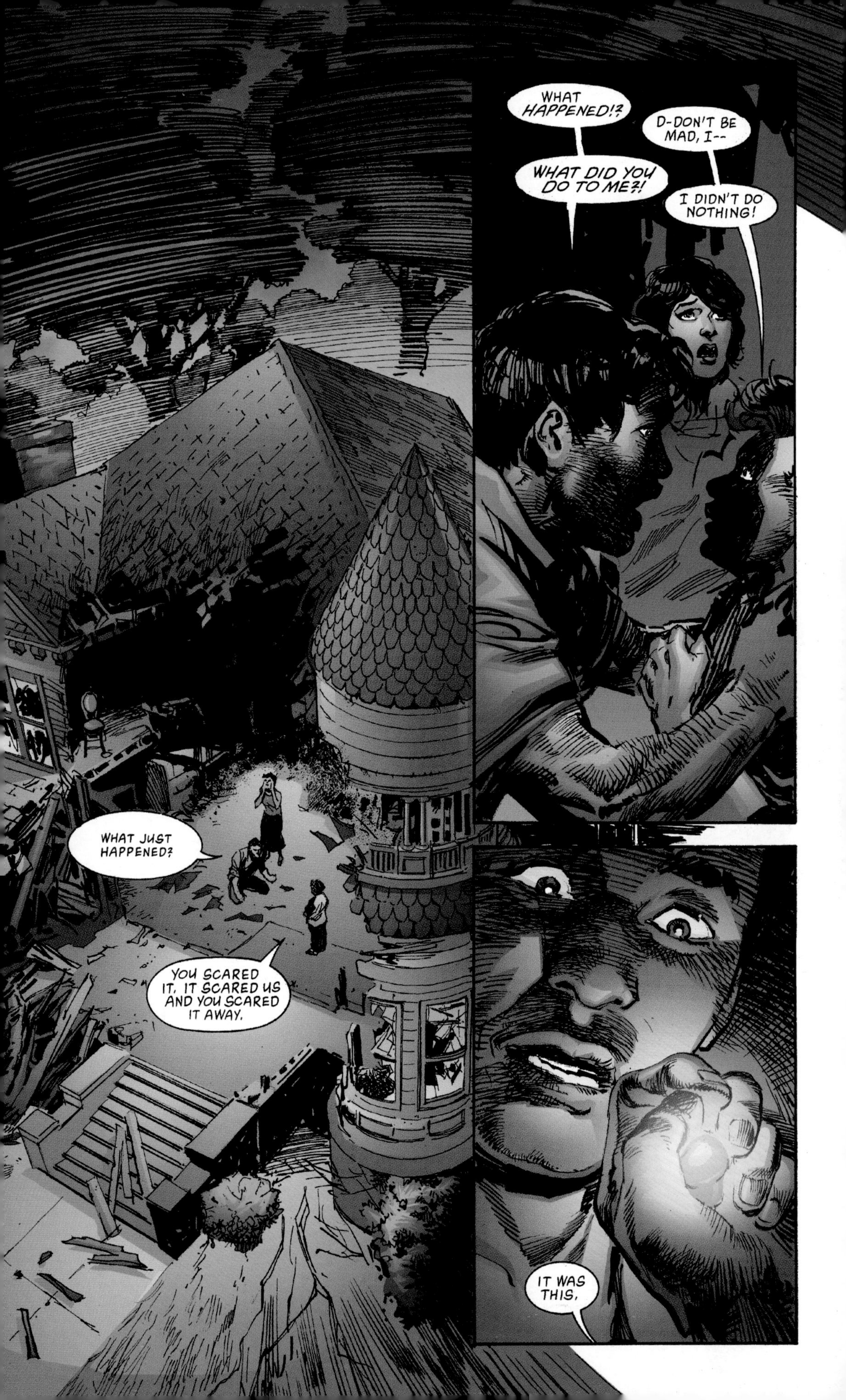
WHAT HAPPENED!?
WHAT DID YOU DO TO ME?!
D-DON'T BE MAD, I--
I DIDN'T DO NOTHING!
WHAT JUST HAPPENED?
YOU SCARED IT. IT SCARED US AND YOU SCARED IT AWAY.
IT WAS THIS.

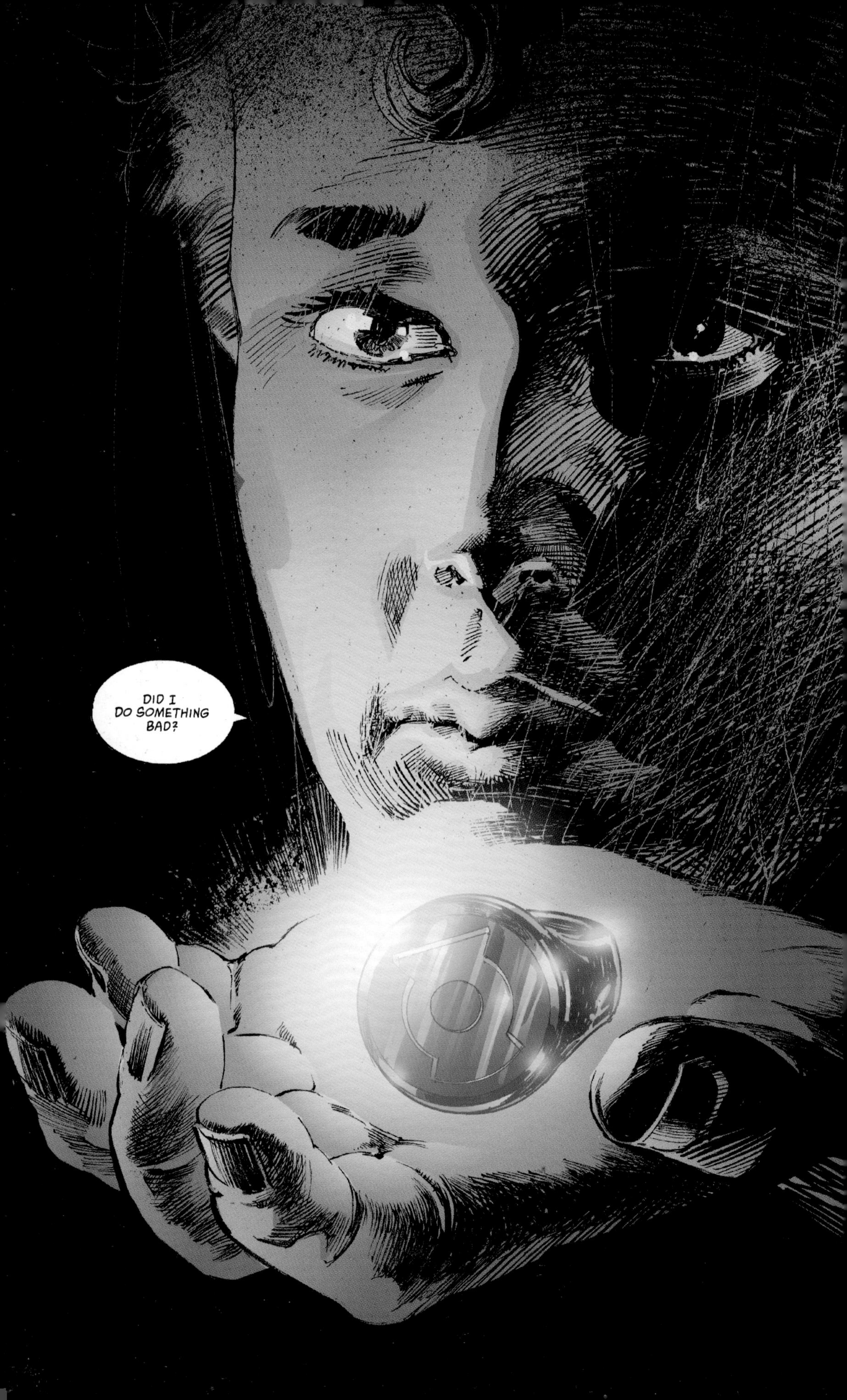
DID I DO SOMETHING BAD?

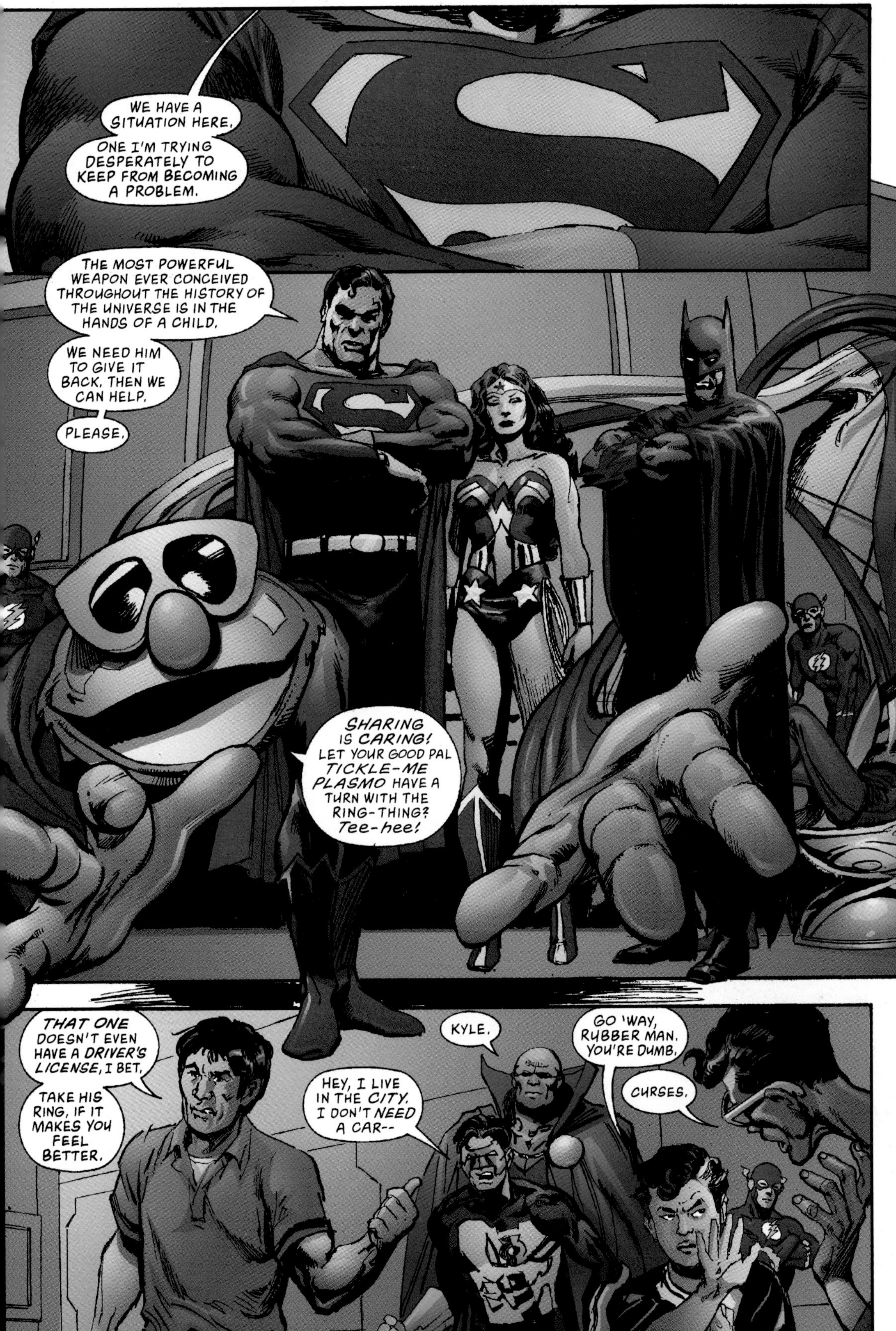
WE HAVE A SITUATION HERE.
ONE I'M TRYING DESPERATELY TO KEEP FROM BECOMING A PROBLEM.
THE MOST POWERFUL WEAPON EVER CONCEIVED THROUGHOUT THE HISTORY OF THE UNIVERSE IS IN THE HANDS OF A CHILD.
WE NEED HIM TO GIVE IT BACK. THEN WE CAN HELP.
PLEASE.
SHARING IS CARING! LET YOUR GOOD PAL TICKLE-ME PLASMO HAVE A TURN WITH THE RING-THING? Tee-hee!
THAT ONE DOESN'T EVEN HAVE A DRIVER'S LICENSE, I BET.
TAKE HIS RING, IF IT MAKES YOU FEEL BETTER.
HEY, I LIVE IN THE CITY. I DON'T NEED A CAR--
KYLE.
GO 'WAY, RUBBER MAN. YOU'RE DUMB.
CURSES.

BETTER YET, ASK-- MARTY.

WE DON'T HAVE TO *ASK*, THIS IS A COURTESY. KNOW THAT.

LOSE THE ATTITUDE, DROP THE PRIDE. HAVE THE BOY GIVE US THE RING.

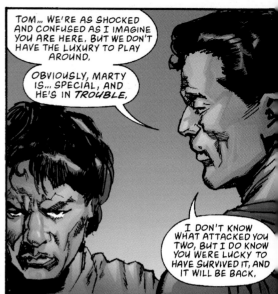

TOM... WE'RE AS SHOCKED AND CONFUSED AS I IMAGINE YOU ARE HERE, BUT WE DON'T HAVE THE LUXURY TO PLAY AROUND.

OBVIOUSLY, MARTY IS... SPECIAL, AND HE'S IN *TROUBLE*.

I DON'T KNOW WHAT ATTACKED YOU TWO, BUT I DO KNOW YOU WERE LUCKY TO HAVE SURVIVED IT, AND IT WILL BE BACK.

DO ME A FAVOR, DON'T *SNOW* ME! THIS ISN'T ABOUT ME. IT'S NOT EVEN ABOUT THE *KID*. IT'S ABOUT *YOU PEOPLE*-- YOUR *KIND*--

AND ONE OF *YOUR* MISTAKES!

FUNNY HOW YOU DIDN'T SHOW UNTIL THE *RING* POPPED UP, ISN'T IT?

M-MISTER TOM?

MISTER TOM? WHERE YOU GOING?

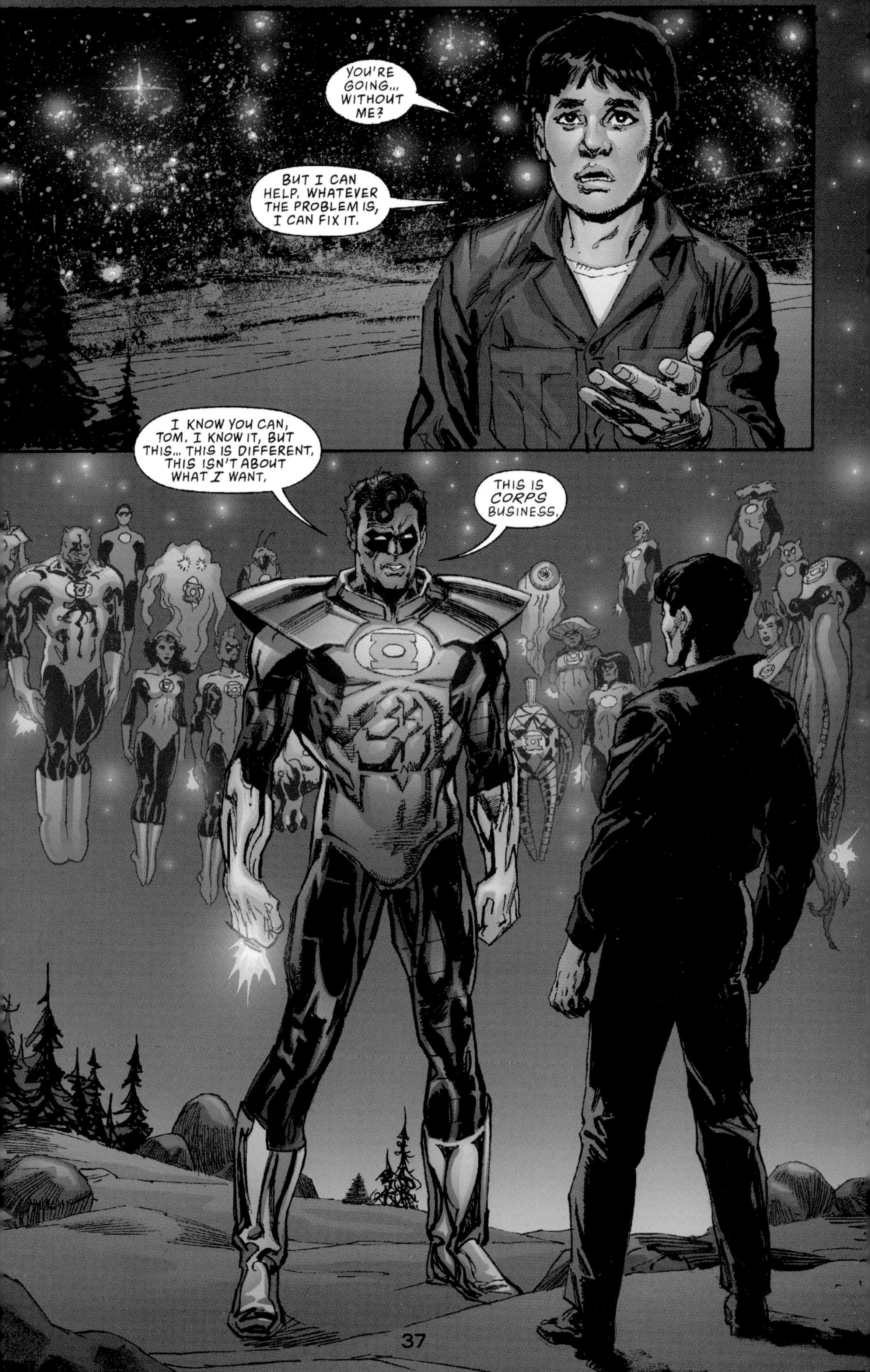
YOU'RE GOING... WITHOUT ME?
BUT I CAN HELP. WHATEVER THE PROBLEM IS, I CAN FIX IT.
I KNOW YOU CAN, TOM. I KNOW IT, BUT THIS... THIS IS DIFFERENT. THIS ISN'T ABOUT WHAT I WANT.
THIS IS CORPS BUSINESS.

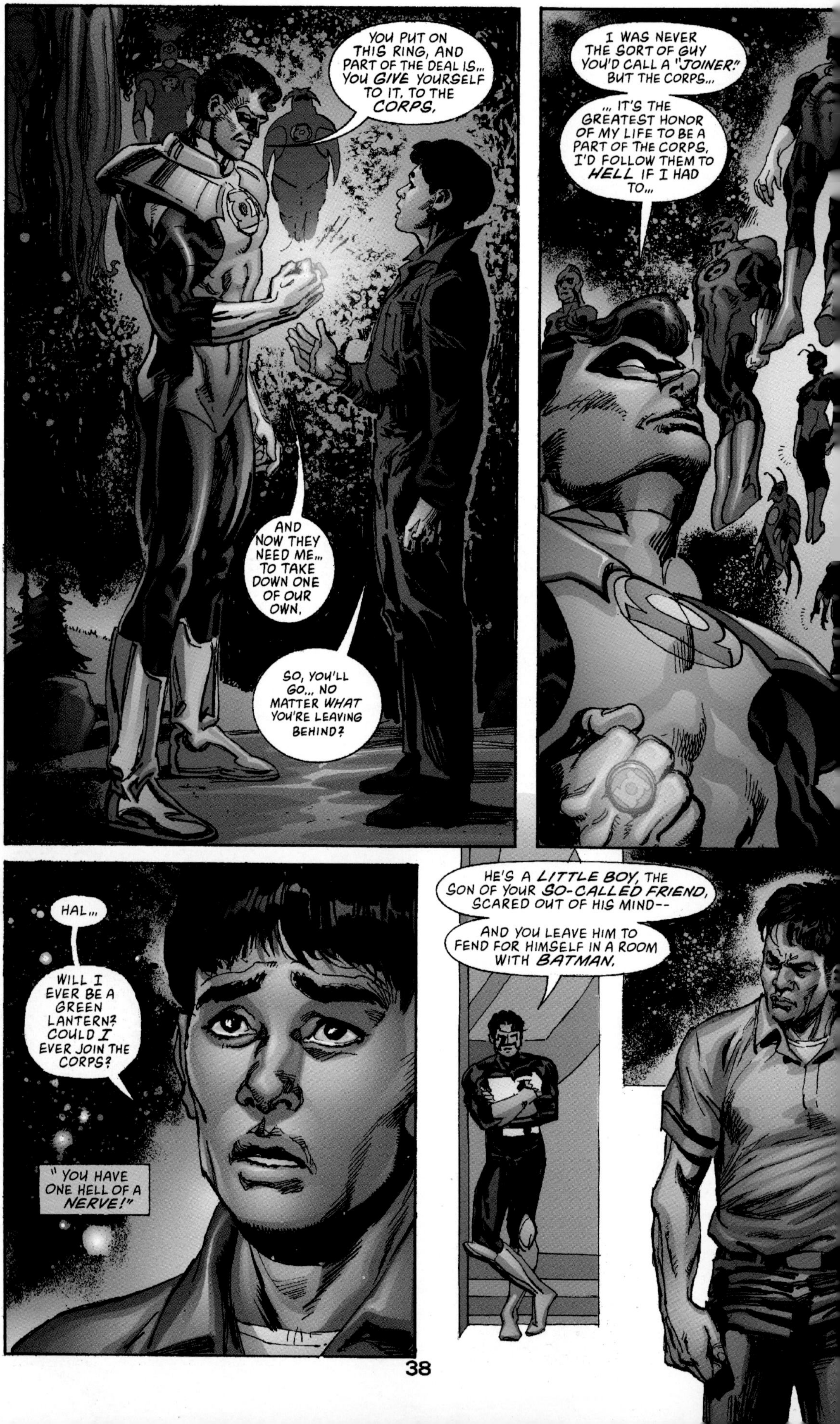
YOU PUT ON THIS RING, AND PART OF THE DEAL IS... YOU GIVE YOURSELF TO IT, TO THE CORPS.
AND NOW THEY NEED ME... TO TAKE DOWN ONE OF OUR OWN.
SO, YOU'LL GO... NO MATTER WHAT YOU'RE LEAVING BEHIND?
I WAS NEVER THE SORT OF GUY YOU'D CALL A "JOINER." BUT THE CORPS...
... IT'S THE GREATEST HONOR OF MY LIFE TO BE A PART OF THE CORPS. I'D FOLLOW THEM TO HELL IF I HAD TO...
HAL...
WILL I EVER BE A GREEN LANTERN? COULD I EVER JOIN THE CORPS?
" YOU HAVE ONE HELL OF A NERVE!"
HE'S A LITTLE BOY, THE SON OF YOUR SO-CALLED FRIEND, SCARED OUT OF HIS MIND--
AND YOU LEAVE HIM TO FEND FOR HIMSELF IN A ROOM WITH BATMAN.

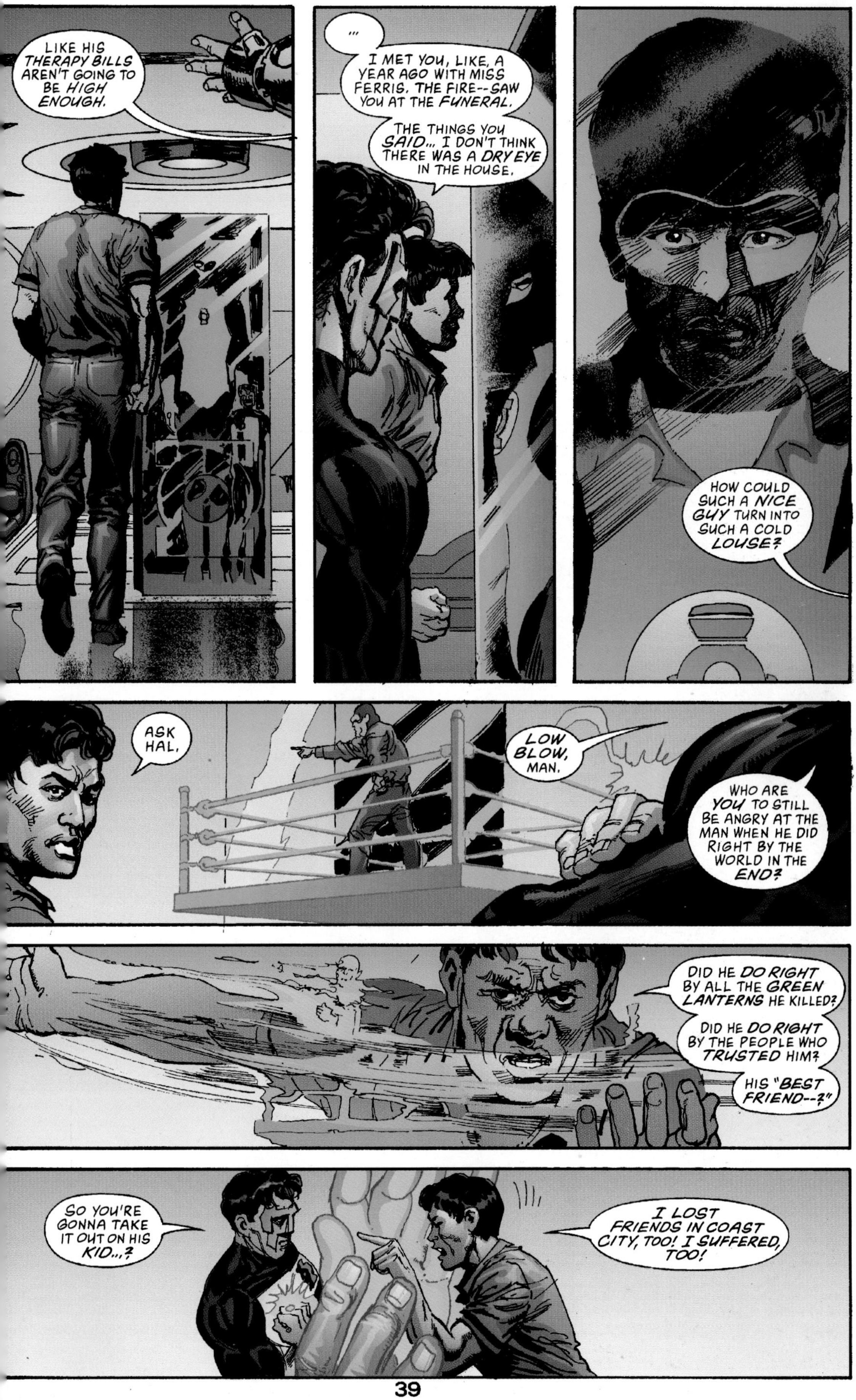
LIKE HIS THERAPY BILLS AREN'T GOING TO BE HIGH ENOUGH.
...
I MET YOU, LIKE, A YEAR AGO WITH MISS FERRIS. THE FIRE--SAW YOU AT THE FUNERAL.
THE THINGS YOU SAID... I DON'T THINK THERE WAS A DRY EYE IN THE HOUSE.
HOW COULD SUCH A NICE GUY TURN INTO SUCH A COLD LOUSE?
ASK HAL.
LOW BLOW, MAN.
WHO ARE YOU TO STILL BE ANGRY AT THE MAN WHEN HE DID RIGHT BY THE WORLD IN THE END?
DID HE DO RIGHT BY ALL THE GREEN LANTERNS HE KILLED?
DID HE DO RIGHT BY THE PEOPLE WHO TRUSTED HIM?
HIS "BEST FRIEND--?"
SO YOU'RE GONNA TAKE IT OUT ON HIS KID...?
I LOST FRIENDS IN COAST CITY, TOO! I SUFFERED, TOO!

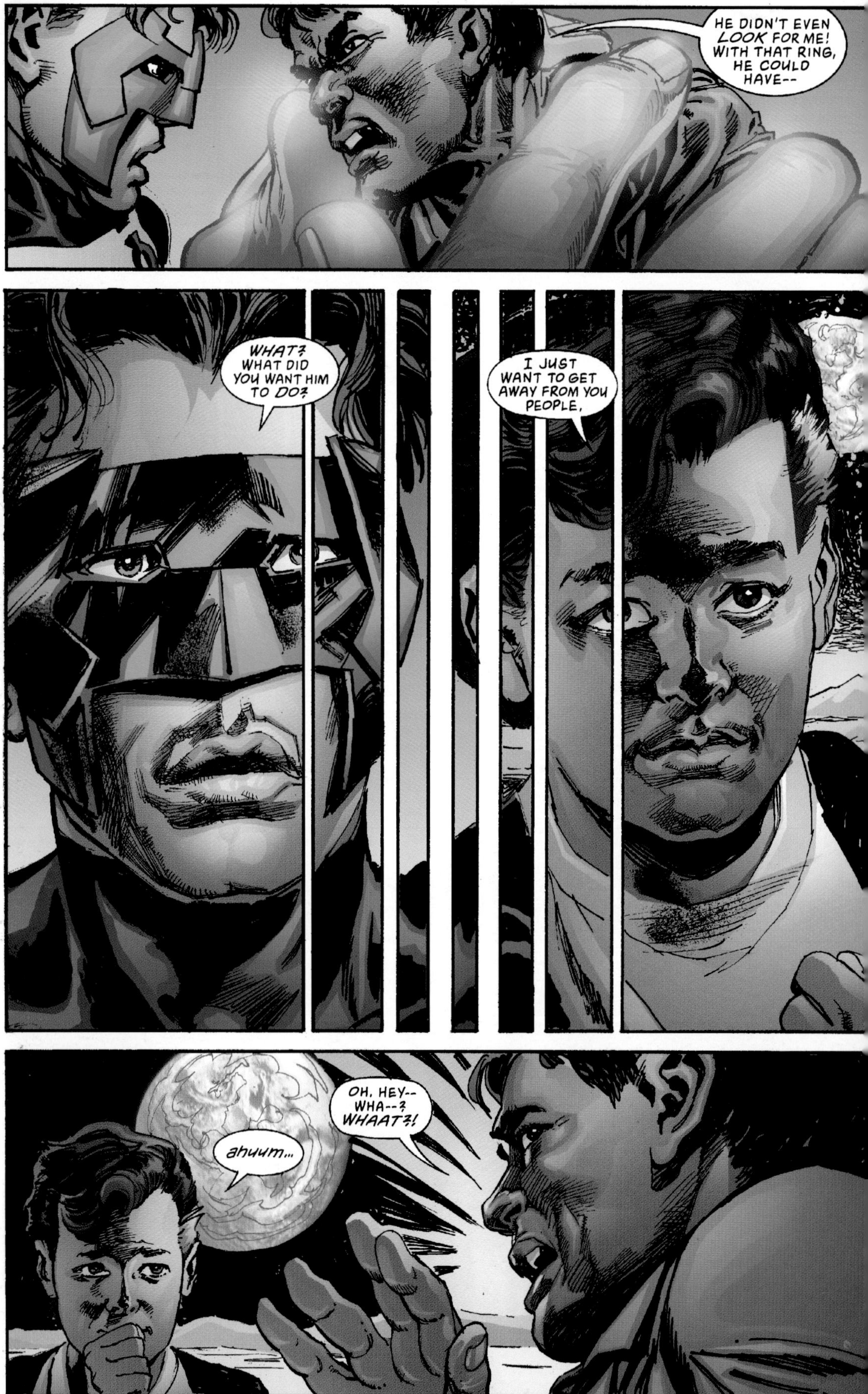
HE DIDN'T EVEN LOOK FOR ME! WITH THAT RING, HE COULD HAVE--
WHAT? WHAT DID YOU WANT HIM TO DO?
I JUST WANT TO GET AWAY FROM YOU PEOPLE.
ahuum...
OH, HEY-- WHA--? WHAAT?!

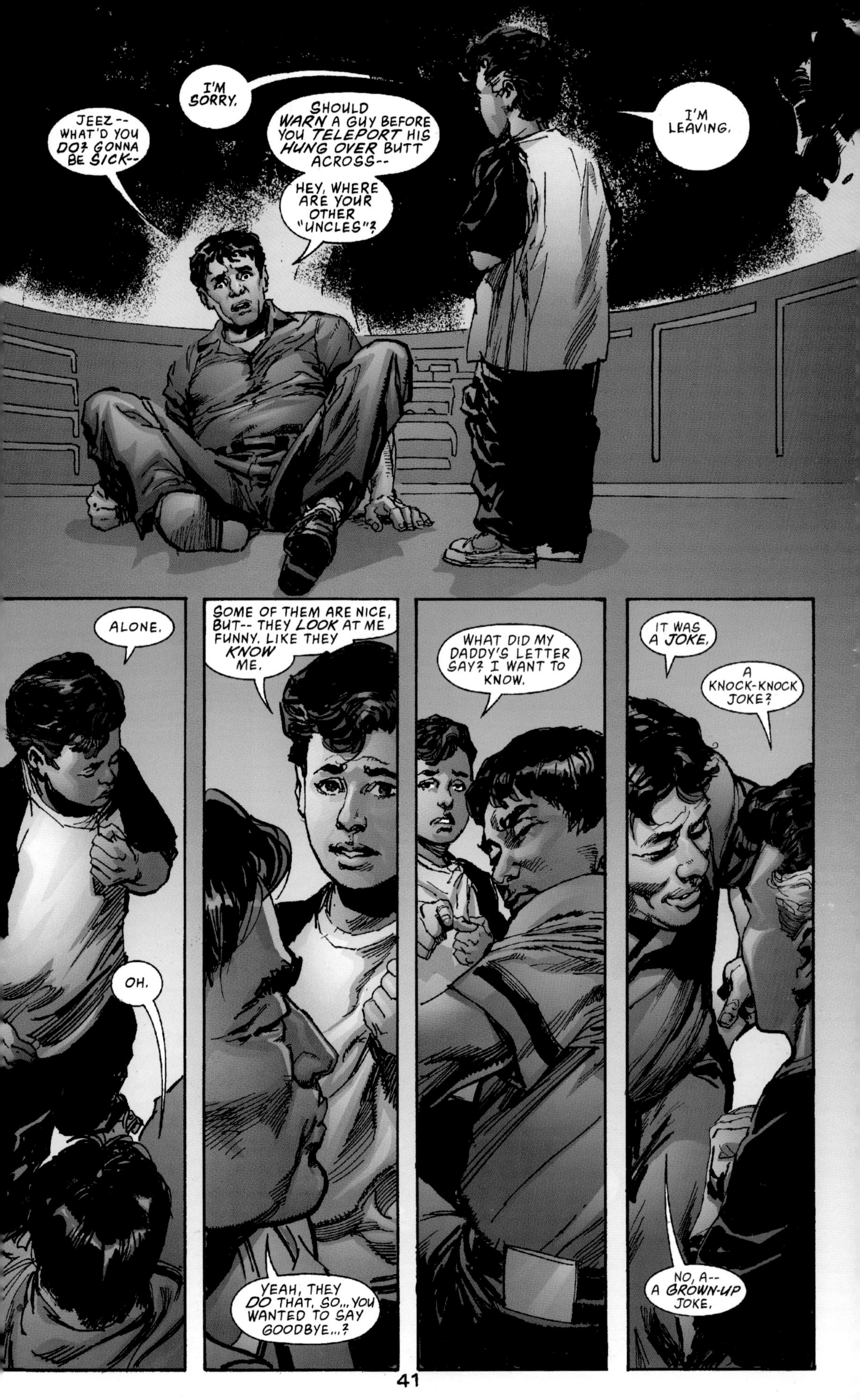
JEEZ -- WHAT'D YOU DO? GONNA BE SICK--
I'M SORRY.
SHOULD WARN A GUY BEFORE YOU TELEPORT HIS HUNG OVER BUTT ACROSS--
HEY, WHERE ARE YOUR OTHER "UNCLES"?
I'M LEAVING.
ALONE.
OH.
SOME OF THEM ARE NICE, BUT-- THEY LOOK AT ME FUNNY. LIKE THEY KNOW ME.
YEAH, THEY DO THAT. SO... YOU WANTED TO SAY GOODBYE...?
WHAT DID MY DADDY'S LETTER SAY? I WANT TO KNOW.
IT WAS A JOKE.
A KNOCK-KNOCK JOKE?
NO, A-- A GROWN-UP JOKE.

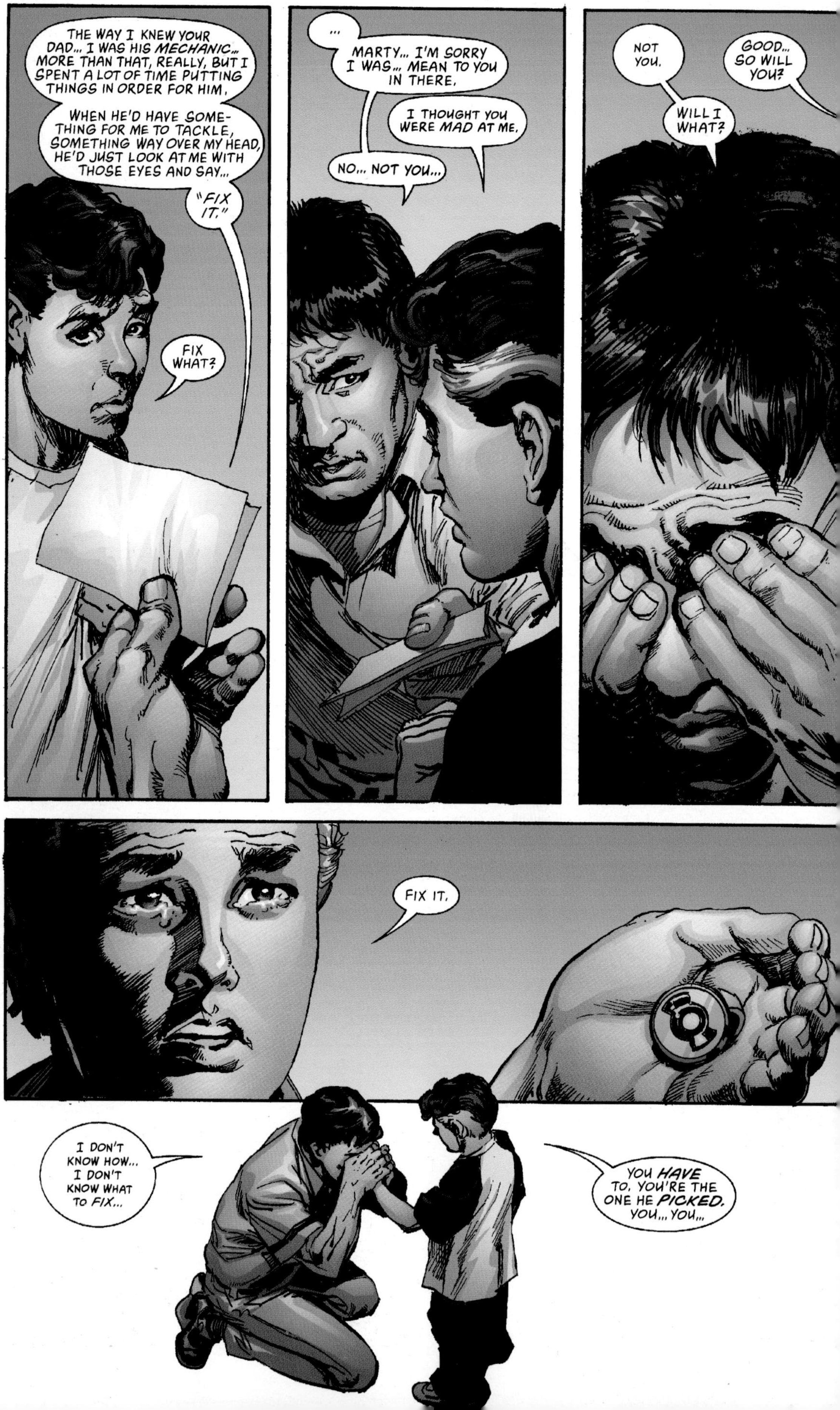
THE WAY I KNEW YOUR DAD... I WAS HIS MECHANIC... MORE THAN THAT, REALLY, BUT I SPENT A LOT OF TIME PUTTING THINGS IN ORDER FOR HIM.
WHEN HE'D HAVE SOMETHING FOR ME TO TACKLE, SOMETHING WAY OVER MY HEAD, HE'D JUST LOOK AT ME WITH THOSE EYES AND SAY...
"FIX IT."
FIX WHAT?
...
MARTY... I'M SORRY I WAS... MEAN TO YOU IN THERE.
I THOUGHT YOU WERE MAD AT ME.
NO... NOT YOU...
NOT YOU.
GOOD... SO WILL YOU?
WILL I WHAT?
FIX IT.
I DON'T KNOW HOW... I DON'T KNOW WHAT TO FIX...
YOU HAVE TO. YOU'RE THE ONE HE PICKED. YOU... YOU...

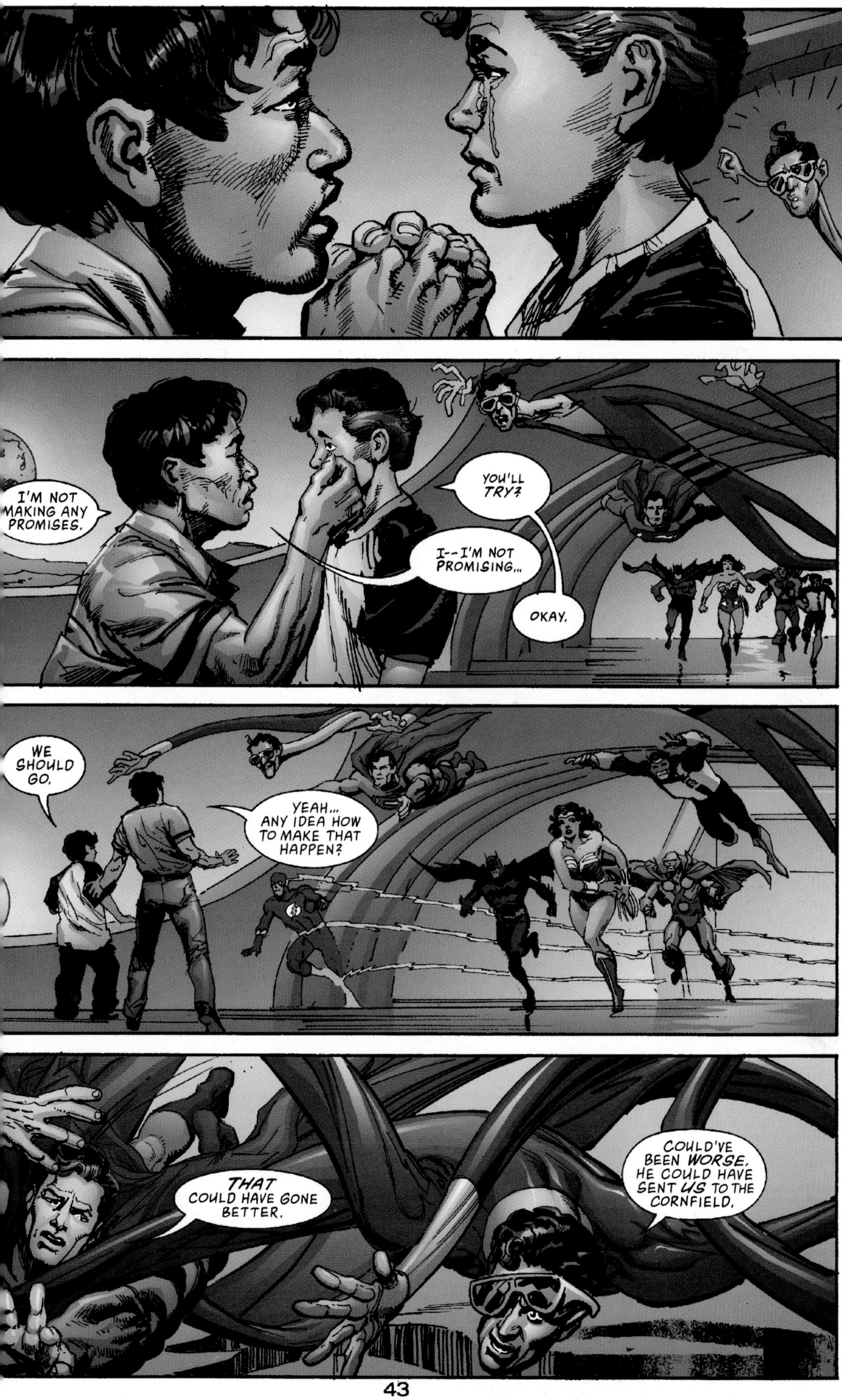
I'M NOT MAKING ANY PROMISES.
YOU'LL TRY?
I--I'M NOT PROMISING...
OKAY.
WE SHOULD GO.
YEAH... ANY IDEA HOW TO MAKE THAT HAPPEN?
THAT COULD HAVE GONE BETTER.
COULD'VE BEEN WORSE. HE COULD HAVE SENT US TO THE CORNFIELD.

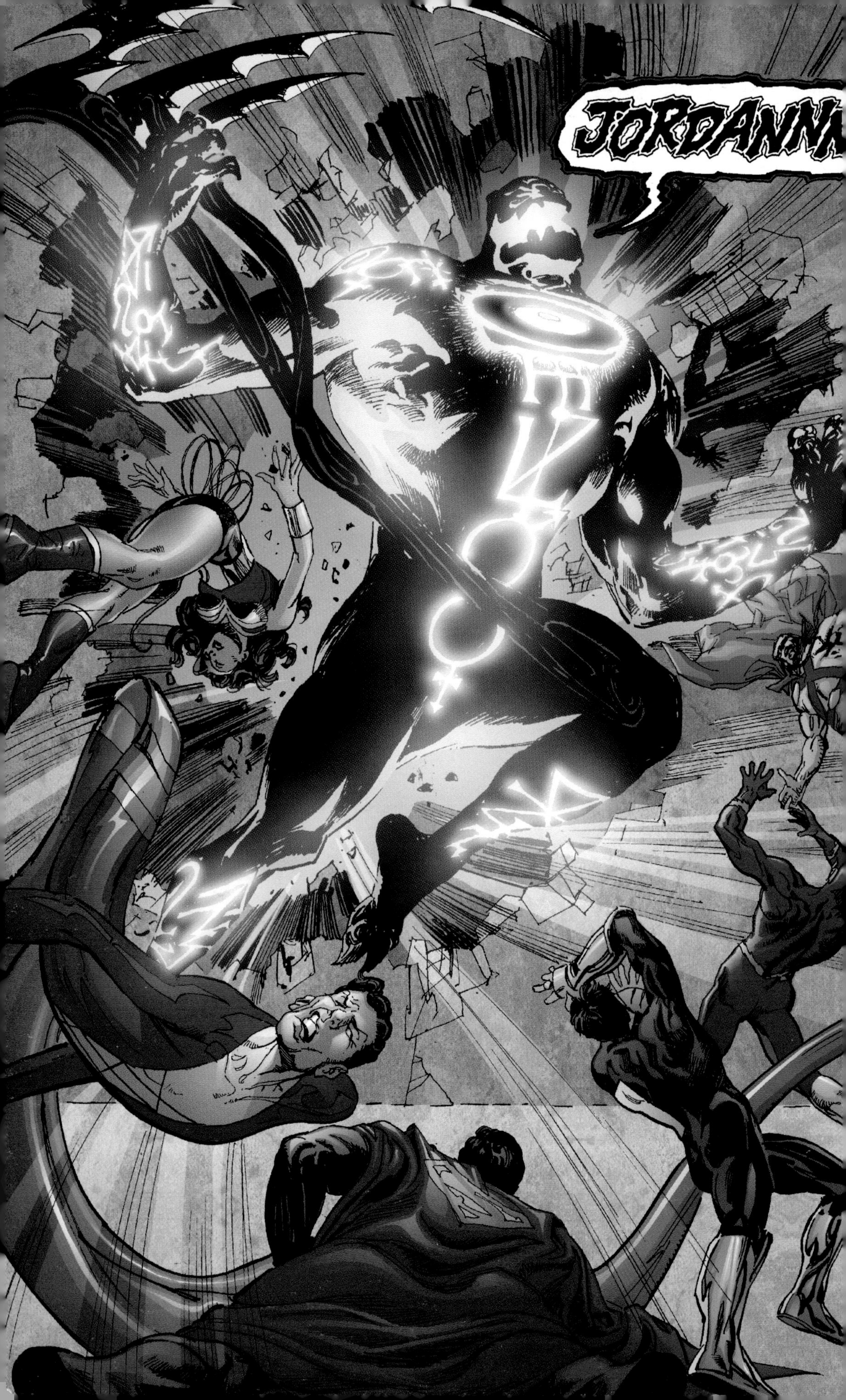
JORDANN

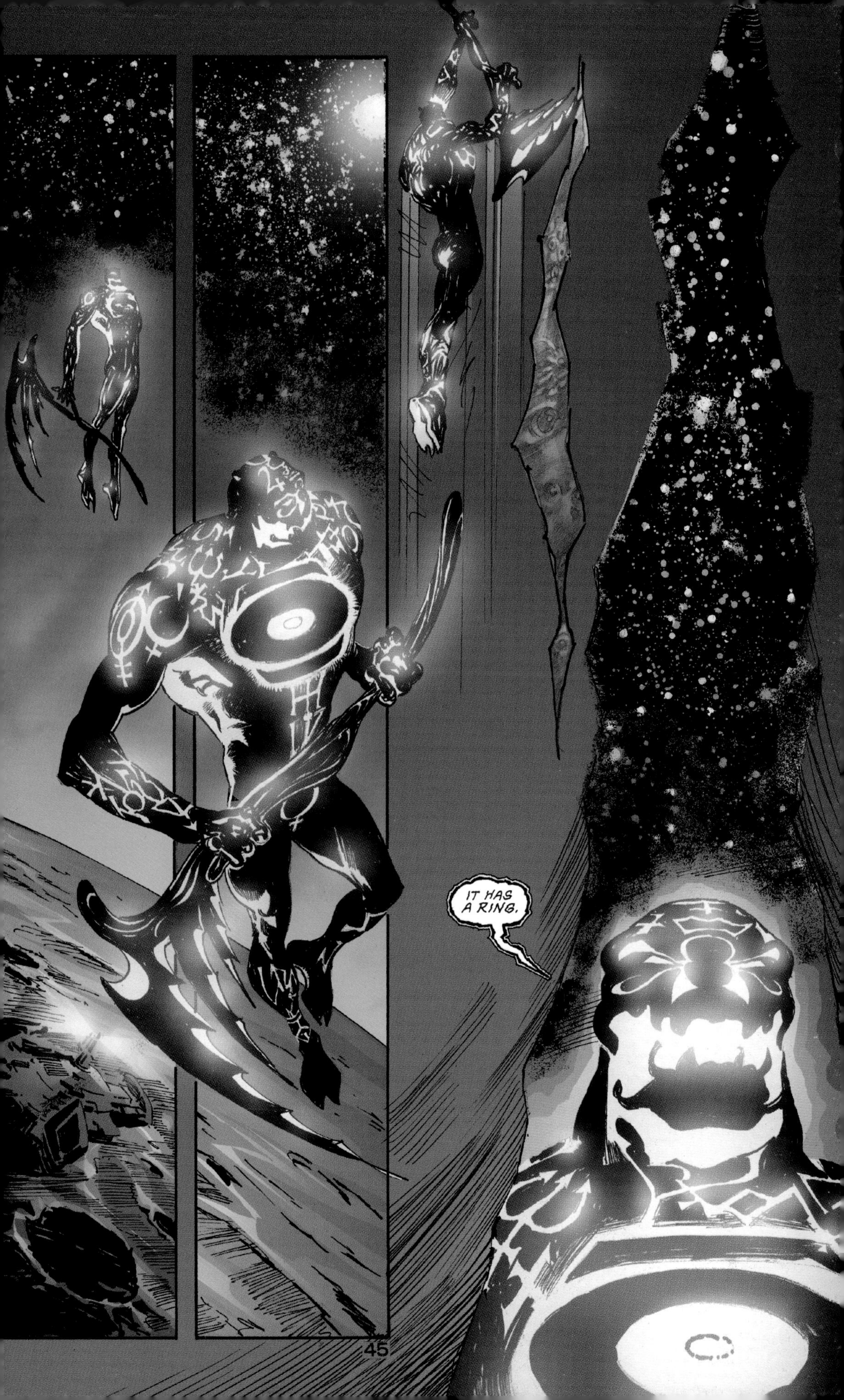
IT HAS A RING.

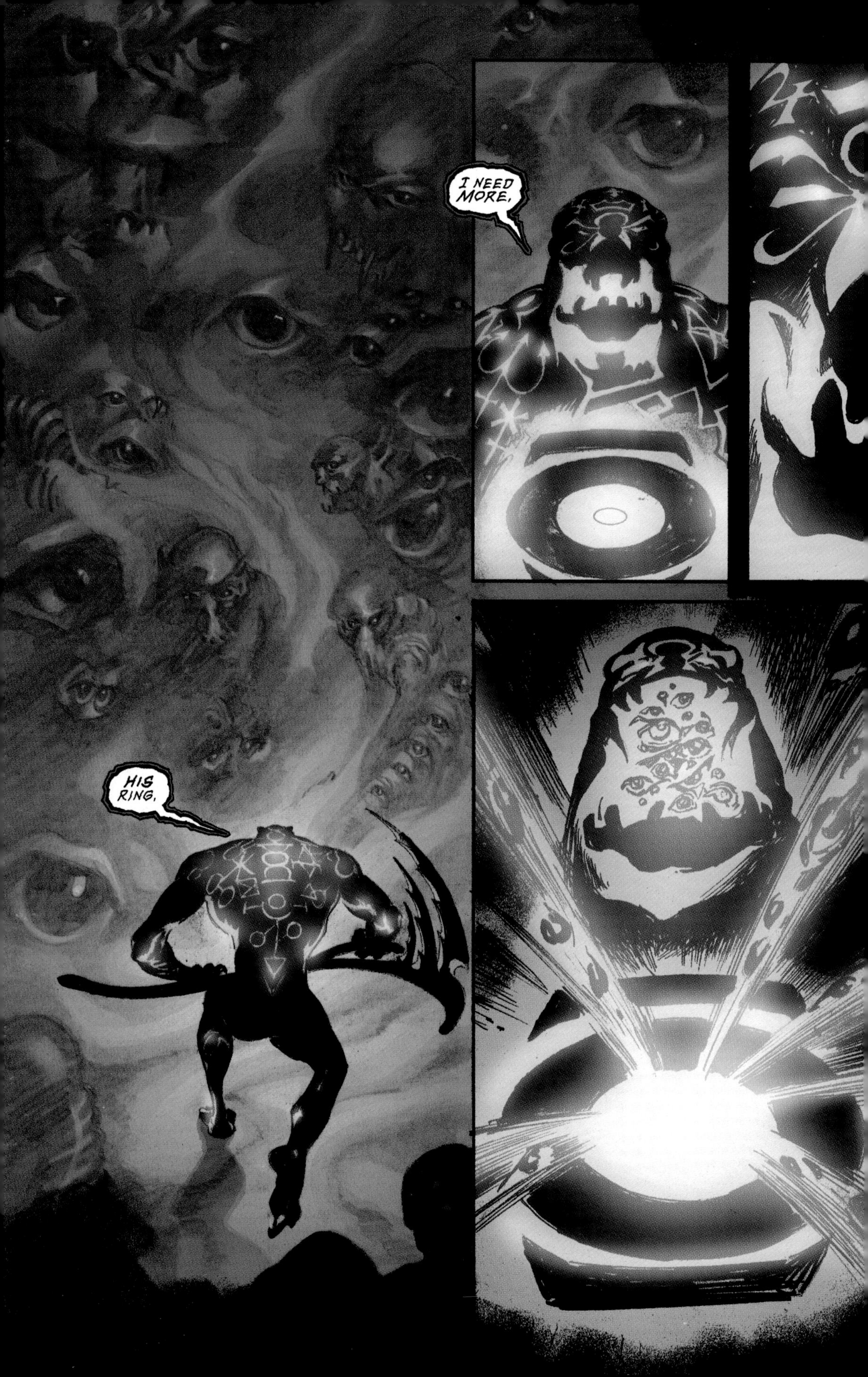
I NEED MORE.
HIS RING.

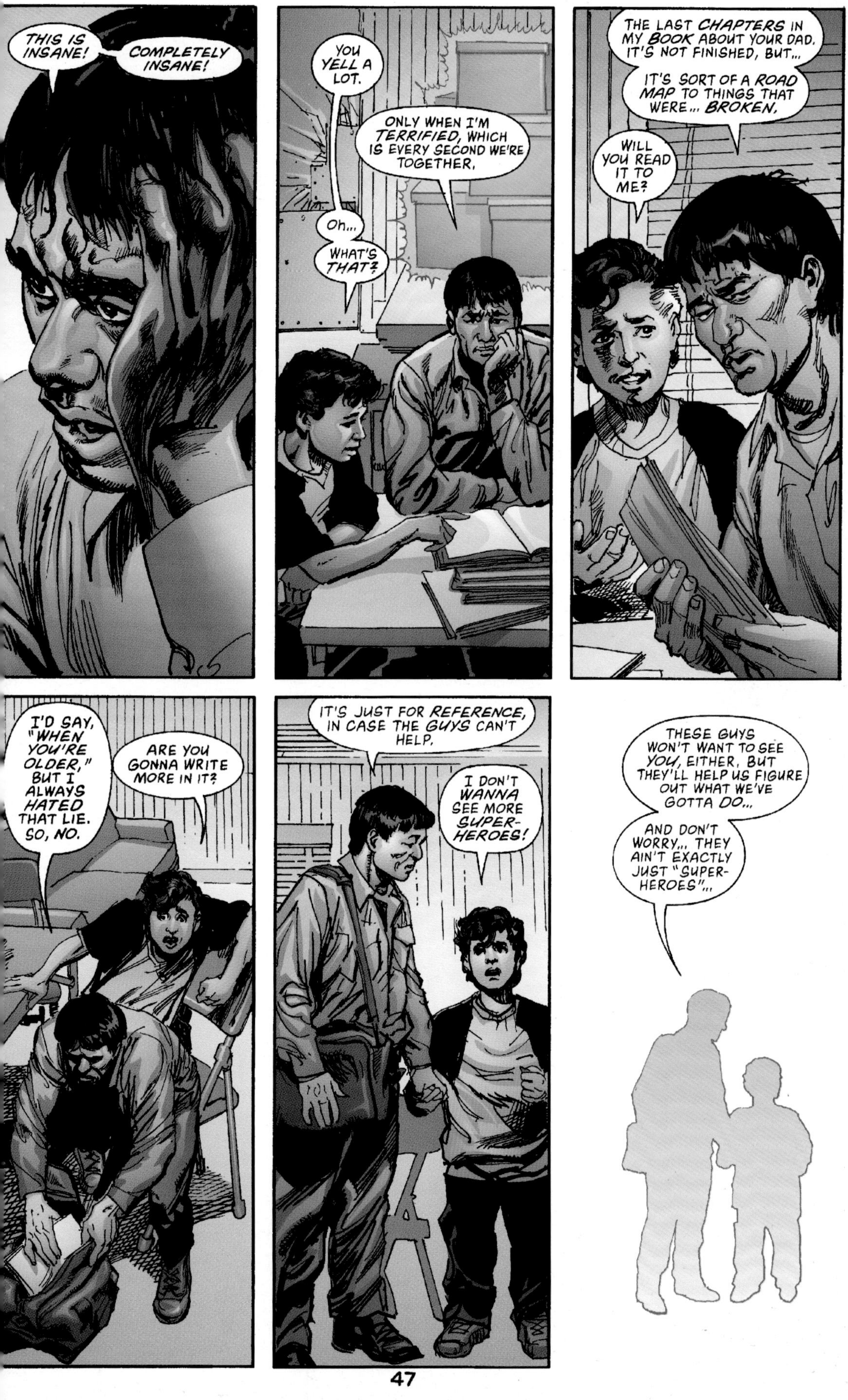
THIS IS INSANE!
COMPLETELY INSANE!
YOU YELL A LOT.
ONLY WHEN I'M TERRIFIED, WHICH IS EVERY SECOND WE'RE TOGETHER.
OH...
WHAT'S THAT?
THE LAST CHAPTERS IN MY BOOK ABOUT YOUR DAD. IT'S NOT FINISHED, BUT...
IT'S SORT OF A ROAD MAP TO THINGS THAT WERE... BROKEN.
WILL YOU READ IT TO ME?
ARE YOU GONNA WRITE MORE IN IT?
I'D SAY, "WHEN YOU'RE OLDER," BUT I ALWAYS HATED THAT LIE. SO, NO.
IT'S JUST FOR REFERENCE, IN CASE THE GUYS CAN'T HELP.
I DON'T WANNA SEE MORE SUPER-HEROES!
THESE GUYS WON'T WANT TO SEE YOU, EITHER, BUT THEY'LL HELP US FIGURE OUT WHAT WE'VE GOTTA DO...
AND DON'T WORRY... THEY AIN'T EXACTLY JUST "SUPER-HEROES"...

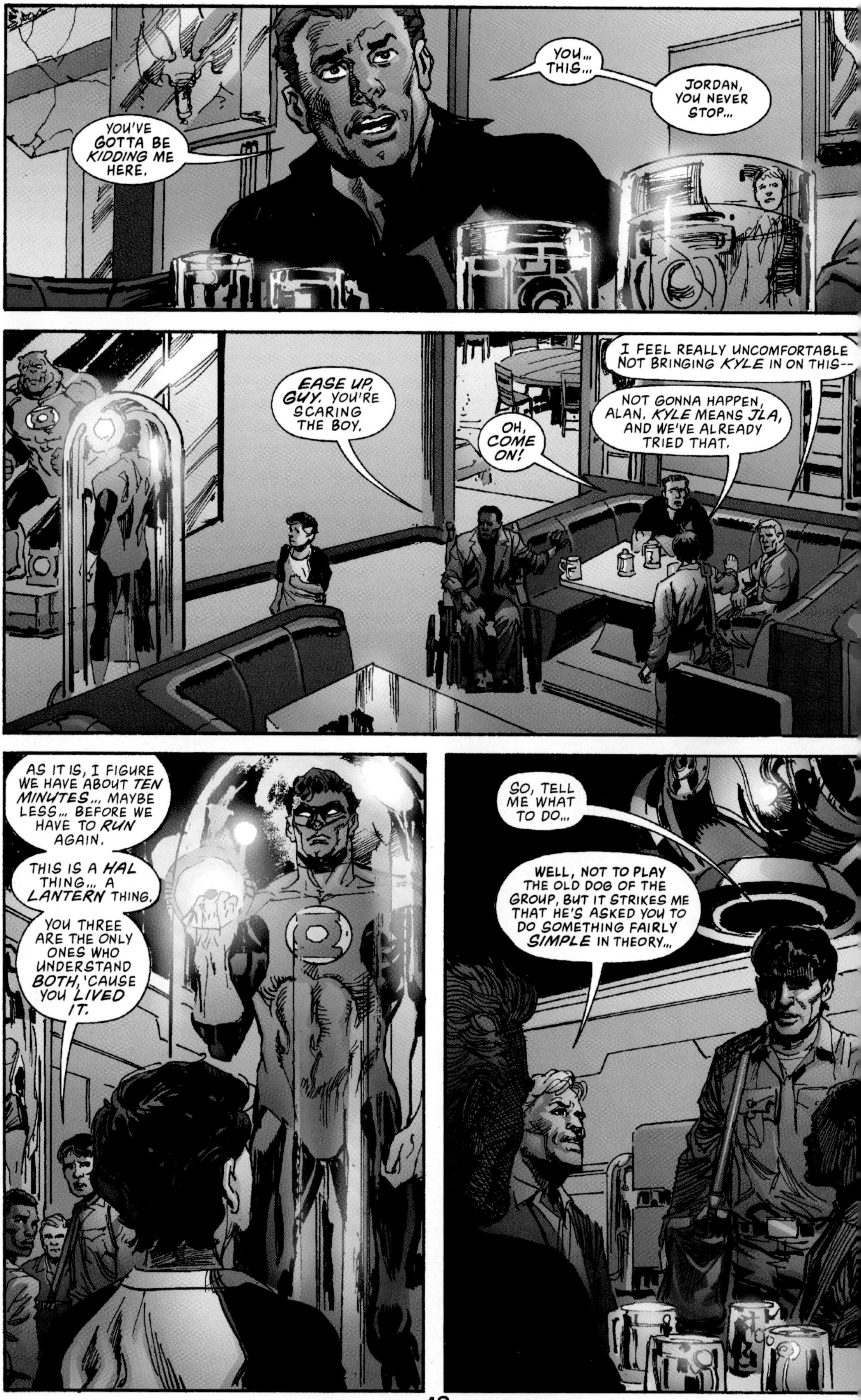
YOU'VE GOTTA BE KIDDING ME HERE.
YOU... THIS...
JORDAN, YOU NEVER STOP...
EASE UP, GUY. YOU'RE SCARING THE BOY.
OH, COME ON!
I FEEL REALLY UNCOMFORTABLE NOT BRINGING KYLE IN ON THIS--
NOT GONNA HAPPEN, ALAN. KYLE MEANS JLA, AND WE'VE ALREADY TRIED THAT.
AS IT IS, I FIGURE WE HAVE ABOUT TEN MINUTES... MAYBE LESS... BEFORE WE HAVE TO RUN AGAIN.
THIS IS A HAL THING... A LANTERN THING.
YOU THREE ARE THE ONLY ONES WHO UNDERSTAND BOTH, 'CAUSE YOU LIVED IT.
SO, TELL ME WHAT TO DO...
WELL, NOT TO PLAY THE OLD DOG OF THE GROUP, BUT IT STRIKES ME THAT HE'S ASKED YOU TO DO SOMETHING FAIRLY SIMPLE IN THEORY...

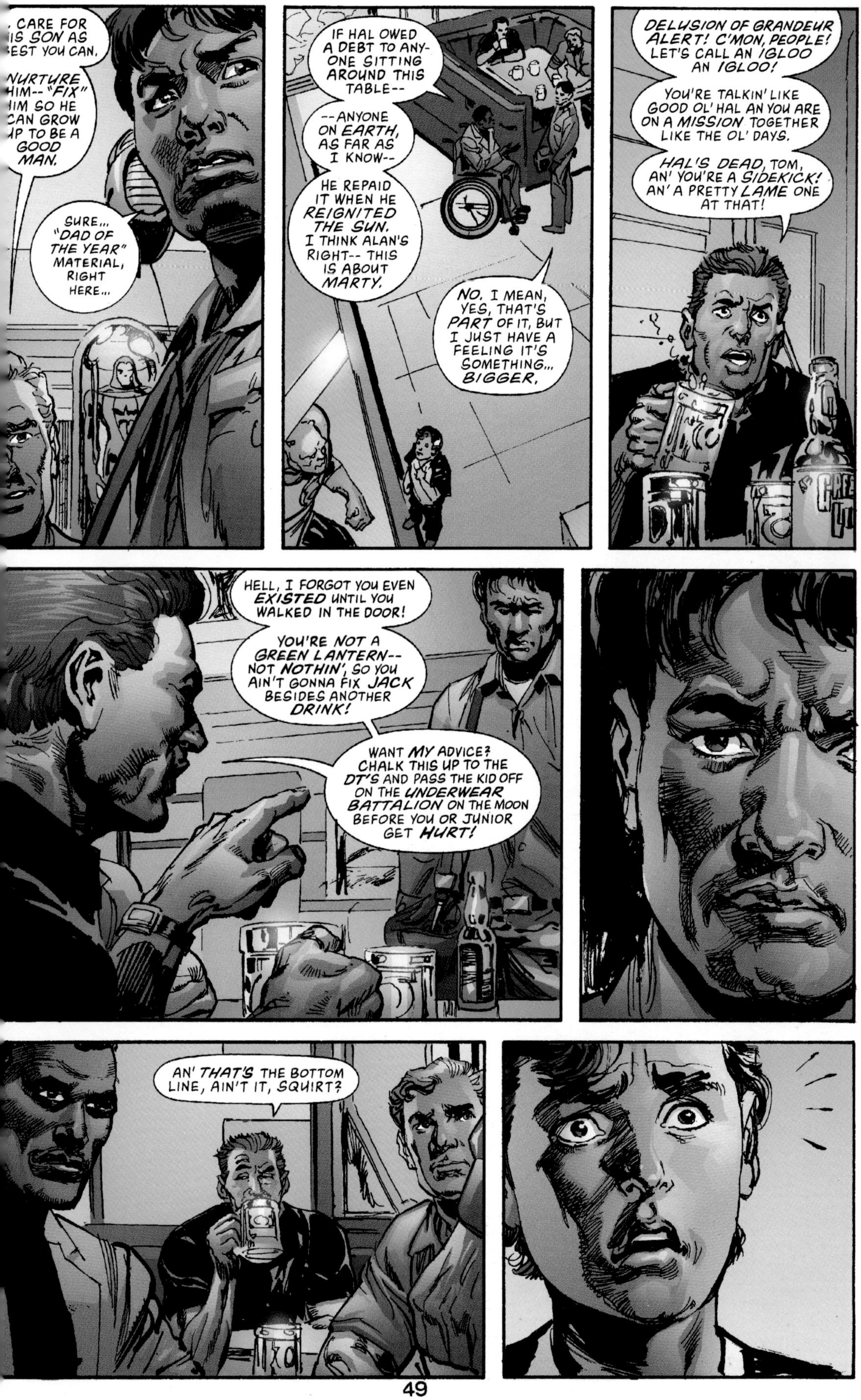

. CARE FOR IS SON AS EST YOU CAN.
NURTURE HIM-- "FIX" IM SO HE CAN GROW P TO BE A GOOD MAN.
SURE... "DAD OF THE YEAR" MATERIAL, RIGHT HERE...
IF HAL OWED A DEBT TO ANY-ONE SITTING AROUND THIS TABLE--
--ANYONE ON EARTH, AS FAR AS I KNOW--
HE REPAID IT WHEN HE REIGNITED THE SUN. I THINK ALAN'S RIGHT-- THIS IS ABOUT MARTY.
NO. I MEAN, YES, THAT'S PART OF IT, BUT I JUST HAVE A FEELING IT'S SOMETHING... BIGGER.
DELUSION OF GRANDEUR ALERT! C'MON, PEOPLE! LET'S CALL AN IGLOO AN IGLOO!
YOU'RE TALKIN' LIKE GOOD OL' HAL AN YOU ARE ON A MISSION TOGETHER LIKE THE OL' DAYS.
HAL'S DEAD, TOM, AN' YOU'RE A SIDEKICK! AN' A PRETTY LAME ONE AT THAT!
HELL, I FORGOT YOU EVEN EXISTED UNTIL YOU WALKED IN THE DOOR!
YOU'RE NOT A GREEN LANTERN-- NOT NOTHIN', SO YOU AIN'T GONNA FIX JACK BESIDES ANOTHER DRINK!
WANT MY ADVICE? CHALK THIS UP TO THE DT'S AND PASS THE KID OFF ON THE UNDERWEAR BATTALION ON THE MOON BEFORE YOU OR JUNIOR GET HURT!
AN' THAT'S THE BOTTOM LINE, AIN'T IT, SQUIRT?

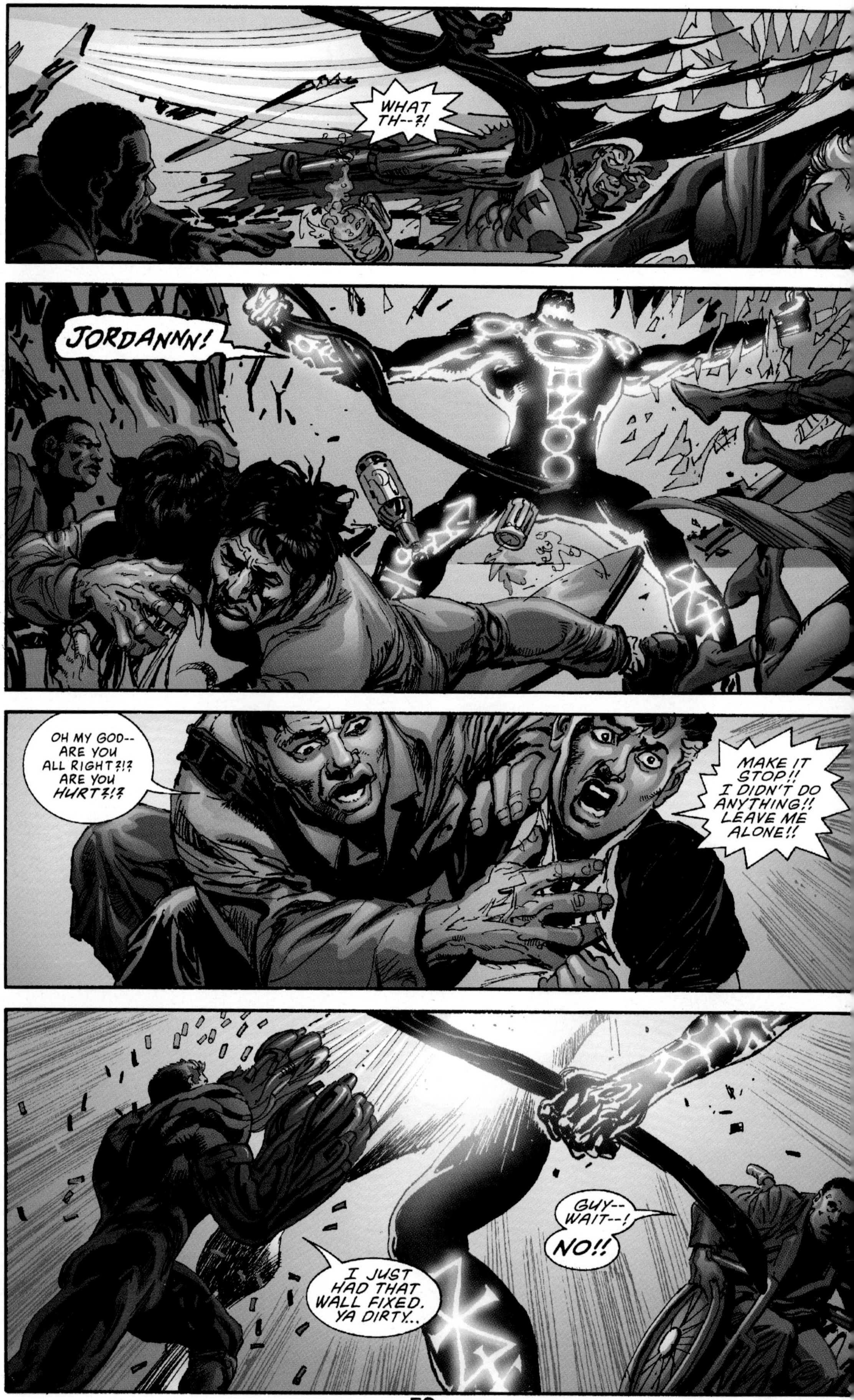
WHAT TH--?!
JORDANNN!
OH MY GOD-- ARE YOU ALL RIGHT?!? ARE YOU HURT?!?
MAKE IT STOP!! I DIDN'T DO ANYTHING!! LEAVE ME ALONE!!
GUY-- WAIT--!
NO!!
I JUST HAD THAT WALL FIXED. YA DIRTY..

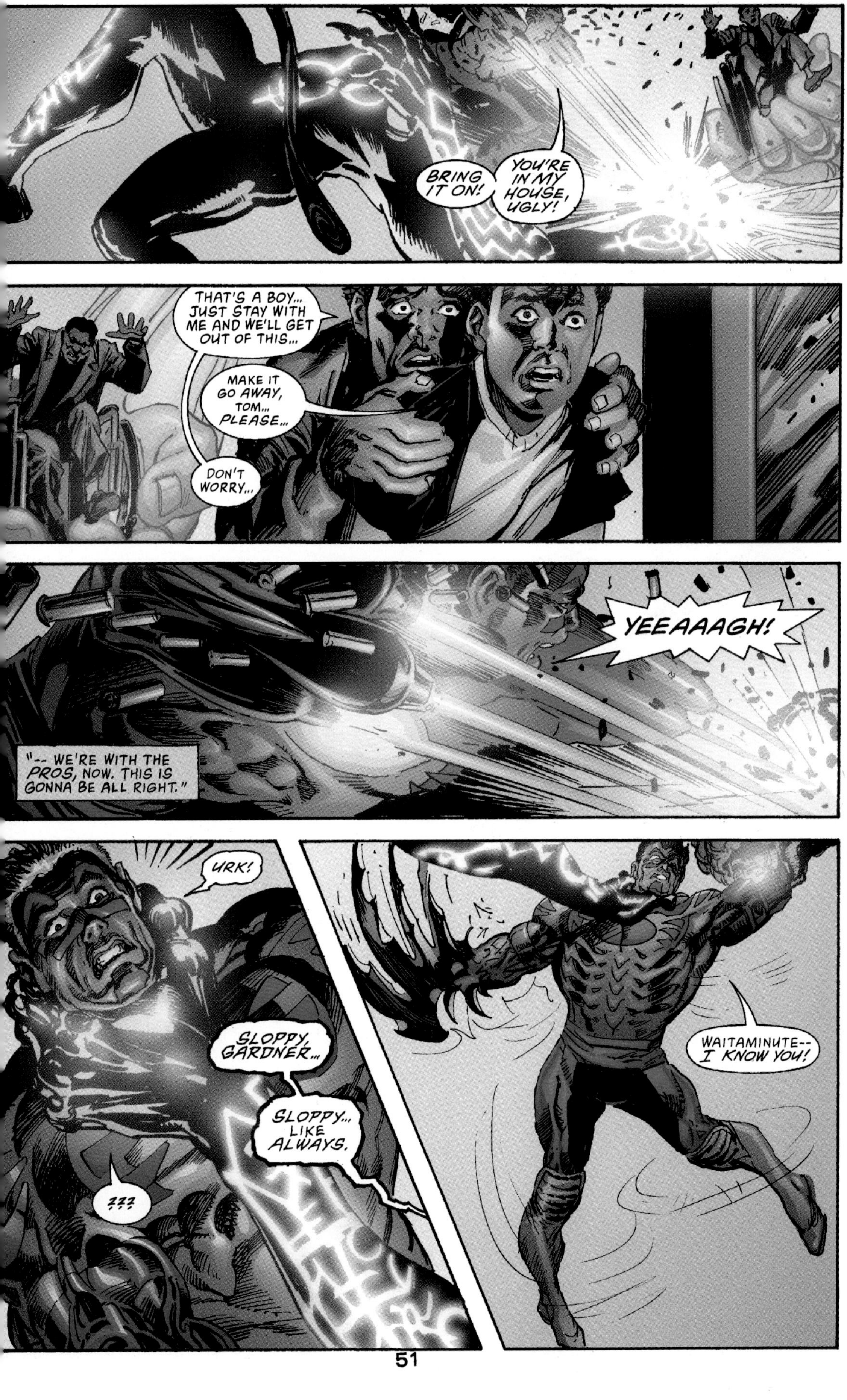

BRING IT ON!
YOU'RE IN MY HOUSE, UGLY!
THAT'S A BOY... JUST STAY WITH ME AND WE'LL GET OUT OF THIS...
MAKE IT GO AWAY, TOM... PLEASE...
DON'T WORRY...
"-- WE'RE WITH THE PROS, NOW. THIS IS GONNA BE ALL RIGHT."
YEEAAAGH!
URK!
SLOPPY, GARDNER...
SLOPPY... LIKE ALWAYS.
???
WAITAMINUTE-- I KNOW YOU!

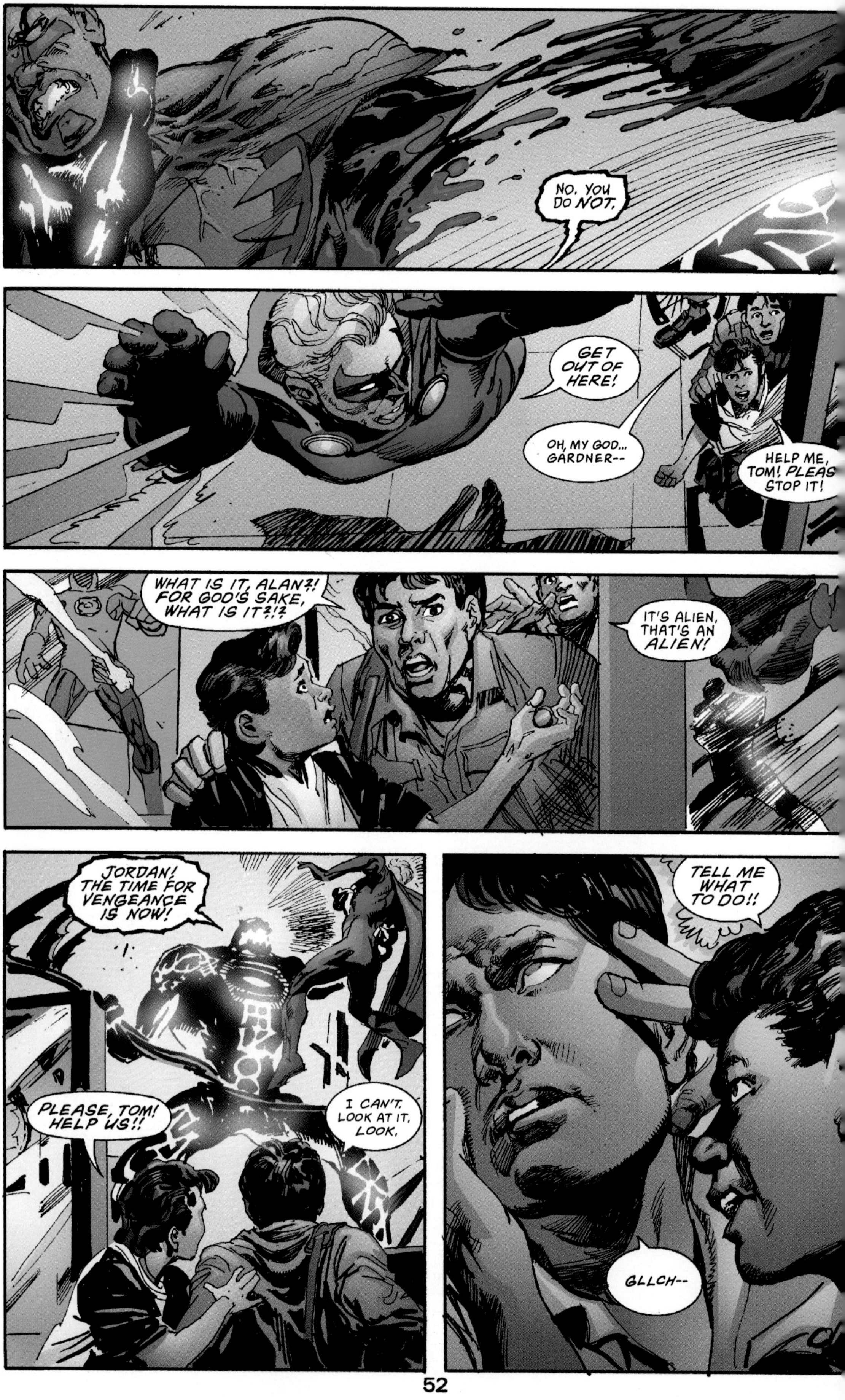
NO, YOU DO NOT.
GET OUT OF HERE!
OH, MY GOD... GARDNER--
HELP ME, TOM! PLEAS STOP IT!
WHAT IS IT, ALAN?! FOR GOD'S SAKE, WHAT IS IT?!?
IT'S ALIEN, THAT'S AN ALIEN!
JORDAN! THE TIME FOR VENGEANCE IS NOW!
PLEASE, TOM! HELP US!!
I CAN'T. LOOK AT IT, LOOK.
TELL ME WHAT TO DO!!
GLLCH--

The ring," Hal said,
"responds to will power.
Simple as that."
"But, what can it do?"
I asked again--
still confused.

"Anything." He said,
"Everything. If you
will it--

"--it happens."

It forges dreams and
thoughts into matter.
It reads minds. It
lets you fly, become
invisible, pass through
walls, teleport through
space— walk through
time."

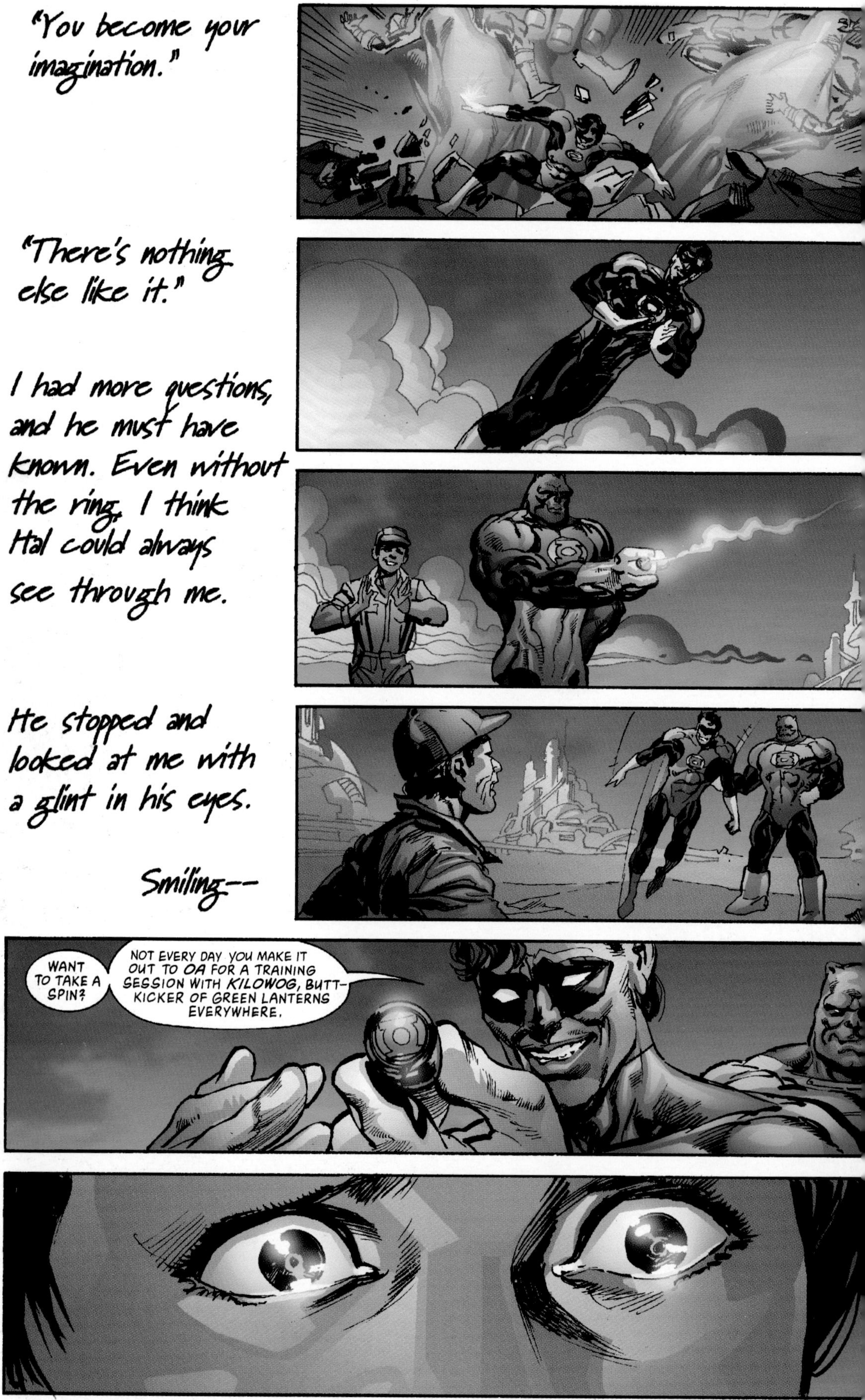
"You become your imagination."
"There's nothing else like it."
I had more questions, and he must have known. Even without the ring, I think Hal could always see through me.
He stopped and looked at me with a glint in his eyes.
Smiling--
WANT TO TAKE A SPIN?
NOT EVERY DAY YOU MAKE IT OUT TO OA FOR A TRAINING SESSION WITH KILOWOG, BUTT-KICKER OF GREEN LANTERNS EVERYWHERE.

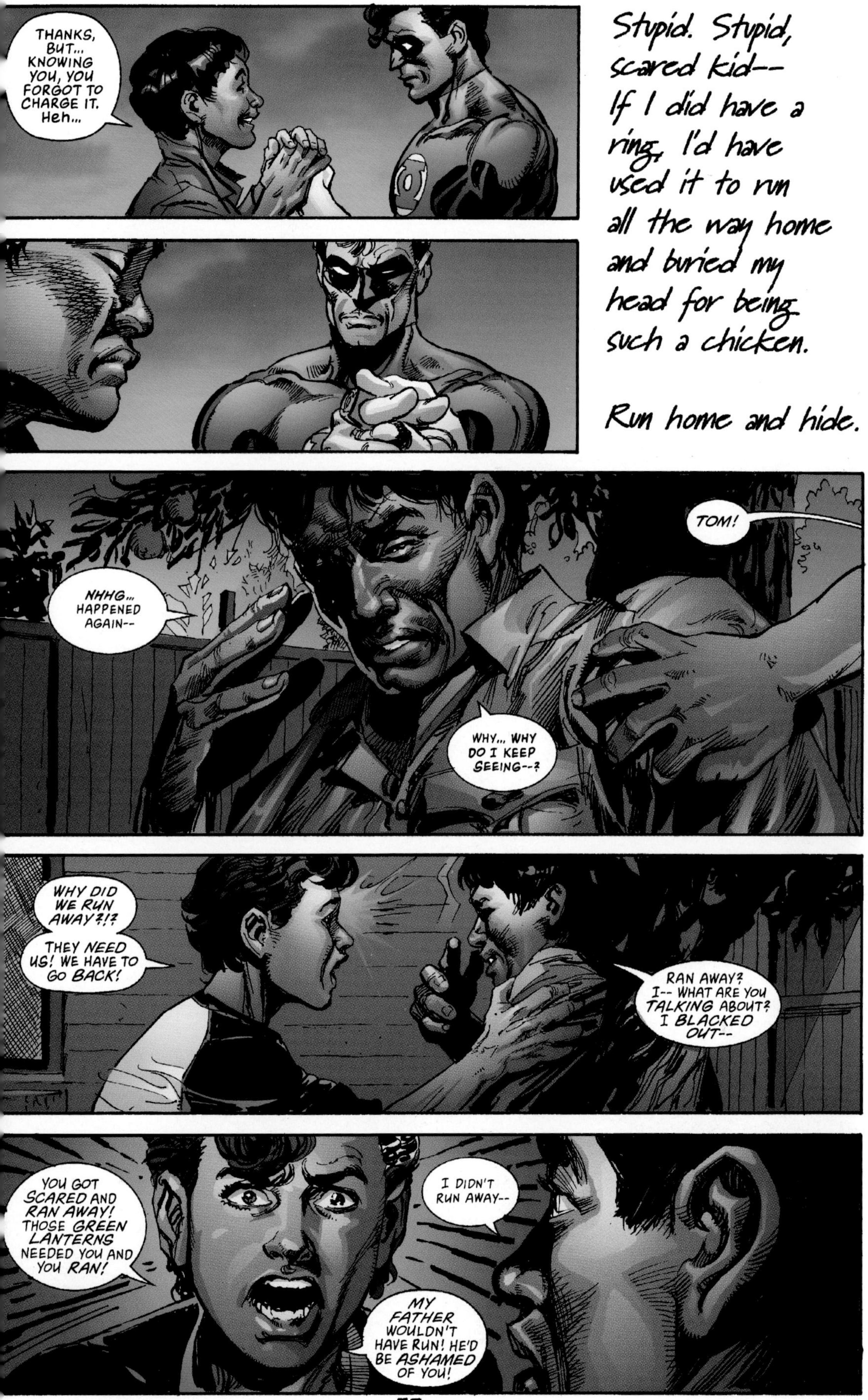
THANKS, BUT... KNOWING YOU, YOU FORGOT TO CHARGE IT. Heh...
Stupid. Stupid, scared kid-- If I did have a ring, I'd have used it to run all the way home and buried my head for being such a chicken.
Run home and hide.
TOM!
NHHG... HAPPENED AGAIN--
WHY... WHY DO I KEEP SEEING--?
WHY DID WE RUN AWAY?!?
THEY NEED US! WE HAVE TO GO BACK!
RAN AWAY? I-- WHAT ARE YOU TALKING ABOUT? I BLACKED OUT--
YOU GOT SCARED AND RAN AWAY! THOSE GREEN LANTERNS NEEDED YOU AND YOU RAN!
I DIDN'T RUN AWAY--
MY FATHER WOULDN'T HAVE RUN! HE'D BE ASHAMED OF YOU!

SHUT UP!

NNGH!

HOW DARE YOU LECTURE ME ABOUT *SHAME* AND YOUR *FATHER!*

YOU DON'T KNOW ANYTHING ABOUT ME-- AND *LESS* ABOUT *HIM!*

HE WAS *GREEN LANTERN!* HE WAS *BRAVE* AND *SMART* AND THE *BEST!* HE WOULDN'T BE *AFRAID* OF A *MONSTER* LIKE YOU ARE!

THERE WAS *NOTHING* HE COULDN'T DO OR *FIX* AND YOU'RE *STUPID!*

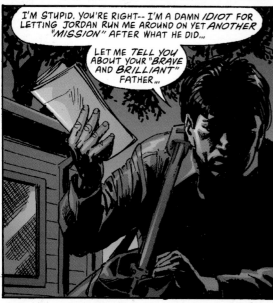

I'M STUPID. YOU'RE RIGHT-- I'M A DAMN *IDIOT* FOR LETTING JORDAN RUN ME AROUND ON YET *ANOTHER* "*MISSION*" AFTER WHAT HE DID...

LET ME *TELL* YOU ABOUT YOUR "*BRAVE* AND *BRILLIANT*" FATHER...

... THE *TRAITOR,* THE *MURDERER,*

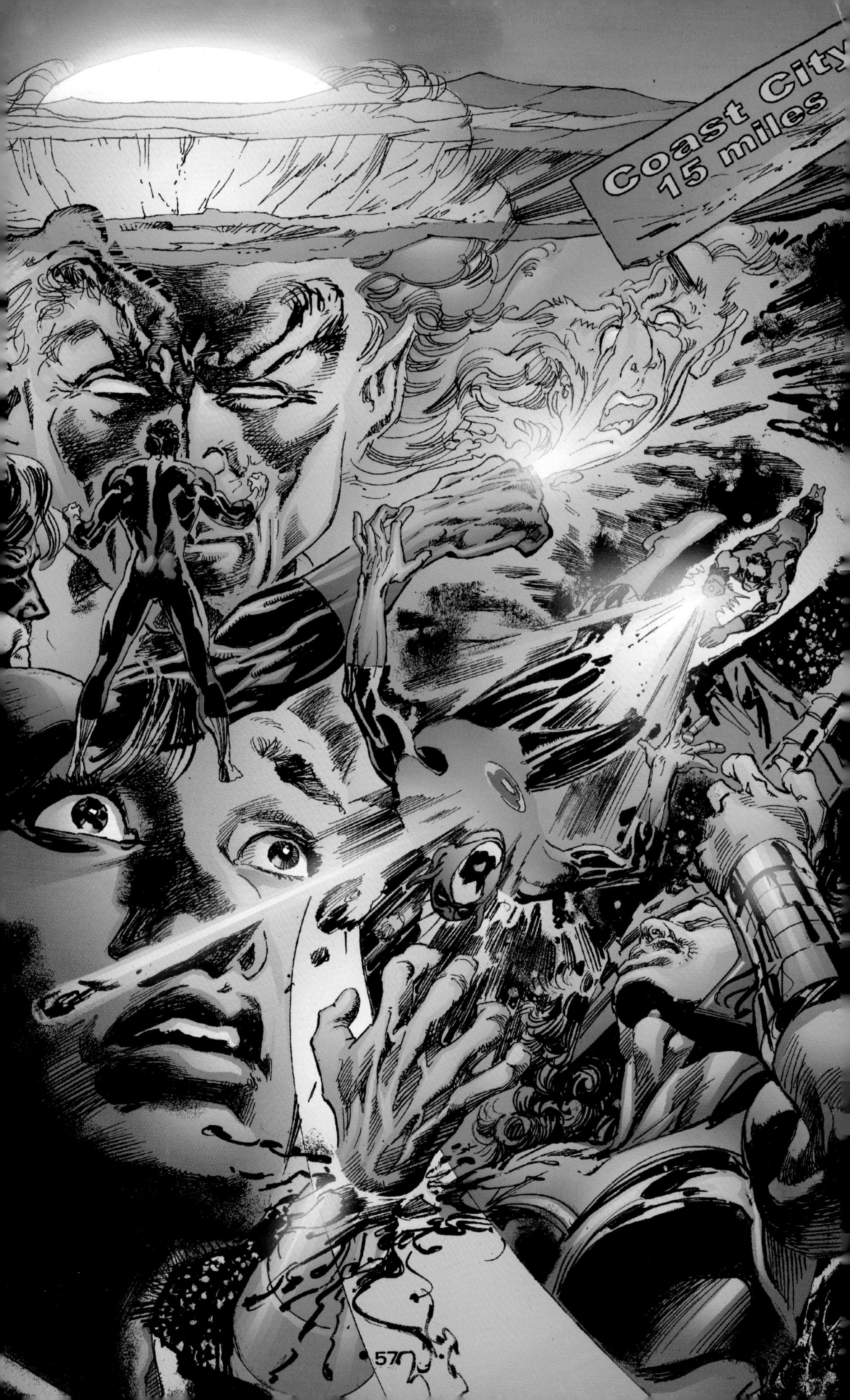
Coast City
15 miles

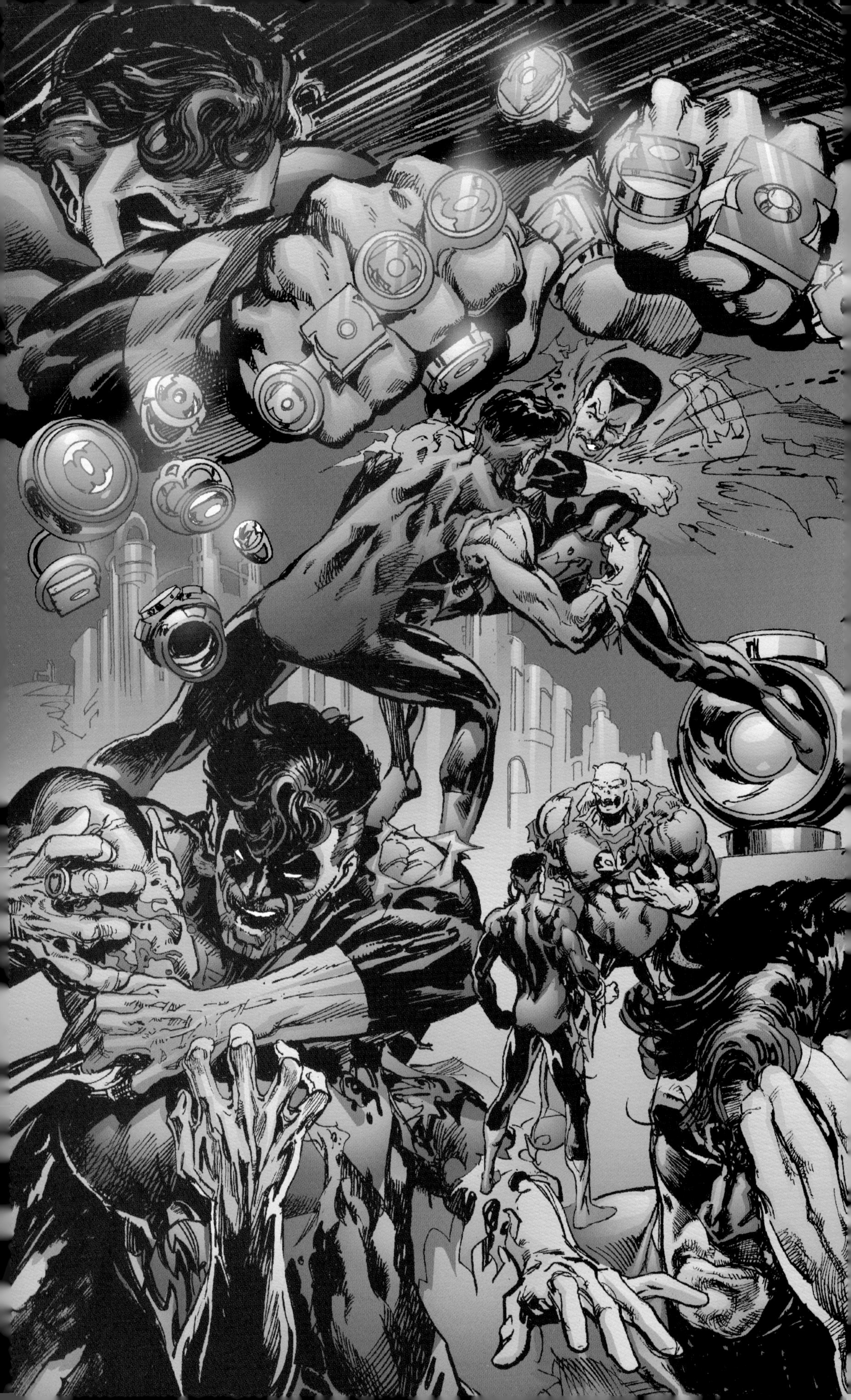

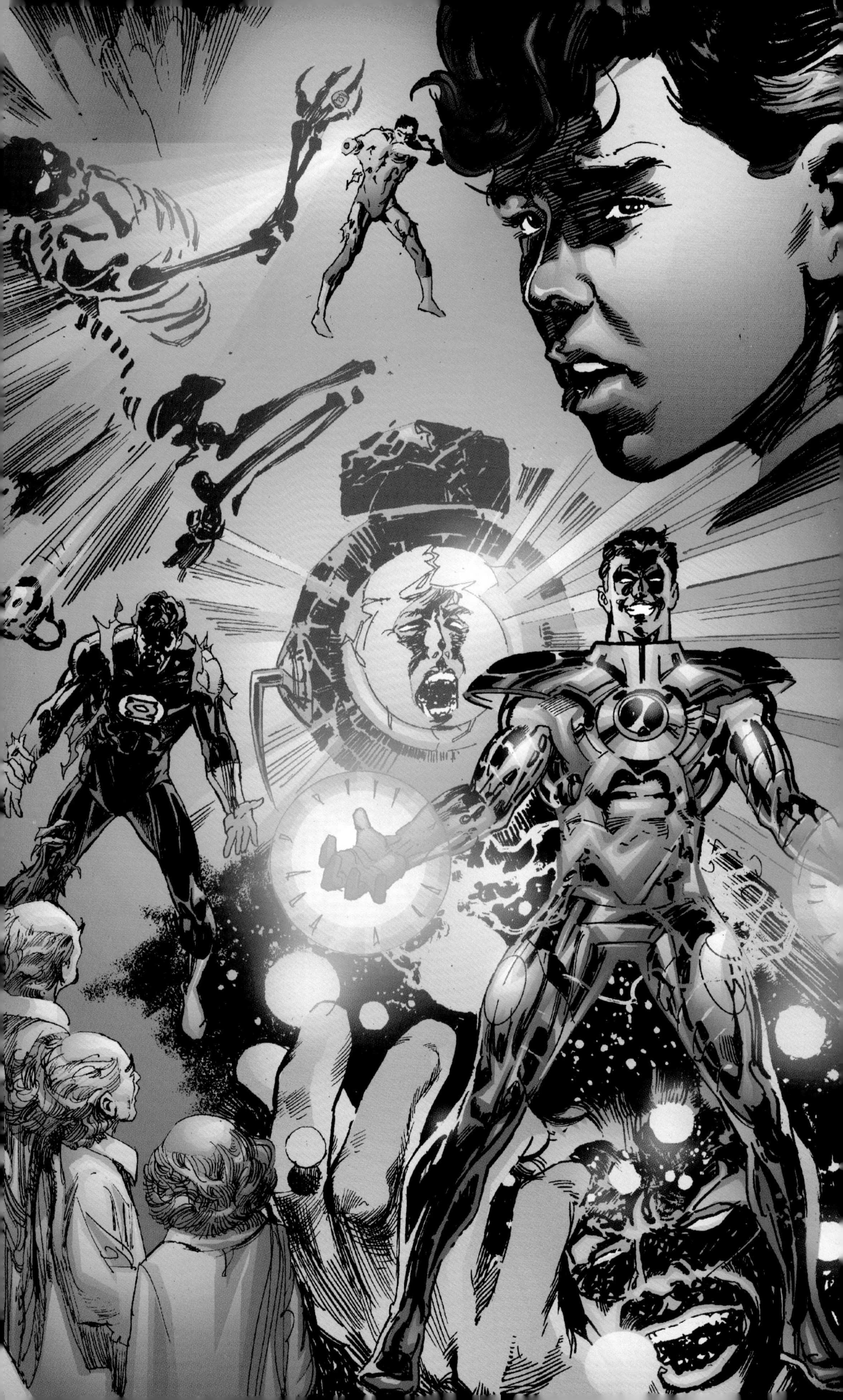

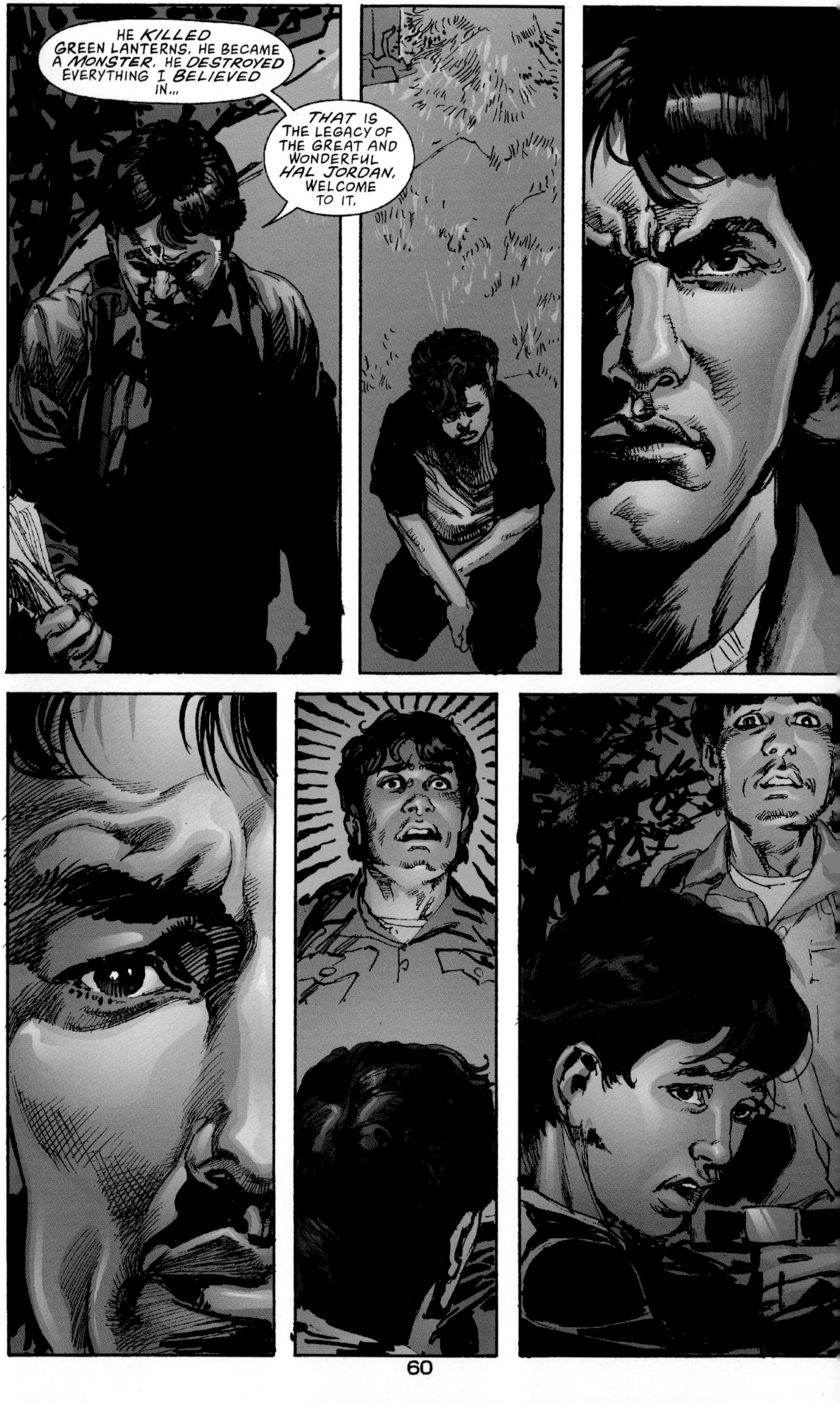
HE KILLED GREEN LANTERNS. HE BECAME A MONSTER. HE DESTROYED EVERYTHING I BELIEVED IN...
THAT IS THE LEGACY OF THE GREAT AND WONDERFUL HAL JORDAN. WELCOME TO IT.

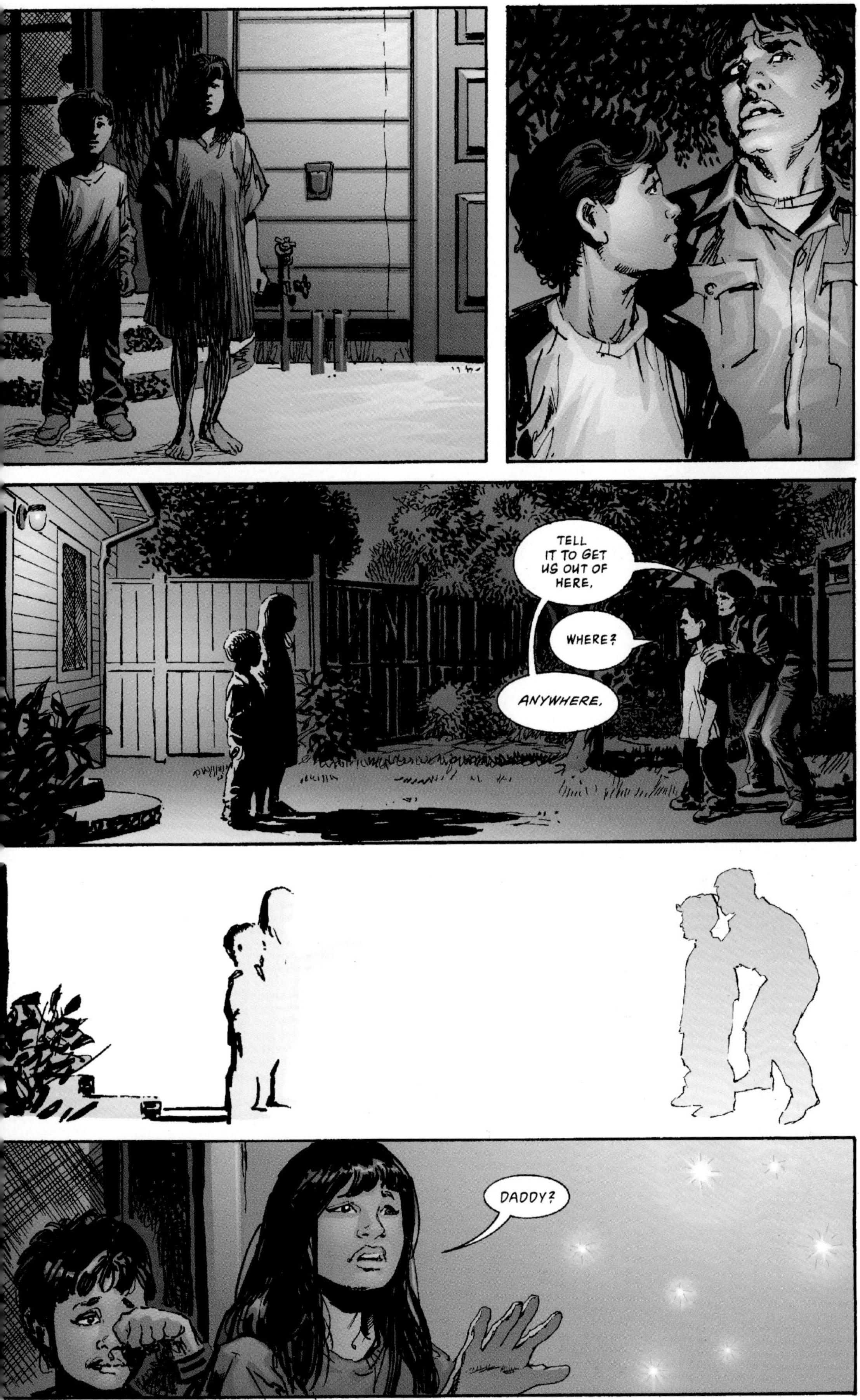
TELL IT TO GET US OUT OF HERE.
WHERE?
ANYWHERE.
DADDY?

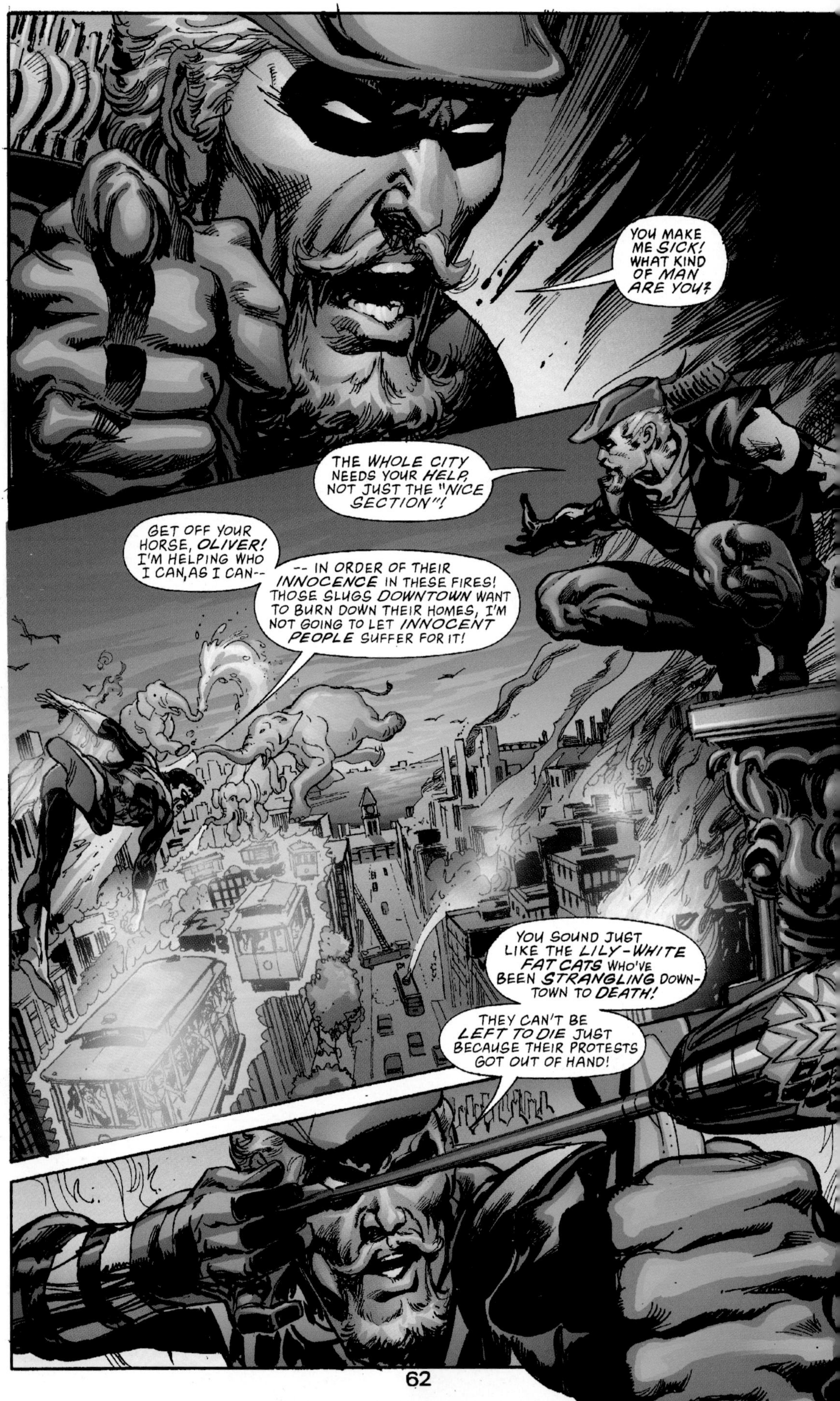
YOU MAKE ME SICK! WHAT KIND OF MAN ARE YOU?
THE WHOLE CITY NEEDS YOUR HELP, NOT JUST THE "NICE SECTION"!
GET OFF YOUR HORSE, OLIVER! I'M HELPING WHO I CAN, AS I CAN--
-- IN ORDER OF THEIR INNOCENCE IN THESE FIRES! THOSE SLUGS DOWNTOWN WANT TO BURN DOWN THEIR HOMES, I'M NOT GOING TO LET INNOCENT PEOPLE SUFFER FOR IT!
YOU SOUND JUST LIKE THE LILY-WHITE FAT CATS WHO'VE BEEN STRANGLING DOWN-TOWN TO DEATH!
THEY CAN'T BE LEFT TO DIE JUST BECAUSE THEIR PROTESTS GOT OUT OF HAND!

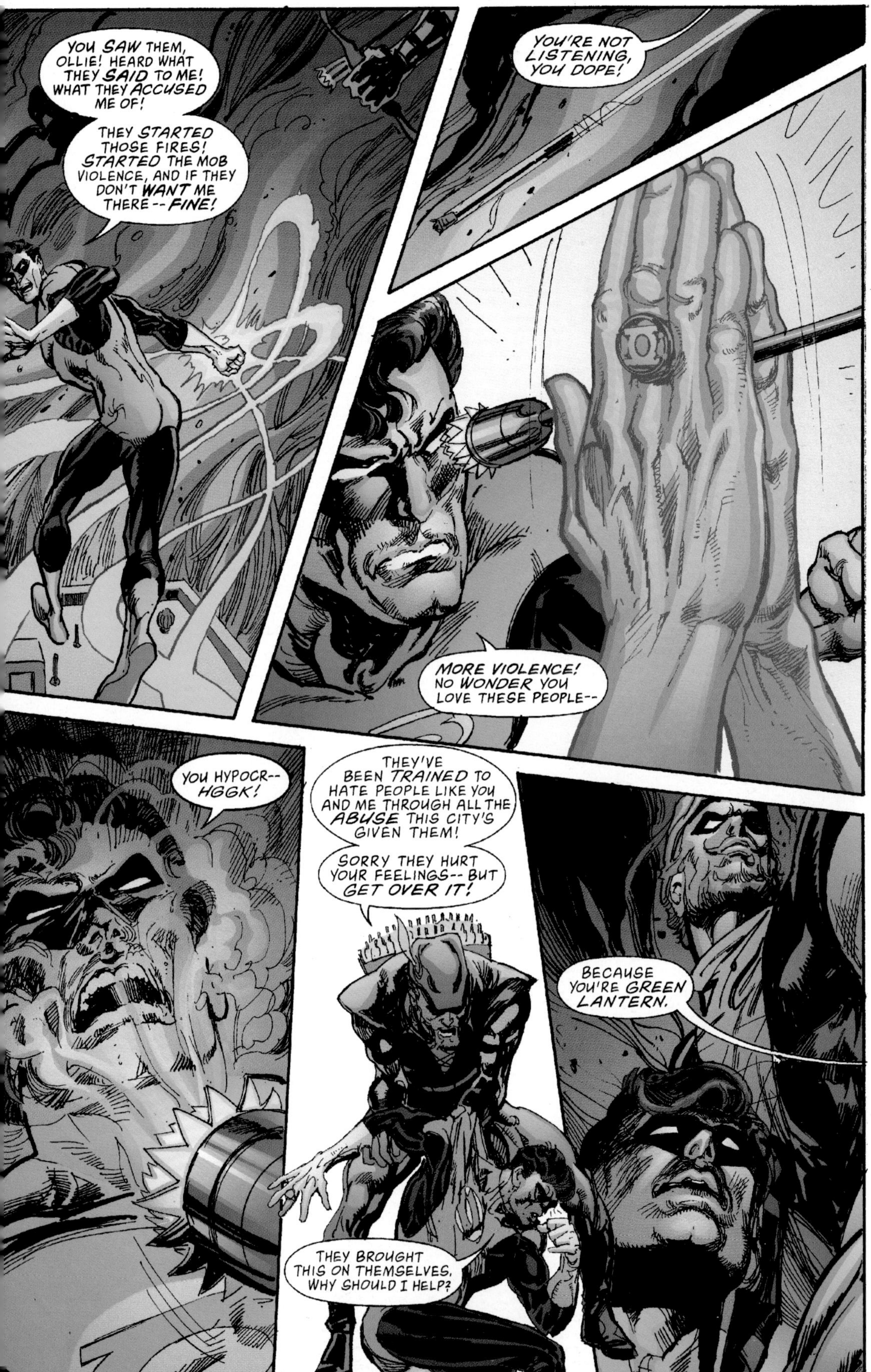
YOU SAW THEM, OLLIE! HEARD WHAT THEY SAID TO ME! WHAT THEY ACCUSED ME OF!
THEY STARTED THOSE FIRES! STARTED THE MOB VIOLENCE, AND IF THEY DON'T WANT ME THERE -- FINE!
YOU'RE NOT LISTENING, YOU DOPE!
MORE VIOLENCE! NO WONDER YOU LOVE THESE PEOPLE--
YOU HYPOCR-- HGGK!
THEY'VE BEEN TRAINED TO HATE PEOPLE LIKE YOU AND ME THROUGH ALL THE ABUSE THIS CITY'S GIVEN THEM!
SORRY THEY HURT YOUR FEELINGS-- BUT GET OVER IT!
THEY BROUGHT THIS ON THEMSELVES. WHY SHOULD I HELP?
BECAUSE YOU'RE GREEN LANTERN.

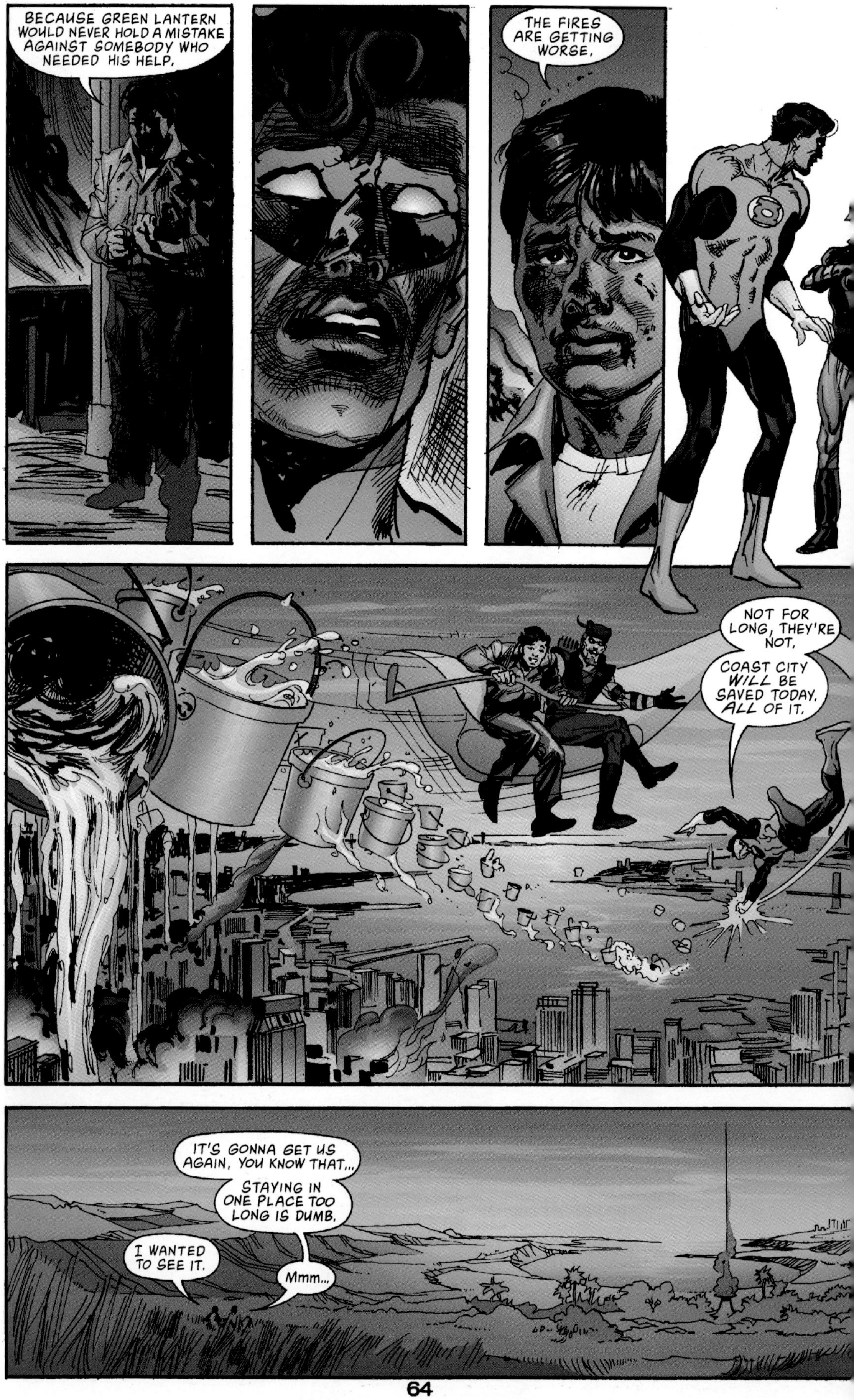

BECAUSE GREEN LANTERN WOULD NEVER HOLD A MISTAKE AGAINST SOMEBODY WHO NEEDED HIS HELP.
THE FIRES ARE GETTING WORSE.
NOT FOR LONG, THEY'RE NOT.
COAST CITY WILL BE SAVED TODAY. ALL OF IT.
IT'S GONNA GET US AGAIN, YOU KNOW THAT...
STAYING IN ONE PLACE TOO LONG IS DUMB.
I WANTED TO SEE IT.
Mmm...

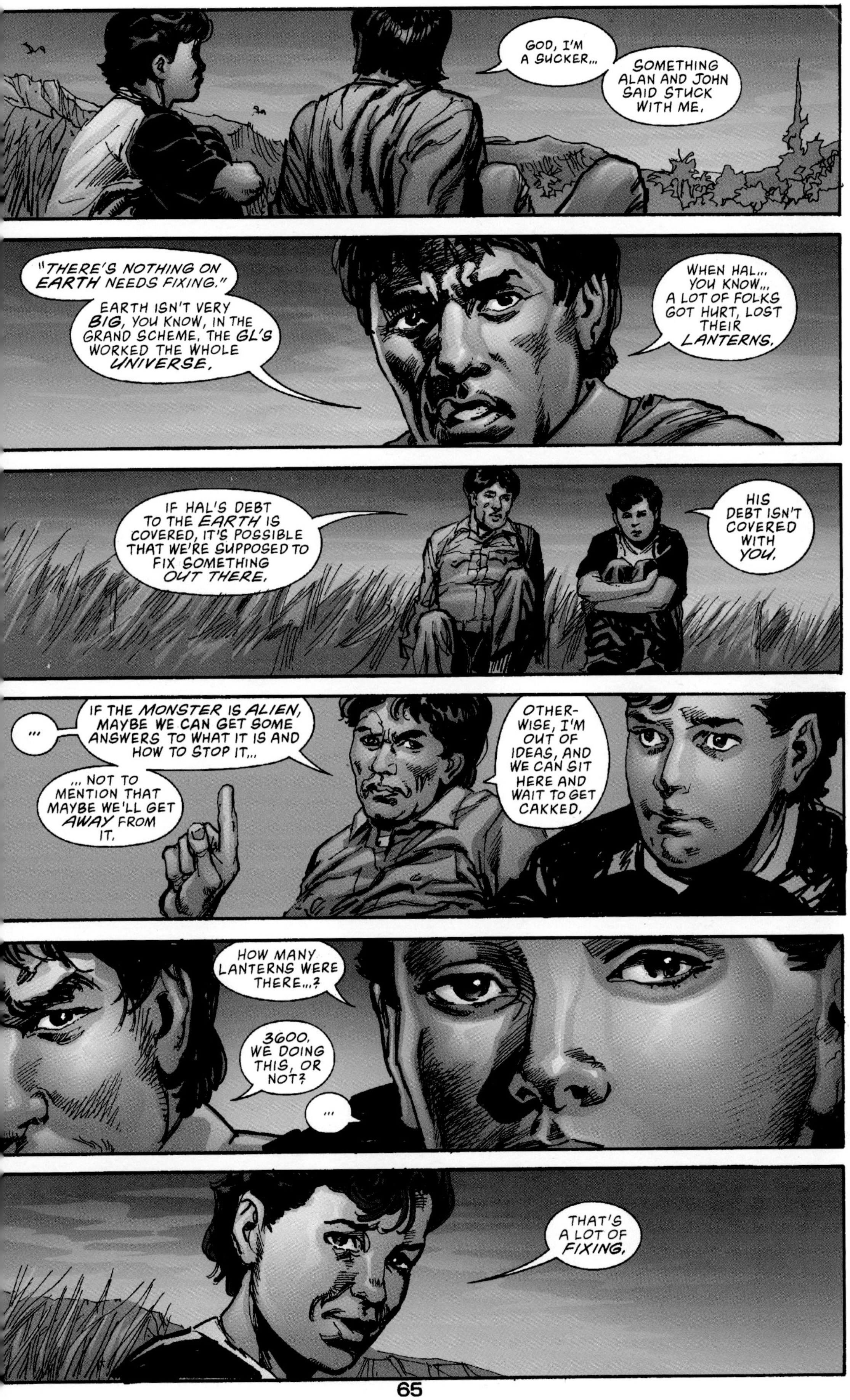
GOD, I'M A SUCKER...
SOMETHING ALAN AND JOHN SAID STUCK WITH ME.
"THERE'S NOTHING ON EARTH NEEDS FIXING."
EARTH ISN'T VERY BIG, YOU KNOW, IN THE GRAND SCHEME. THE GL'S WORKED THE WHOLE UNIVERSE.
WHEN HAL... YOU KNOW... A LOT OF FOLKS GOT HURT, LOST THEIR LANTERNS.
IF HAL'S DEBT TO THE EARTH IS COVERED, IT'S POSSIBLE THAT WE'RE SUPPOSED TO FIX SOMETHING OUT THERE.
HIS DEBT ISN'T COVERED WITH YOU.
...
IF THE MONSTER IS ALIEN, MAYBE WE CAN GET SOME ANSWERS TO WHAT IT IS AND HOW TO STOP IT...
... NOT TO MENTION THAT MAYBE WE'LL GET AWAY FROM IT.
OTHER-WISE, I'M OUT OF IDEAS, AND WE CAN SIT HERE AND WAIT TO GET CAKKED.
HOW MANY LANTERNS WERE THERE...?
3600. WE DOING THIS, OR NOT?
...
THAT'S A LOT OF FIXING.

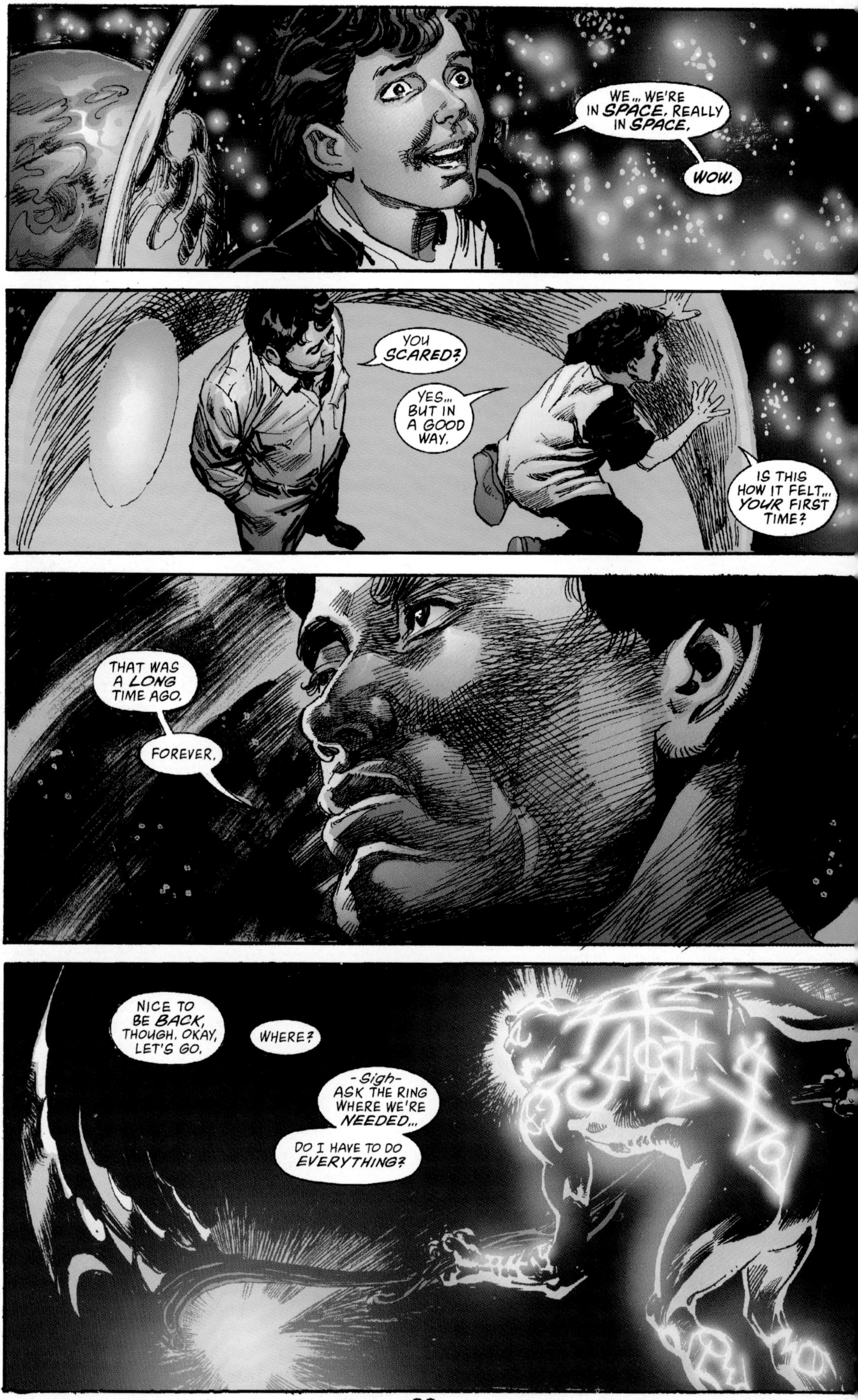
WE... WE'RE IN SPACE. REALLY IN SPACE.
WOW.
YOU SCARED?
YES... BUT IN A GOOD WAY.
IS THIS HOW IT FELT... YOUR FIRST TIME?
THAT WAS A LONG TIME AGO.
FOREVER.
NICE TO BE BACK, THOUGH. OKAY, LET'S GO.
WHERE?
-Sigh- ASK THE RING WHERE WE'RE NEEDED...
DO I HAVE TO DO EVERYTHING?

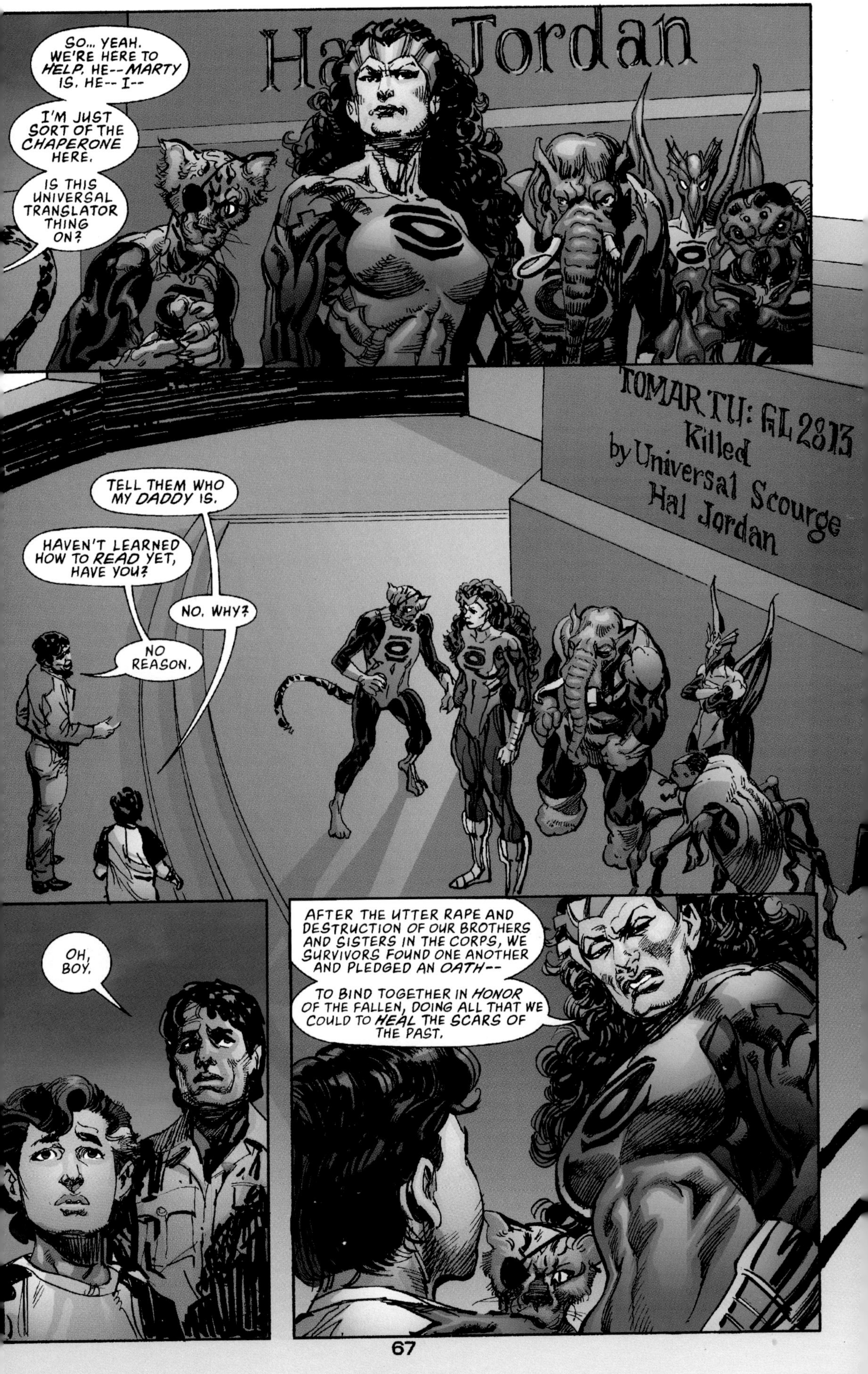
Hal Jordan
SO... YEAH. WE'RE HERE TO HELP. HE-- MARTY IS. HE-- I--
I'M JUST SORT OF THE CHAPERONE HERE.
IS THIS UNIVERSAL TRANSLATOR THING ON?
TOMAR TU: GL 2813 Killed by Universal Scourge Hal Jordan
TELL THEM WHO MY DADDY IS.
HAVEN'T LEARNED HOW TO READ YET, HAVE YOU?
NO. WHY?
NO REASON.
OH, BOY.
AFTER THE UTTER RAPE AND DESTRUCTION OF OUR BROTHERS AND SISTERS IN THE CORPS, WE SURVIVORS FOUND ONE ANOTHER AND PLEDGED AN OATH--
TO BIND TOGETHER IN HONOR OF THE FALLEN, DOING ALL THAT WE COULD TO HEAL THE SCARS OF THE PAST.

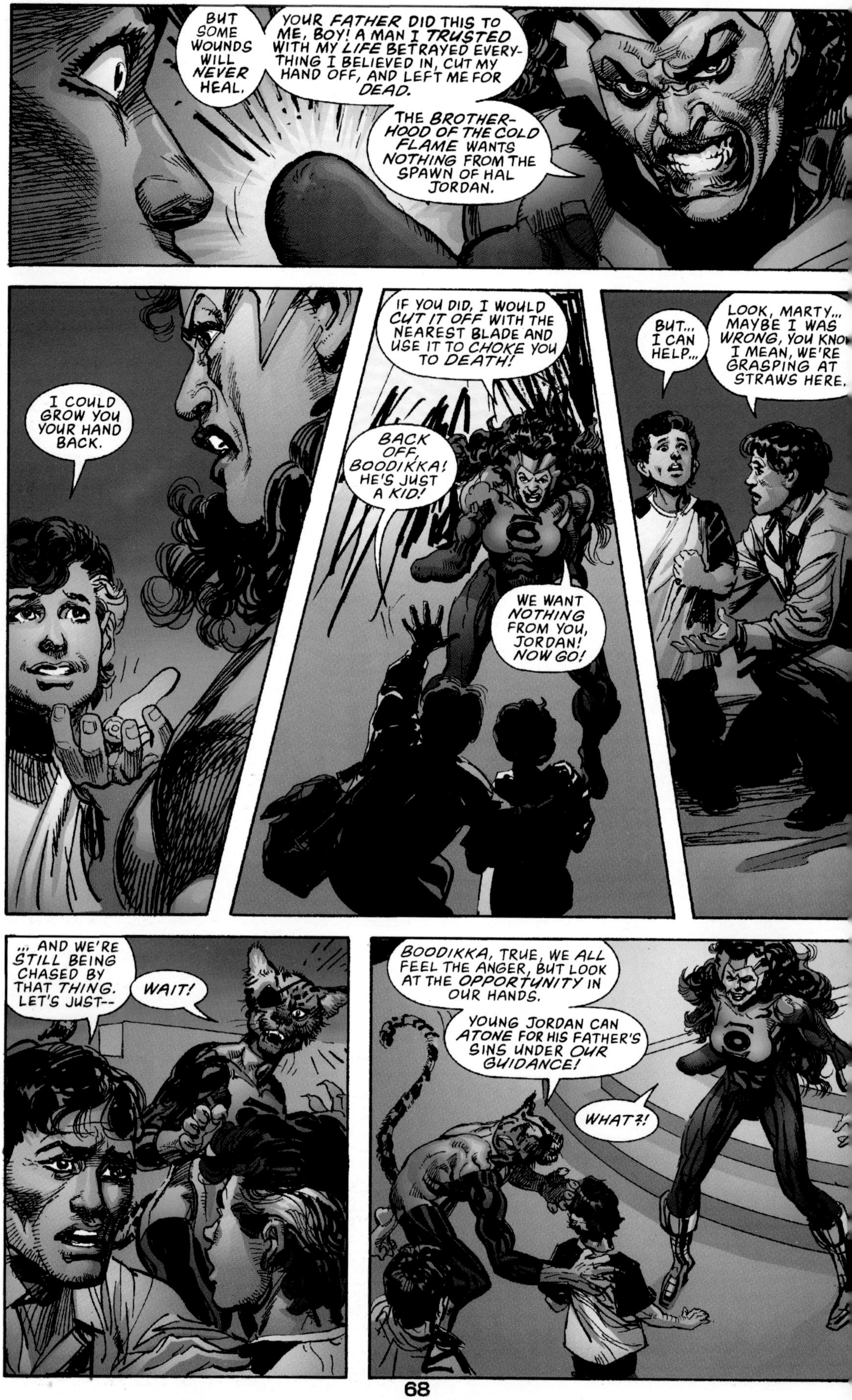
BUT SOME WOUNDS WILL NEVER HEAL.
YOUR FATHER DID THIS TO ME, BOY! A MAN I TRUSTED WITH MY LIFE BETRAYED EVERYTHING I BELIEVED IN, CUT MY HAND OFF, AND LEFT ME FOR DEAD.
THE BROTHERHOOD OF THE COLD FLAME WANTS NOTHING FROM THE SPAWN OF HAL JORDAN.
I COULD GROW YOU YOUR HAND BACK.
IF YOU DID, I WOULD CUT IT OFF WITH THE NEAREST BLADE AND USE IT TO CHOKE YOU TO DEATH!
BACK OFF, BOODIKKA! HE'S JUST A KID!
WE WANT NOTHING FROM YOU, JORDAN! NOW GO!
BUT... I CAN HELP...
LOOK, MARTY... MAYBE I WAS WRONG, YOU KNOW I MEAN, WE'RE GRASPING AT STRAWS HERE.
... AND WE'RE STILL BEING CHASED BY THAT THING. LET'S JUST--
WAIT!
BOODIKKA, TRUE, WE ALL FEEL THE ANGER, BUT LOOK AT THE OPPORTUNITY IN OUR HANDS.
YOUNG JORDAN CAN ATONE FOR HIS FATHER'S SINS UNDER OUR GUIDANCE!
WHAT?!

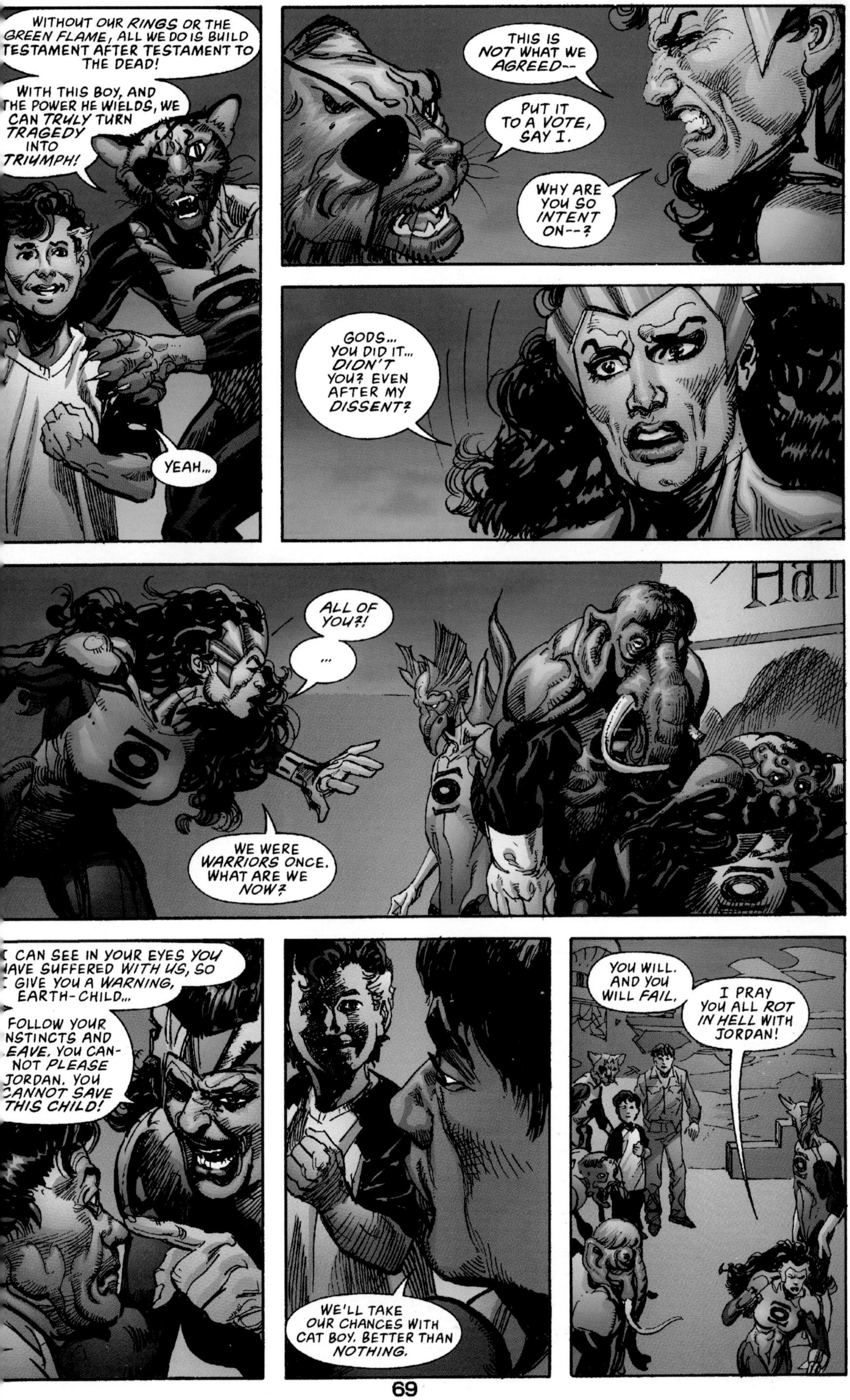
WITHOUT OUR RINGS OR THE GREEN FLAME, ALL WE DO IS BUILD TESTAMENT AFTER TESTAMENT TO THE DEAD!
WITH THIS BOY, AND THE POWER HE WIELDS, WE CAN TRULY TURN TRAGEDY INTO TRIUMPH!
YEAH...
THIS IS NOT WHAT WE AGREED--
PUT IT TO A VOTE, SAY I.
WHY ARE YOU SO INTENT ON--?
GODS... YOU DID IT... DIDN'T YOU? EVEN AFTER MY DISSENT?
ALL OF YOU?!
...
WE WERE WARRIORS ONCE. WHAT ARE WE NOW?
I CAN SEE IN YOUR EYES YOU HAVE SUFFERED WITH US, SO I GIVE YOU A WARNING, EARTH-CHILD...
FOLLOW YOUR INSTINCTS AND LEAVE. YOU CANNOT PLEASE JORDAN. YOU CANNOT SAVE THIS CHILD!
WE'LL TAKE OUR CHANCES WITH CAT BOY. BETTER THAN NOTHING.
YOU WILL. AND YOU WILL FAIL.
I PRAY YOU ALL ROT IN HELL WITH JORDAN!

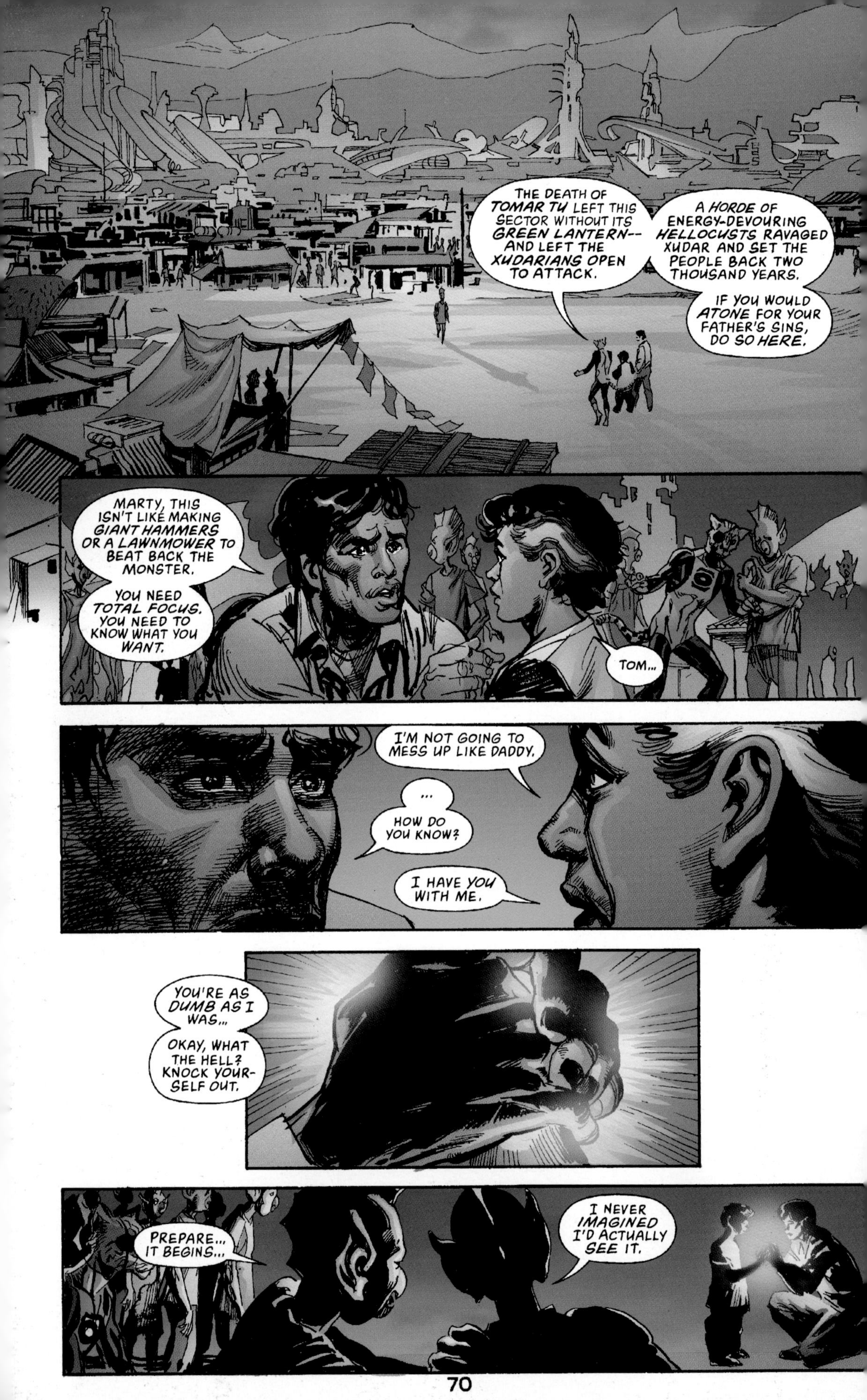
THE DEATH OF TOMAR TU LEFT THIS SECTOR WITHOUT ITS GREEN LANTERN-- AND LEFT THE XUDARIANS OPEN TO ATTACK.
A HORDE OF ENERGY-DEVOURING HELLOCUSTS RAVAGED XUDAR AND SET THE PEOPLE BACK TWO THOUSAND YEARS.
IF YOU WOULD ATONE FOR YOUR FATHER'S SINS, DO SO HERE.
MARTY, THIS ISN'T LIKE MAKING GIANT HAMMERS OR A LAWNMOWER TO BEAT BACK THE MONSTER.
YOU NEED TOTAL FOCUS. YOU NEED TO KNOW WHAT YOU WANT.
TOM...
I'M NOT GOING TO MESS UP LIKE DADDY.
...
HOW DO YOU KNOW?
I HAVE YOU WITH ME.
YOU'RE AS DUMB AS I WAS...
OKAY, WHAT THE HELL? KNOCK YOUR-SELF OUT.
PREPARE... IT BEGINS...
I NEVER IMAGINED I'D ACTUALLY SEE IT.

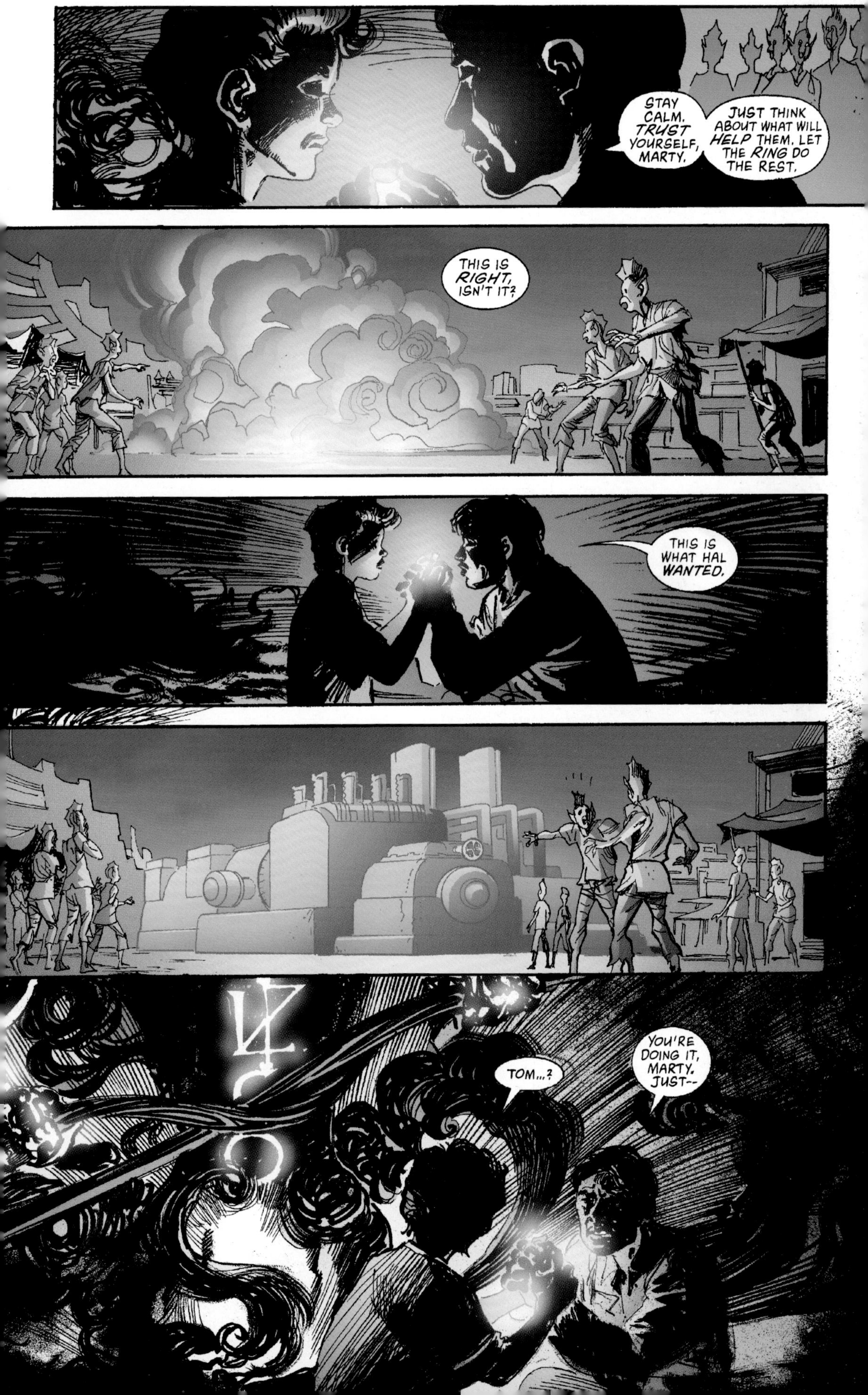
STAY CALM. TRUST YOURSELF, MARTY.
JUST THINK ABOUT WHAT WILL HELP THEM. LET THE RING DO THE REST.
THIS IS RIGHT, ISN'T IT?
THIS IS WHAT HAL WANTED.
TOM...?
YOU'RE DOING IT, MARTY. JUST--

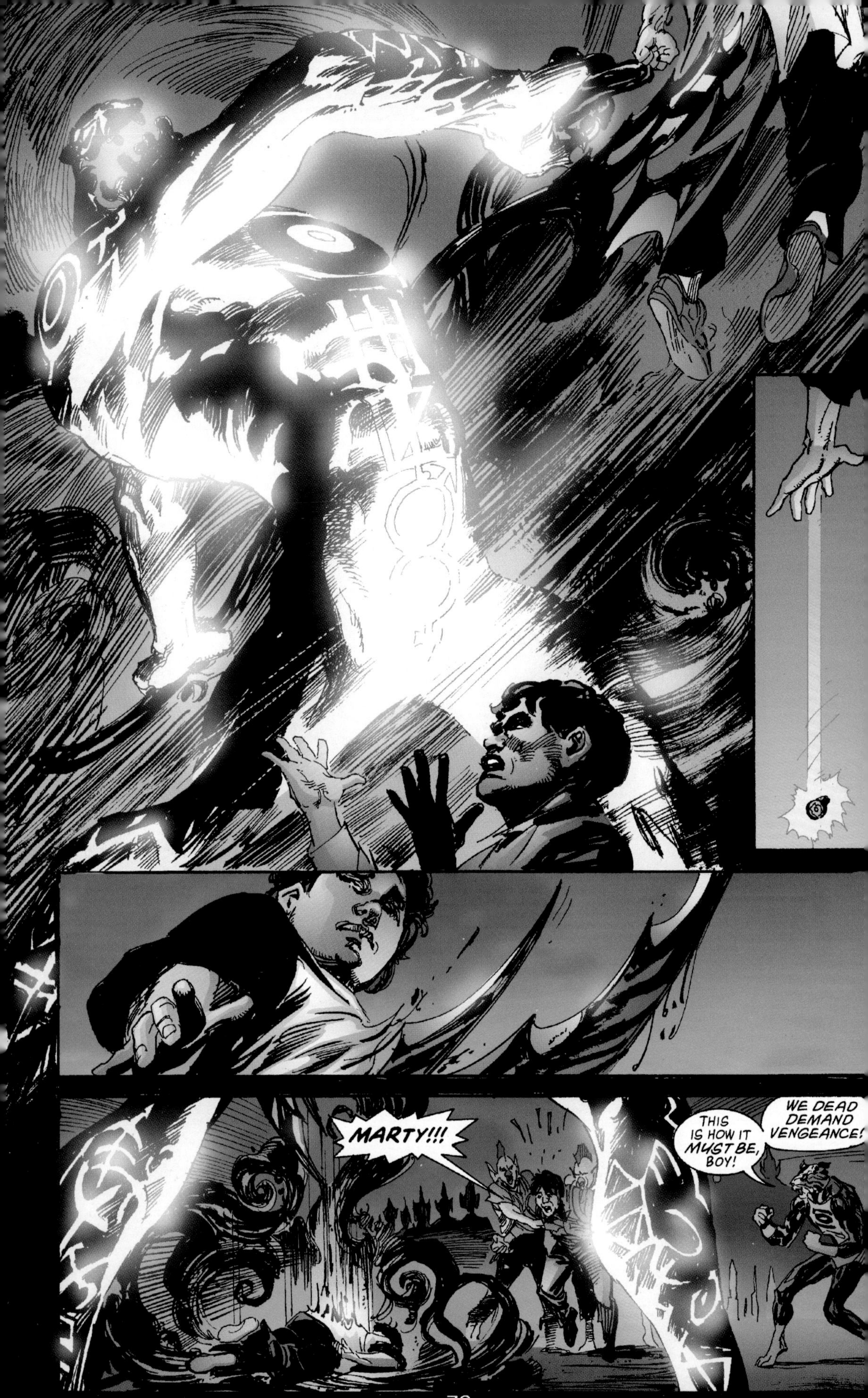
MARTY!!!
THIS IS HOW IT MUST BE, BOY!
WE DEAD DEMAND VENGEANCE!

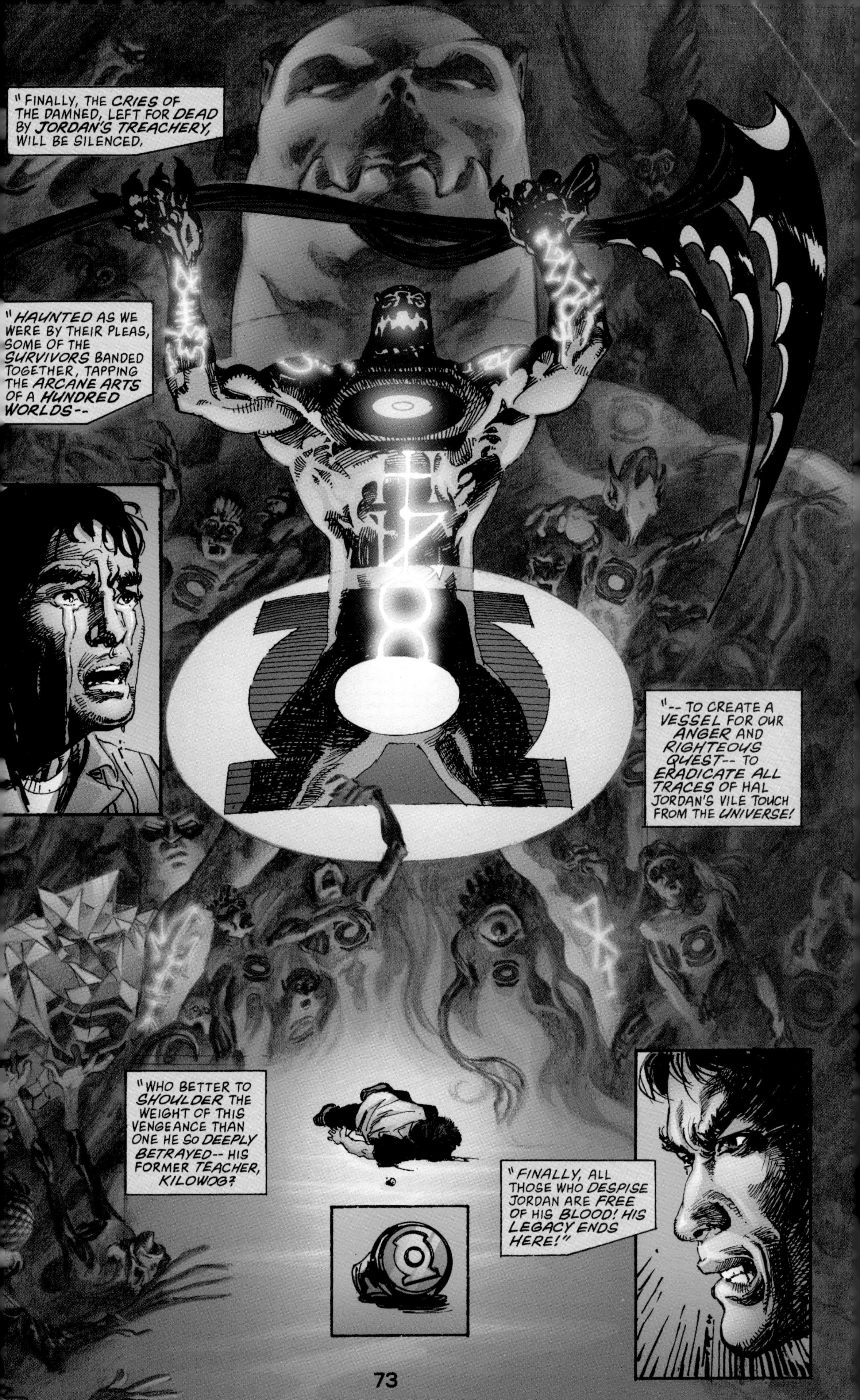
"FINALLY, THE CRIES OF THE DAMNED, LEFT FOR DEAD BY JORDAN'S TREACHERY, WILL BE SILENCED.
"HAUNTED AS WE WERE BY THEIR PLEAS, SOME OF THE SURVIVORS BANDED TOGETHER, TAPPING THE ARCANE ARTS OF A HUNDRED WORLDS--
"-- TO CREATE A VESSEL FOR OUR ANGER AND RIGHTEOUS QUEST-- TO ERADICATE ALL TRACES OF HAL JORDAN'S VILE TOUCH FROM THE UNIVERSE!
"WHO BETTER TO SHOULDER THE WEIGHT OF THIS VENGEANCE THAN ONE HE SO DEEPLY BETRAYED-- HIS FORMER TEACHER, KILOWOG?
"FINALLY, ALL THOSE WHO DESPISE JORDAN ARE FREE OF HIS BLOOD! HIS LEGACY ENDS HERE!"

MARTY!!!

ZK TU:GL 2913
Killed
...versal Scourge
...H-1 Jordan...

MARTY.

I... OH, GOD.

FINALLY... THE D-DAY OF ATONEMENT... AND A RING--!

NO! NO!!!

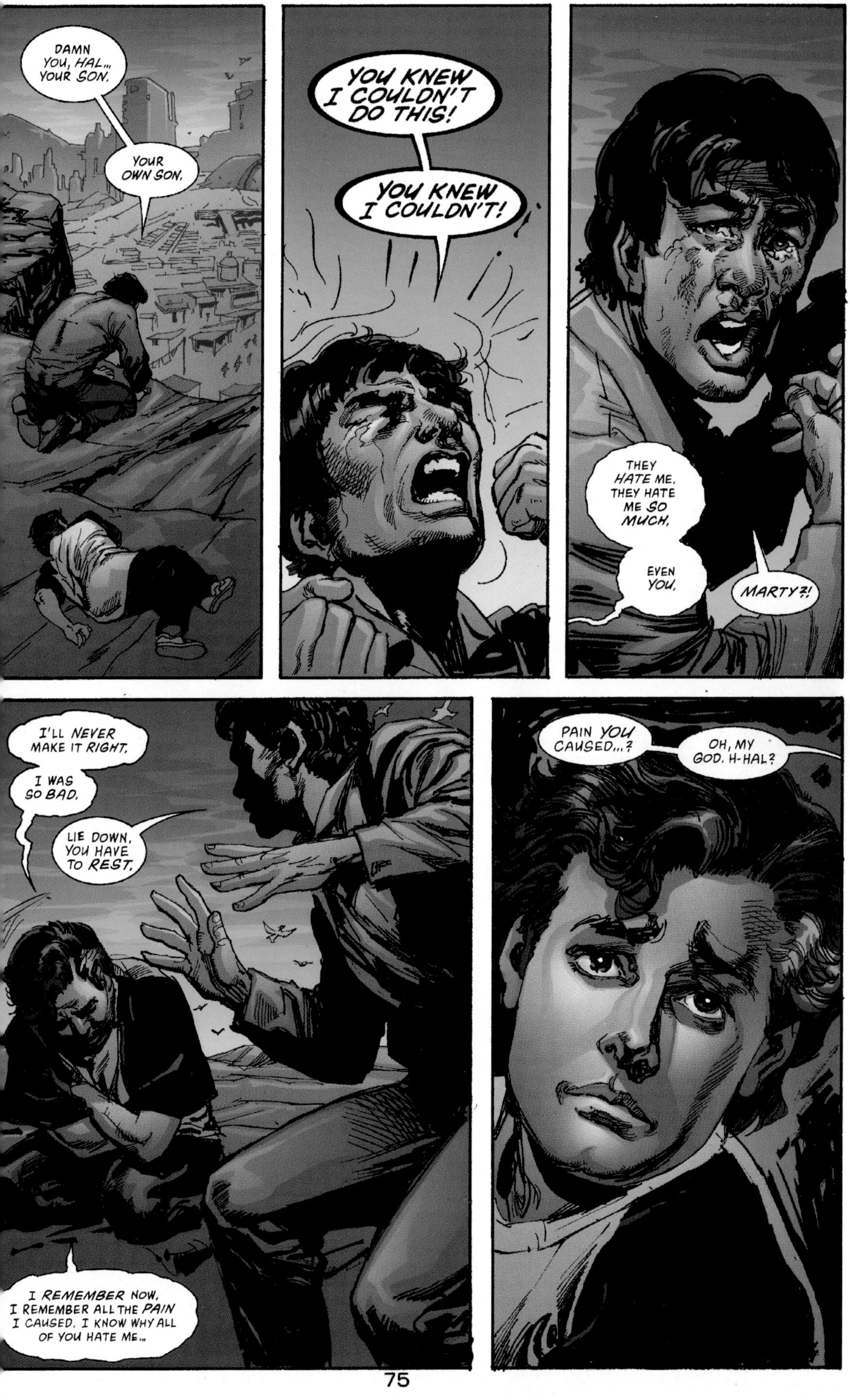
DAMN YOU, HAL... YOUR SON.
YOUR OWN SON.
YOU KNEW I COULDN'T DO THIS!
YOU KNEW I COULDN'T!
THEY HATE ME. THEY HATE ME SO MUCH.
EVEN YOU.
MARTY?!
I'LL NEVER MAKE IT RIGHT.
I WAS SO BAD.
LIE DOWN. YOU HAVE TO REST.
I REMEMBER NOW. I REMEMBER ALL THE PAIN I CAUSED. I KNOW WHY ALL OF YOU HATE ME...
PAIN YOU CAUSED...?
OH, MY GOD. H-HAL?

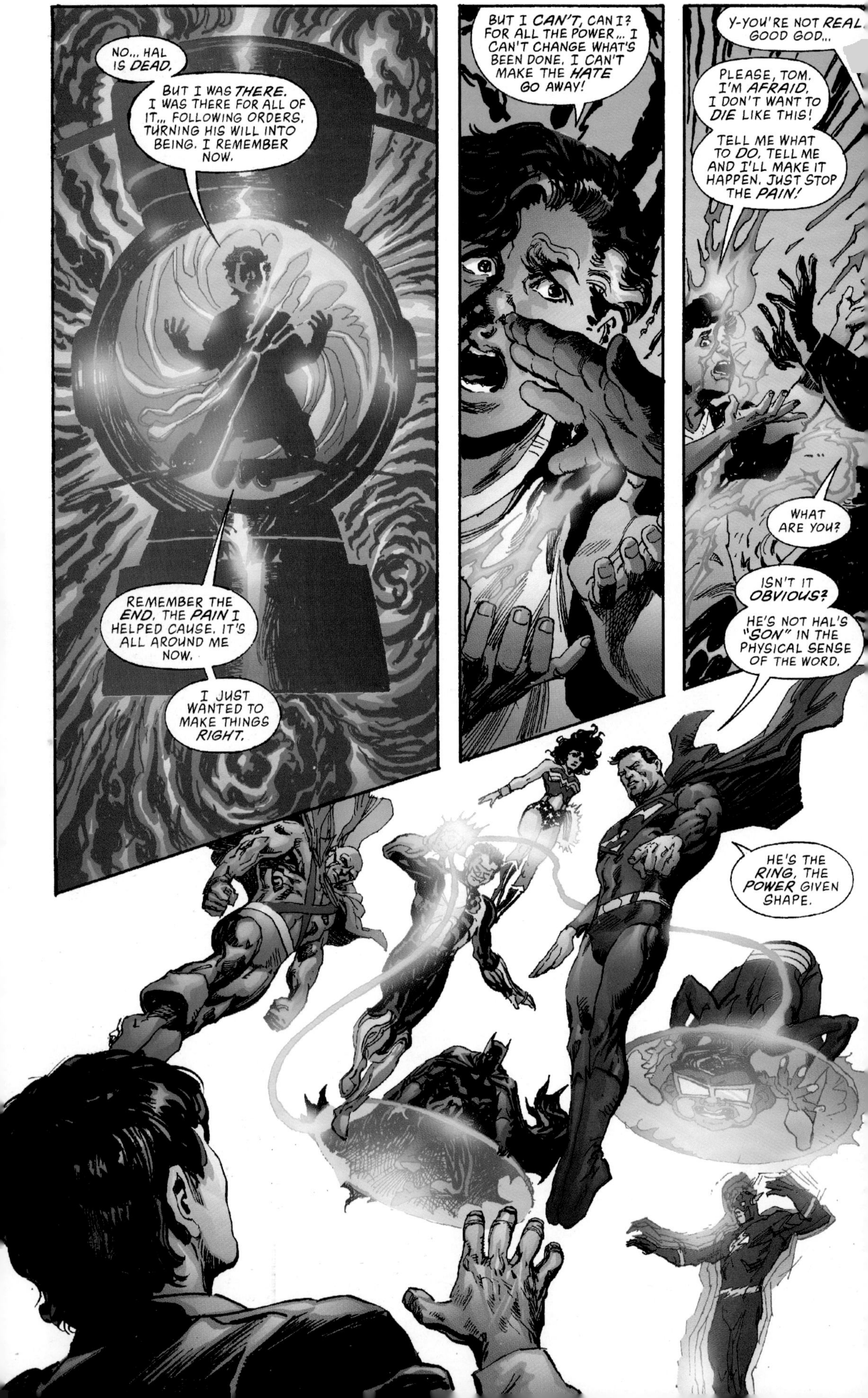
NO... HAL IS DEAD.
BUT I WAS THERE. I WAS THERE FOR ALL OF IT... FOLLOWING ORDERS, TURNING HIS WILL INTO BEING. I REMEMBER NOW.
REMEMBER THE END. THE PAIN I HELPED CAUSE. IT'S ALL AROUND ME NOW.
I JUST WANTED TO MAKE THINGS RIGHT.
BUT I CAN'T, CAN I? FOR ALL THE POWER... I CAN'T CHANGE WHAT'S BEEN DONE. I CAN'T MAKE THE HATE GO AWAY!
Y-YOU'RE NOT REAL GOOD GOD...
PLEASE, TOM. I'M AFRAID. I DON'T WANT TO DIE LIKE THIS!
TELL ME WHAT TO DO. TELL ME AND I'LL MAKE IT HAPPEN. JUST STOP THE PAIN!
WHAT ARE YOU?
ISN'T IT OBVIOUS?
HE'S NOT HAL'S "SON" IN THE PHYSICAL SENSE OF THE WORD.
HE'S THE RING, THE POWER GIVEN SHAPE.

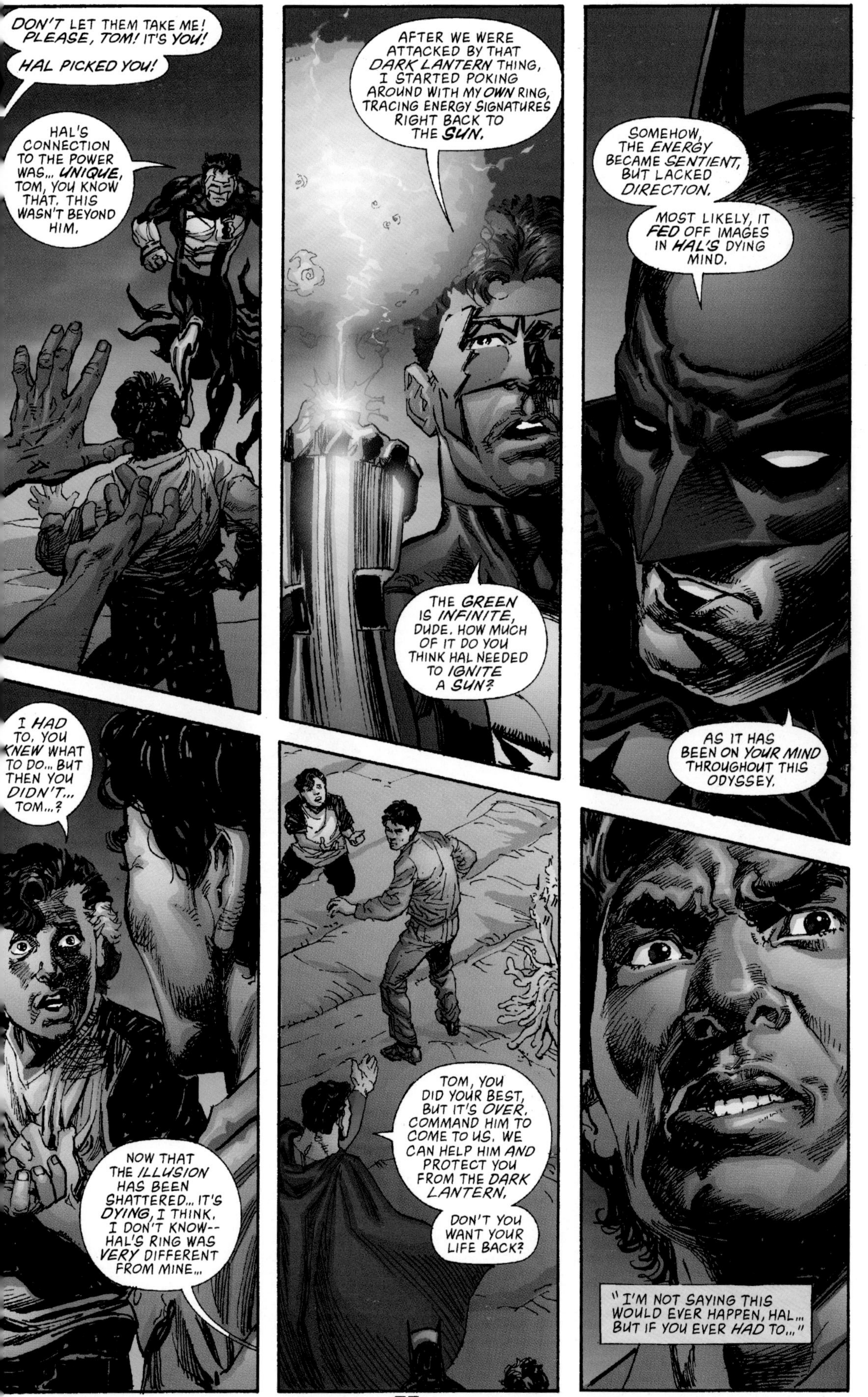
DON'T LET THEM TAKE ME! PLEASE, TOM! IT'S YOU!
HAL PICKED YOU!
HAL'S CONNECTION TO THE POWER WAS... UNIQUE, TOM, YOU KNOW THAT. THIS WASN'T BEYOND HIM.
AFTER WE WERE ATTACKED BY THAT DARK LANTERN THING, I STARTED POKING AROUND WITH MY OWN RING, TRACING ENERGY SIGNATURES RIGHT BACK TO THE SUN.
THE GREEN IS INFINITE, DUDE. HOW MUCH OF IT DO YOU THINK HAL NEEDED TO IGNITE A SUN?
SOMEHOW, THE ENERGY BECAME SENTIENT, BUT LACKED DIRECTION.
MOST LIKELY, IT FED OFF IMAGES IN HAL'S DYING MIND.
AS IT HAS BEEN ON YOUR MIND THROUGHOUT THIS ODYSSEY.
I HAD TO. YOU KNEW WHAT TO DO... BUT THEN YOU DIDN'T... TOM...?
NOW THAT THE ILLUSION HAS BEEN SHATTERED... IT'S DYING, I THINK. I DON'T KNOW-- HAL'S RING WAS VERY DIFFERENT FROM MINE...
TOM, YOU DID YOUR BEST, BUT IT'S OVER. COMMAND HIM TO COME TO US. WE CAN HELP HIM AND PROTECT YOU FROM THE DARK LANTERN.
DON'T YOU WANT YOUR LIFE BACK?
"I'M NOT SAYING THIS WOULD EVER HAPPEN, HAL... BUT IF YOU EVER HAD TO..."

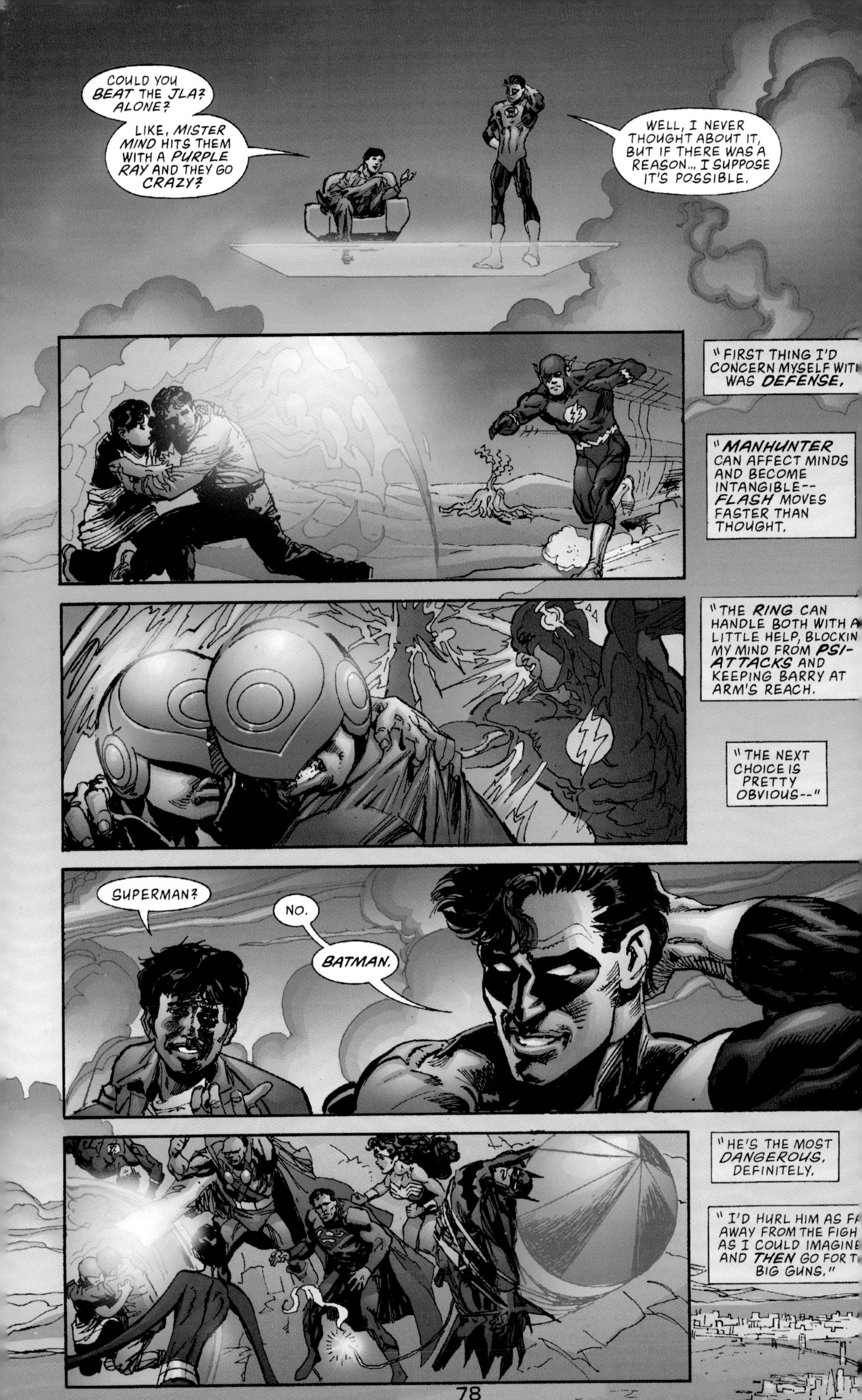
COULD YOU BEAT THE JLA? ALONE?
LIKE, MISTER MIND HITS THEM WITH A PURPLE RAY AND THEY GO CRAZY?
WELL, I NEVER THOUGHT ABOUT IT, BUT IF THERE WAS A REASON... I SUPPOSE IT'S POSSIBLE.
"FIRST THING I'D CONCERN MYSELF WIT WAS DEFENSE.
"MANHUNTER CAN AFFECT MINDS AND BECOME INTANGIBLE-- FLASH MOVES FASTER THAN THOUGHT.
"THE RING CAN HANDLE BOTH WITH A LITTLE HELP, BLOCKIN MY MIND FROM PSI-ATTACKS AND KEEPING BARRY AT ARM'S REACH.
"THE NEXT CHOICE IS PRETTY OBVIOUS--"
SUPERMAN?
NO.
BATMAN.
"HE'S THE MOST DANGEROUS, DEFINITELY.
"I'D HURL HIM AS F AWAY FROM THE FIGH AS I COULD IMAGINE AND THEN GO FOR T BIG GUNS."

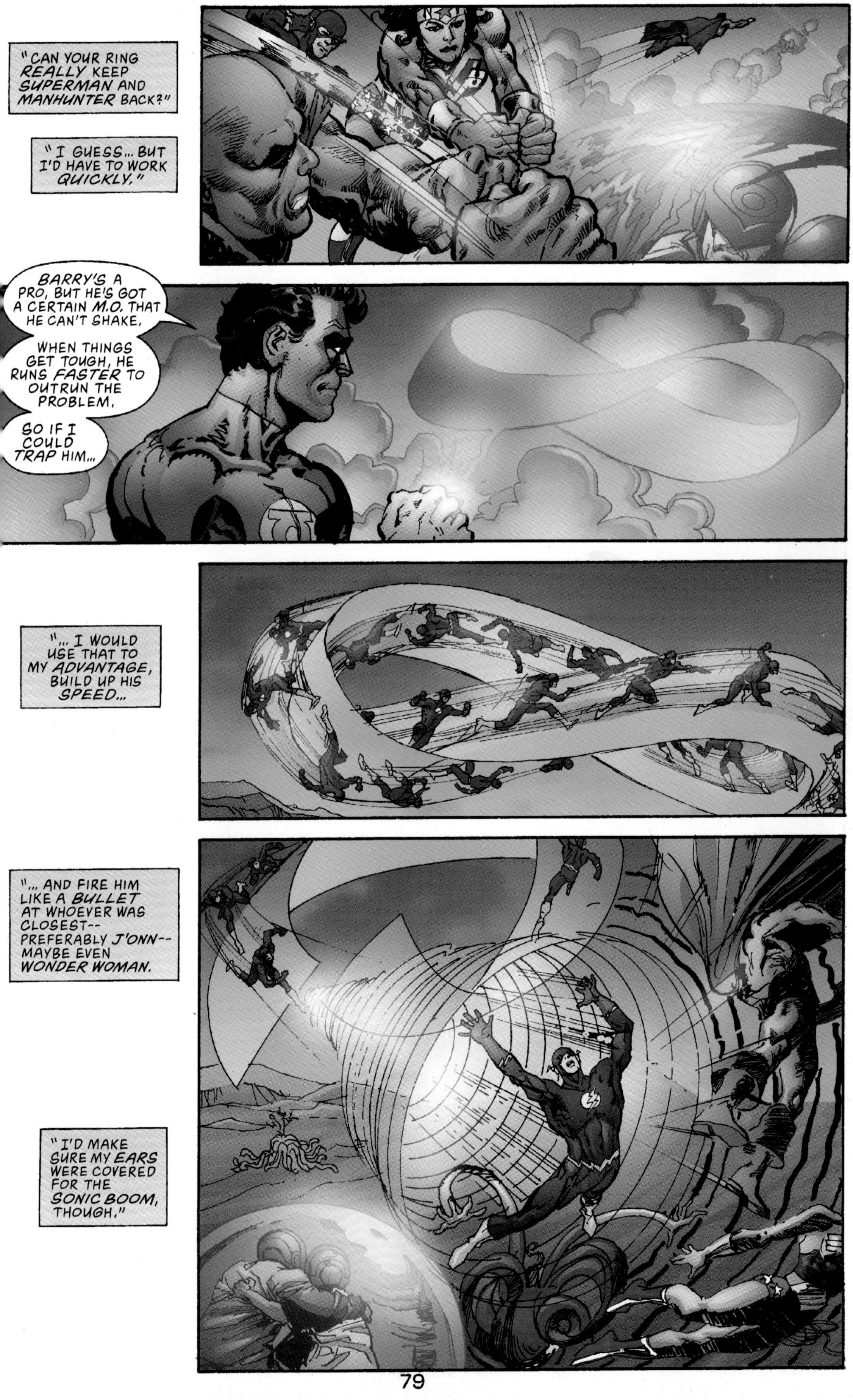

"CAN YOUR RING REALLY KEEP SUPERMAN AND MANHUNTER BACK?"
"I GUESS... BUT I'D HAVE TO WORK QUICKLY."
BARRY'S A PRO, BUT HE'S GOT A CERTAIN M.O. THAT HE CAN'T SHAKE.
WHEN THINGS GET TOUGH, HE RUNS FASTER TO OUTRUN THE PROBLEM.
SO IF I COULD TRAP HIM...
"... I WOULD USE THAT TO MY ADVANTAGE, BUILD UP HIS SPEED...
"... AND FIRE HIM LIKE A BULLET AT WHOEVER WAS CLOSEST-- PREFERABLY J'ONN-- MAYBE EVEN WONDER WOMAN.
"I'D MAKE SURE MY EARS WERE COVERED FOR THE SONIC BOOM, THOUGH."

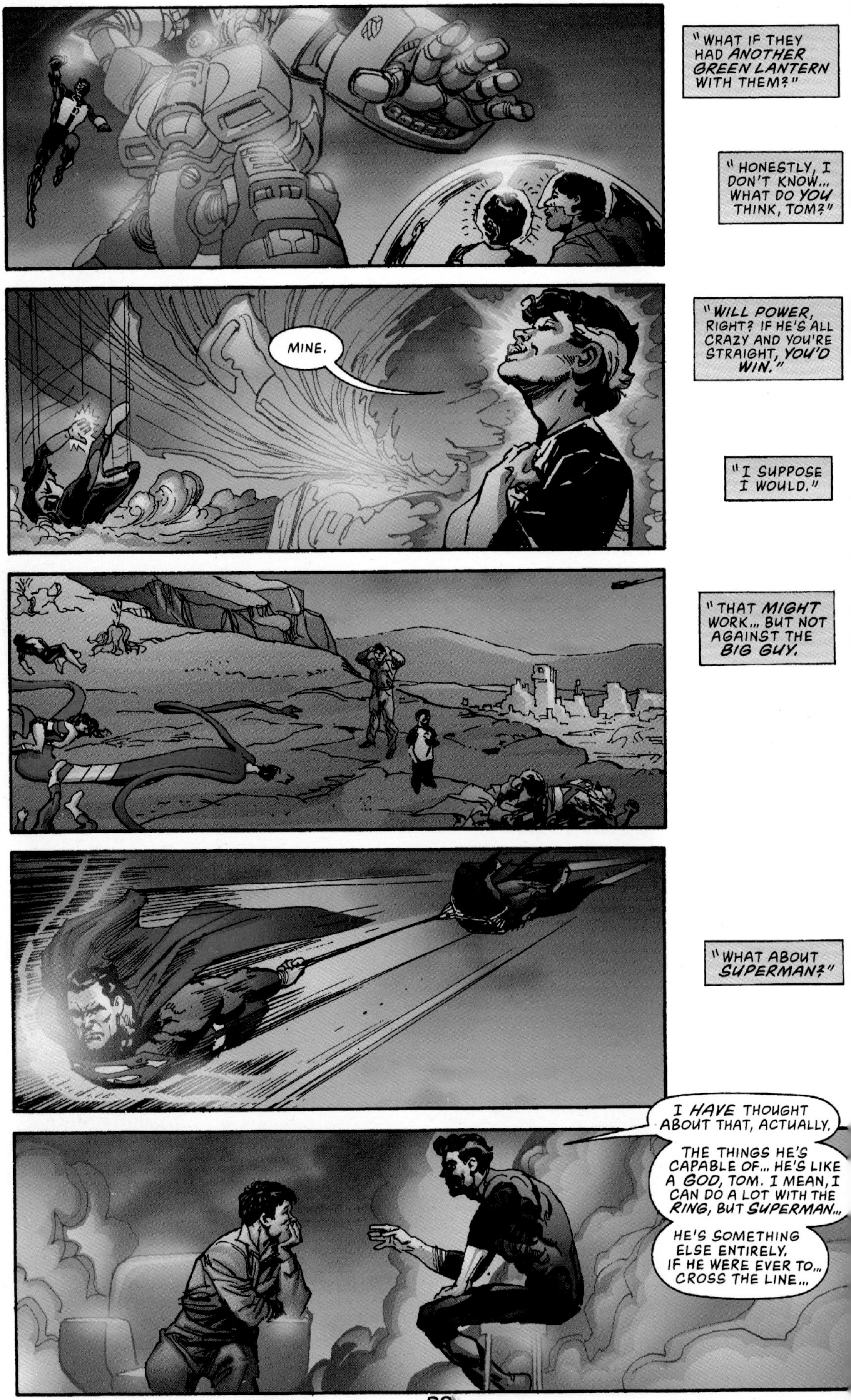
"WHAT IF THEY HAD ANOTHER GREEN LANTERN WITH THEM?"
"HONESTLY, I DON'T KNOW... WHAT DO YOU THINK, TOM?"
MINE.
"WILL POWER, RIGHT? IF HE'S ALL CRAZY AND YOU'RE STRAIGHT, YOU'D WIN."
"I SUPPOSE I WOULD."
"THAT MIGHT WORK... BUT NOT AGAINST THE BIG GUY.
"WHAT ABOUT SUPERMAN?"
I HAVE THOUGHT ABOUT THAT, ACTUALLY.
THE THINGS HE'S CAPABLE OF... HE'S LIKE A GOD, TOM. I MEAN, I CAN DO A LOT WITH THE RING, BUT SUPERMAN...
HE'S SOMETHING ELSE ENTIRELY. IF HE WERE EVER TO... CROSS THE LINE...

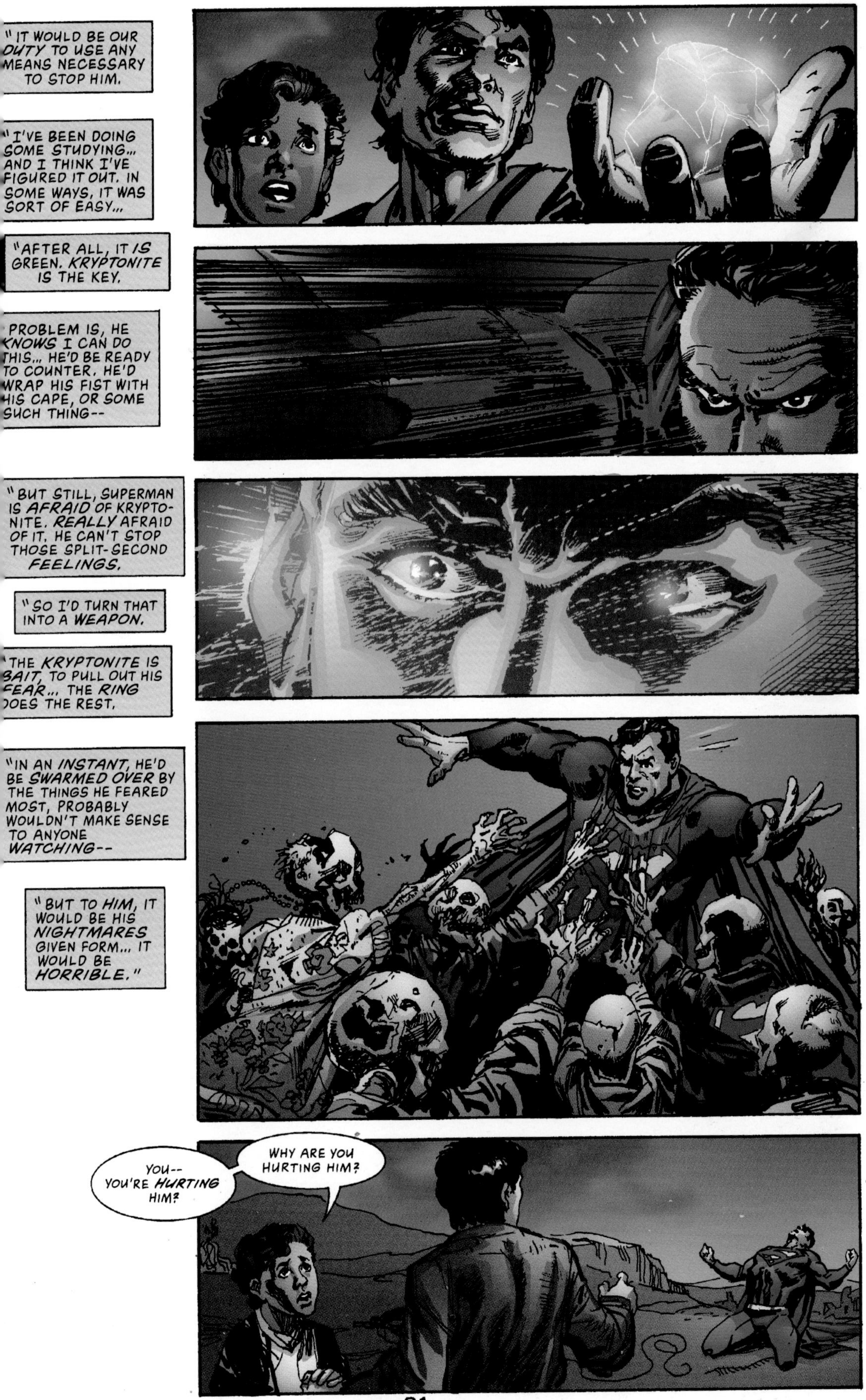
"IT WOULD BE OUR DUTY TO USE ANY MEANS NECESSARY TO STOP HIM.
"I'VE BEEN DOING SOME STUDYING... AND I THINK I'VE FIGURED IT OUT. IN SOME WAYS, IT WAS SORT OF EASY...
"AFTER ALL, IT IS GREEN. KRYPTONITE IS THE KEY.
"PROBLEM IS, HE KNOWS I CAN DO THIS... HE'D BE READY TO COUNTER. HE'D WRAP HIS FIST WITH HIS CAPE, OR SOME SUCH THING--
"BUT STILL, SUPERMAN IS AFRAID OF KRYPTONITE. REALLY AFRAID OF IT. HE CAN'T STOP THOSE SPLIT-SECOND FEELINGS.
"SO I'D TURN THAT INTO A WEAPON.
"THE KRYPTONITE IS BAIT, TO PULL OUT HIS FEAR... THE RING DOES THE REST.
"IN AN INSTANT, HE'D BE SWARMED OVER BY THE THINGS HE FEARED MOST, PROBABLY WOULDN'T MAKE SENSE TO ANYONE WATCHING--
"BUT TO HIM, IT WOULD BE HIS NIGHTMARES GIVEN FORM... IT WOULD BE HORRIBLE."
YOU-- YOU'RE HURTING HIM?
WHY ARE YOU HURTING HIM?

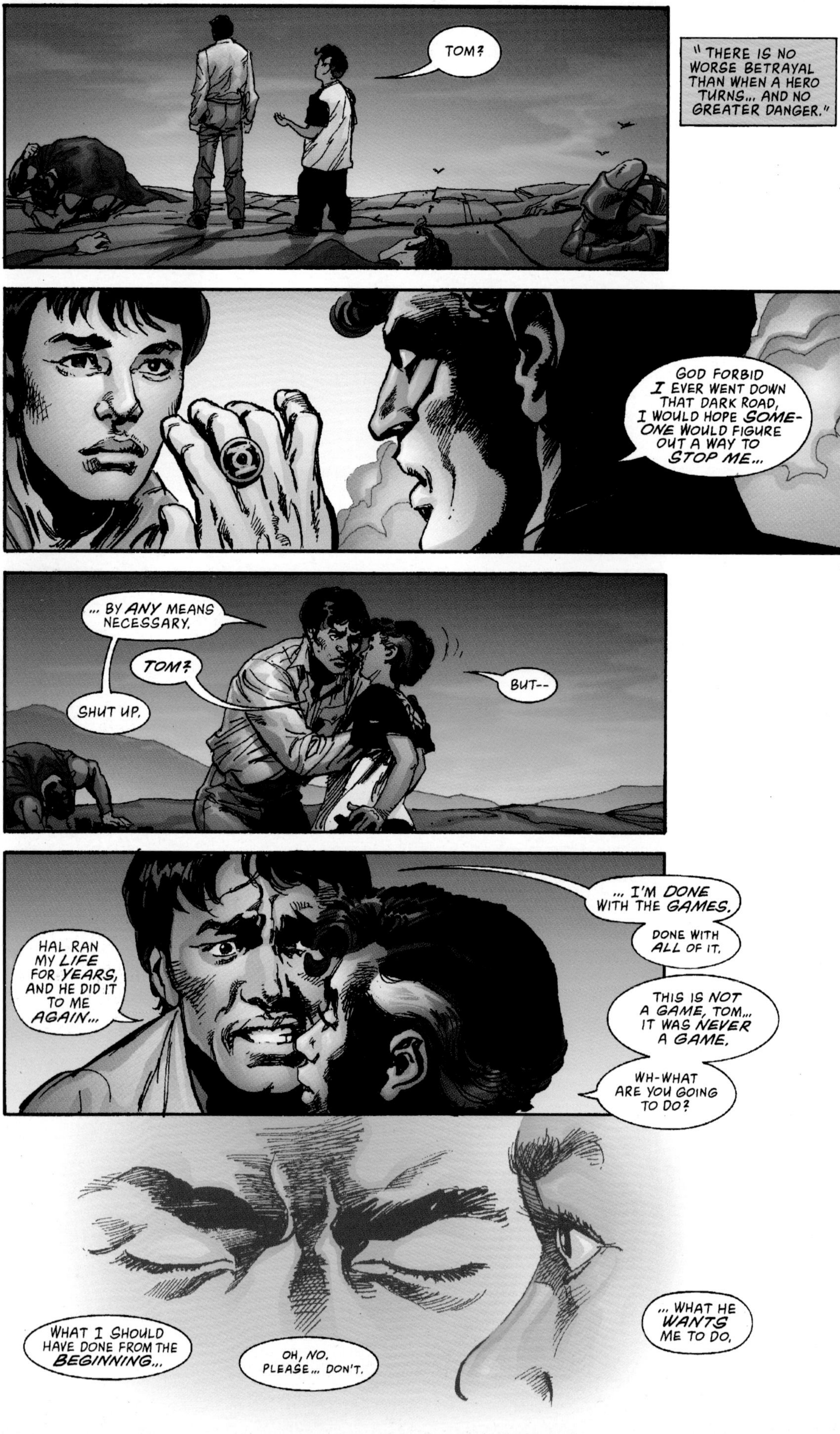
TOM?
"THERE IS NO WORSE BETRAYAL THAN WHEN A HERO TURNS... AND NO GREATER DANGER."
GOD FORBID I EVER WENT DOWN THAT DARK ROAD, I WOULD HOPE SOMEONE WOULD FIGURE OUT A WAY TO STOP ME...
... BY ANY MEANS NECESSARY.
TOM?
BUT--
SHUT UP.
... I'M DONE WITH THE GAMES.
DONE WITH ALL OF IT.
HAL RAN MY LIFE FOR YEARS, AND HE DID IT TO ME AGAIN...
THIS IS NOT A GAME, TOM... IT WAS NEVER A GAME.
WH-WHAT ARE YOU GOING TO DO?
WHAT I SHOULD HAVE DONE FROM THE BEGINNING...
OH, NO. PLEASE... DON'T.
... WHAT HE WANTS ME TO DO.

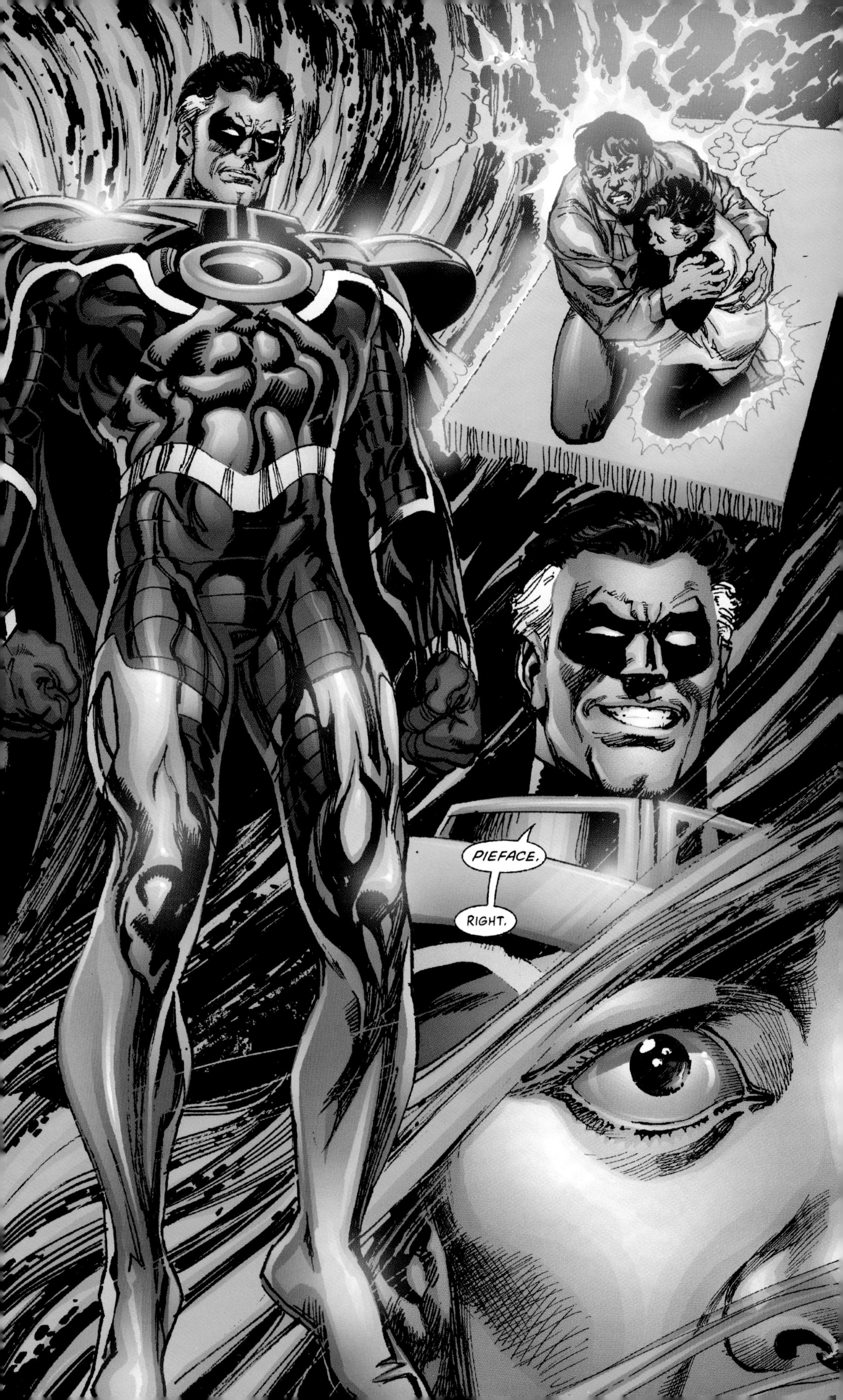
PIEFACE.
RIGHT.

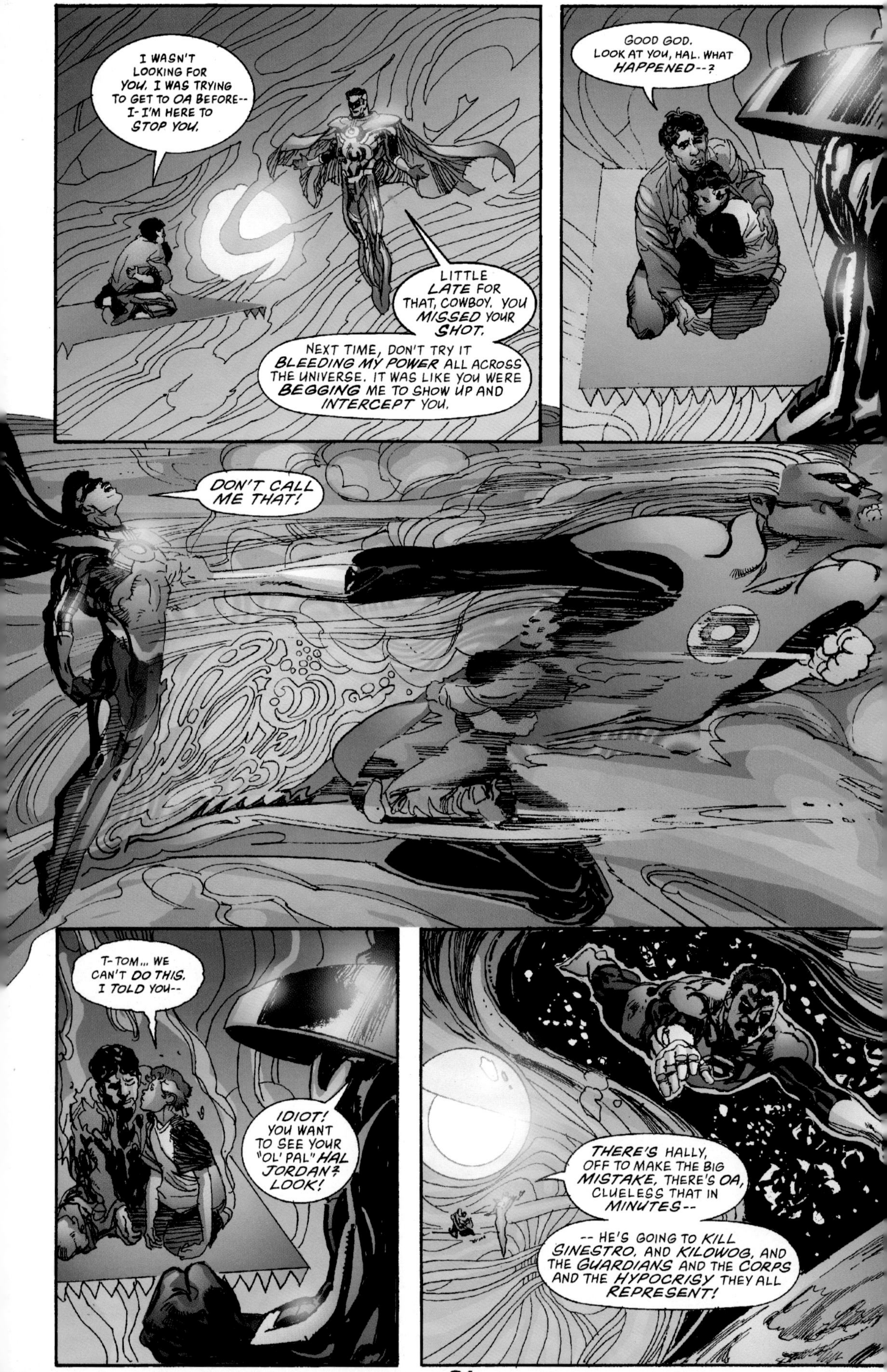
I WASN'T LOOKING FOR YOU. I WAS TRYING TO GET TO OA BEFORE-- I- I'M HERE TO STOP YOU.
LITTLE LATE FOR THAT, COWBOY. YOU MISSED YOUR SHOT.
NEXT TIME, DON'T TRY IT BLEEDING MY POWER ALL ACROSS THE UNIVERSE. IT WAS LIKE YOU WERE BEGGING ME TO SHOW UP AND INTERCEPT YOU.
GOOD GOD. LOOK AT YOU, HAL. WHAT HAPPENED--?
DON'T CALL ME THAT!
T-TOM... WE CAN'T DO THIS. I TOLD YOU--
IDIOT! YOU WANT TO SEE YOUR "OL' PAL" HAL JORDAN? LOOK!
THERE'S HALLY, OFF TO MAKE THE BIG MISTAKE, THERE'S OA, CLUELESS THAT IN MINUTES--
-- HE'S GOING TO KILL SINESTRO, AND KILOWOG, AND THE GUARDIANS AND THE CORPS AND THE HYPOCRISY THEY ALL REPRESENT!

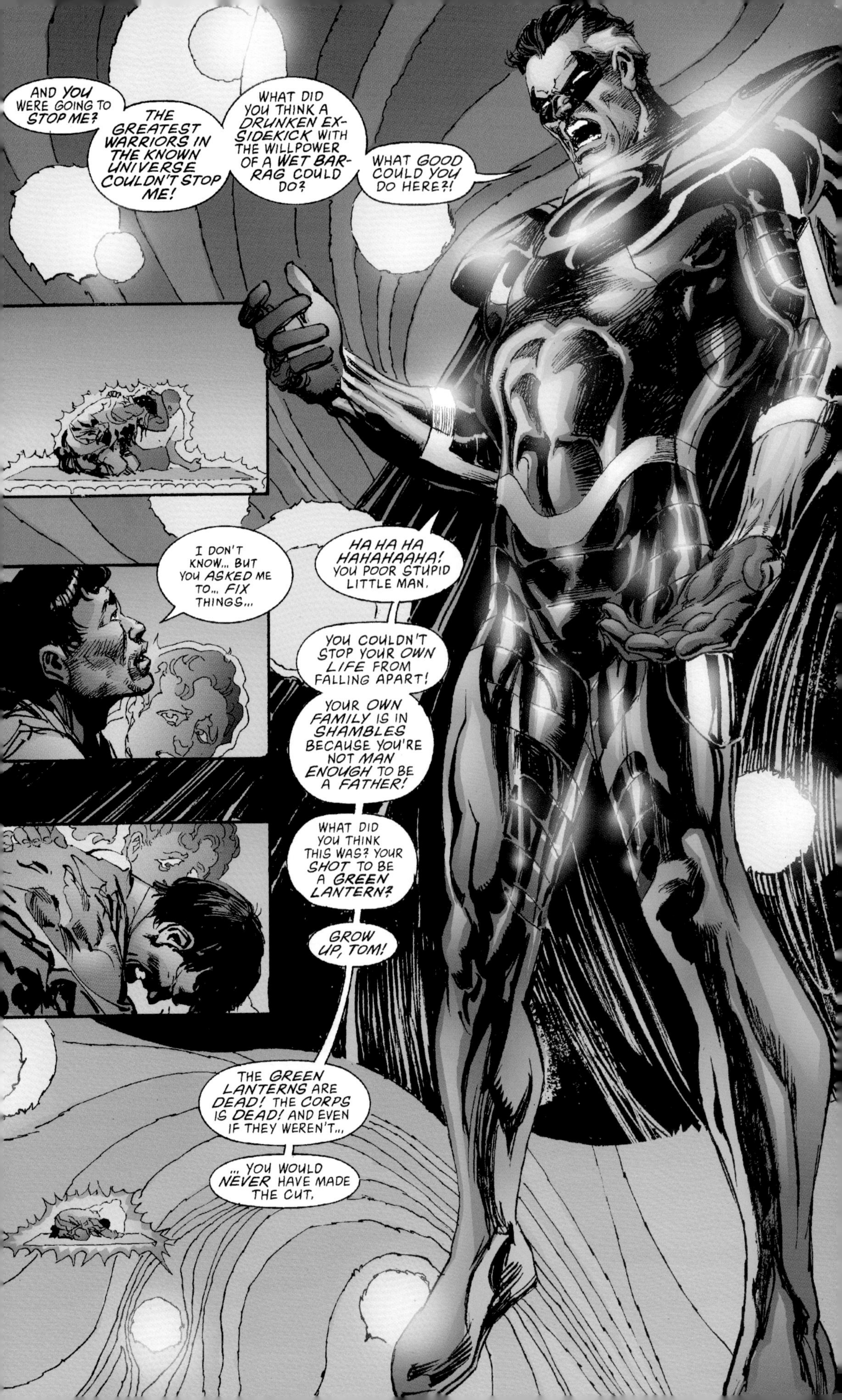

AND YOU WERE GOING TO STOP ME?
THE GREATEST WARRIORS IN THE KNOWN UNIVERSE COULDN'T STOP ME!
WHAT DID YOU THINK A DRUNKEN EX-SIDEKICK WITH THE WILLPOWER OF A WET BAR-RAG COULD DO?
WHAT GOOD COULD YOU DO HERE?!
I DON'T KNOW... BUT YOU ASKED ME TO... FIX THINGS...
HA HA HA HAHAHAAHA! YOU POOR STUPID LITTLE MAN.
YOU COULDN'T STOP YOUR OWN LIFE FROM FALLING APART!
YOUR OWN FAMILY IS IN SHAMBLES BECAUSE YOU'RE NOT MAN ENOUGH TO BE A FATHER!
WHAT DID YOU THINK THIS WAS? YOUR SHOT TO BE A GREEN LANTERN?
GROW UP, TOM!
THE GREEN LANTERNS ARE DEAD! THE CORPS IS DEAD! AND EVEN IF THEY WEREN'T...
... YOU WOULD NEVER HAVE MADE THE CUT.

TELL YOU WHAT, *TOM.* I DON'T KNOW *HOW* YOU GOT MY *POWER* THERE, AND FRANKLY, I DON'T *CARE*--

YOU'RE GOING TO *DIE* OUT HERE UNLESS YOU GET SOME HELP, SO FOR *OLD TIMES' SAKE,* I'LL MAKE YOU A *DEAL.*

GIVE ME THE *POWER.* JUST GIVE IT OVER TO ME AND I'LL *USE IT* TO *FINISH* WHAT I STARTED.

I'LL SET YOU UP IN A NICE *WATERING HOLE* SOMEWHERE, AND YOU CAN GET BACK TO FORGETTING YOUR OWN NAME.

NO... HE CHOSE *YOU,* TOM...

... HE CHOSE... YOU...

HE MADE A *MISTAKE.*

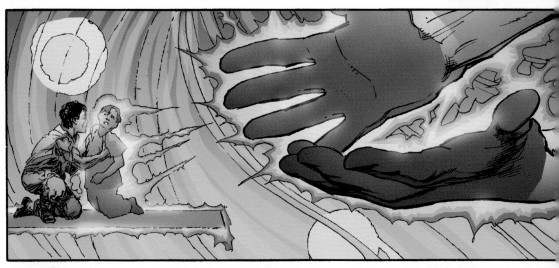

WHY DIDN'T YOU COME LOOKING FOR ME AFTER COAST CITY? BEFORE ALL OF *THIS?*

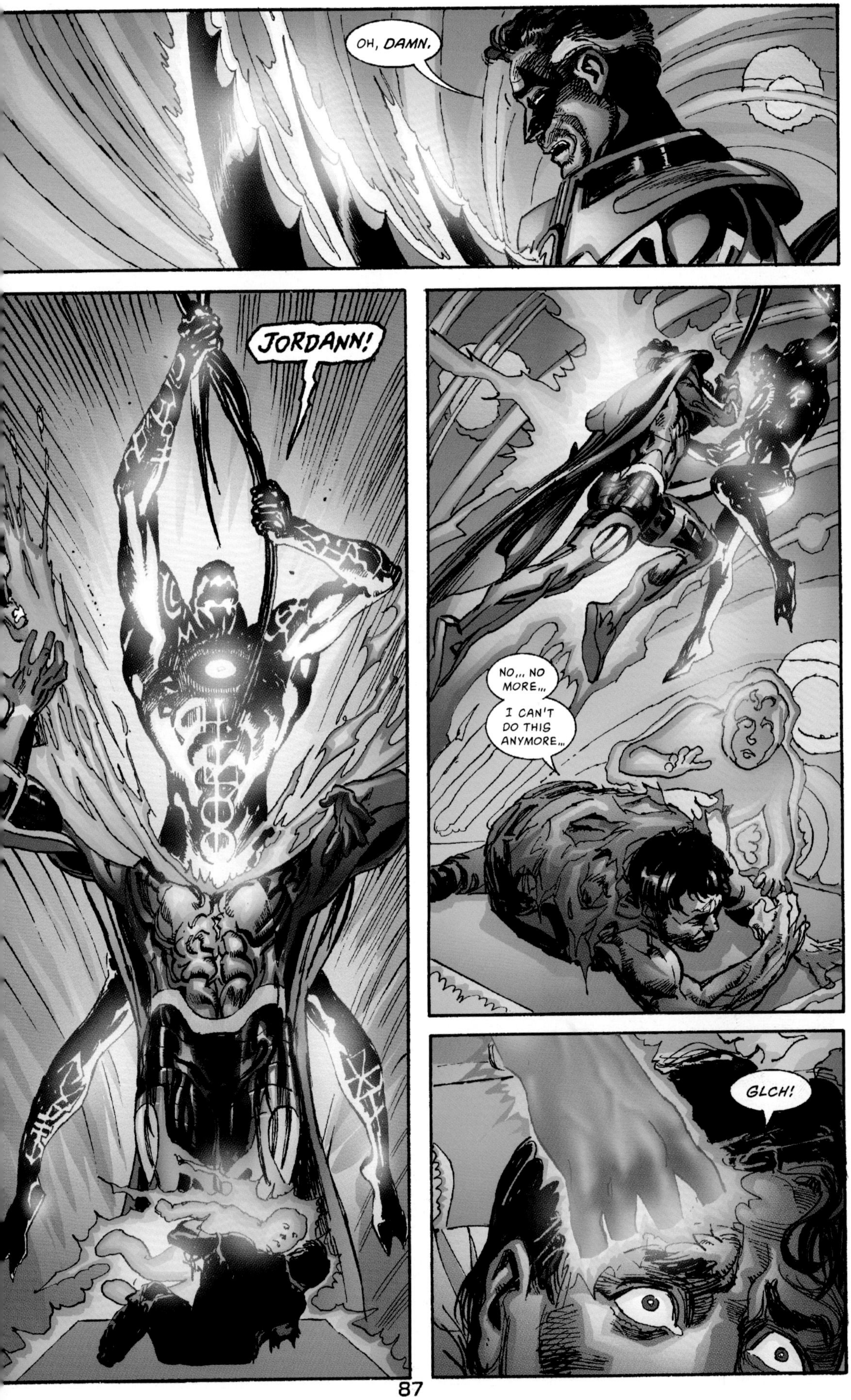

OH, DAMN.
JORDANN!
NO... NO MORE...
I CAN'T DO THIS ANYMORE...
GLCH!

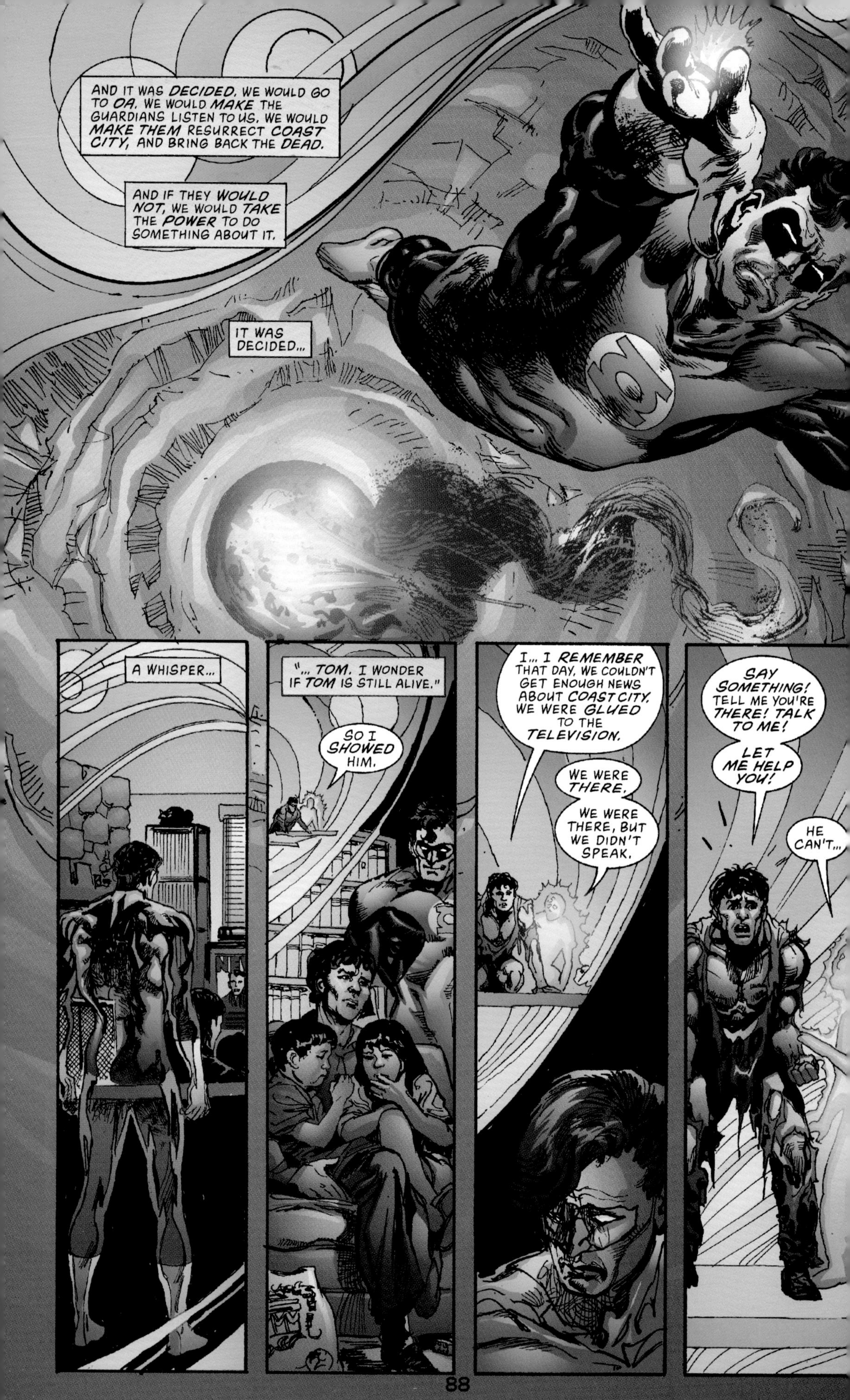
AND IT WAS DECIDED. WE WOULD GO TO OA. WE WOULD MAKE THE GUARDIANS LISTEN TO US. WE WOULD MAKE THEM RESURRECT COAST CITY, AND BRING BACK THE DEAD.
AND IF THEY WOULD NOT, WE WOULD TAKE THE POWER TO DO SOMETHING ABOUT IT.
IT WAS DECIDED...
A WHISPER...
"... TOM. I WONDER IF TOM IS STILL ALIVE."
SO I SHOWED HIM.
I... I REMEMBER THAT DAY. WE COULDN'T GET ENOUGH NEWS ABOUT COAST CITY. WE WERE GLUED TO THE TELEVISION.
WE WERE THERE.
WE WERE THERE, BUT WE DIDN'T SPEAK.
SAY SOMETHING! TELL ME YOU'RE THERE! TALK TO ME!
LET ME HELP YOU!
HE CAN'T...

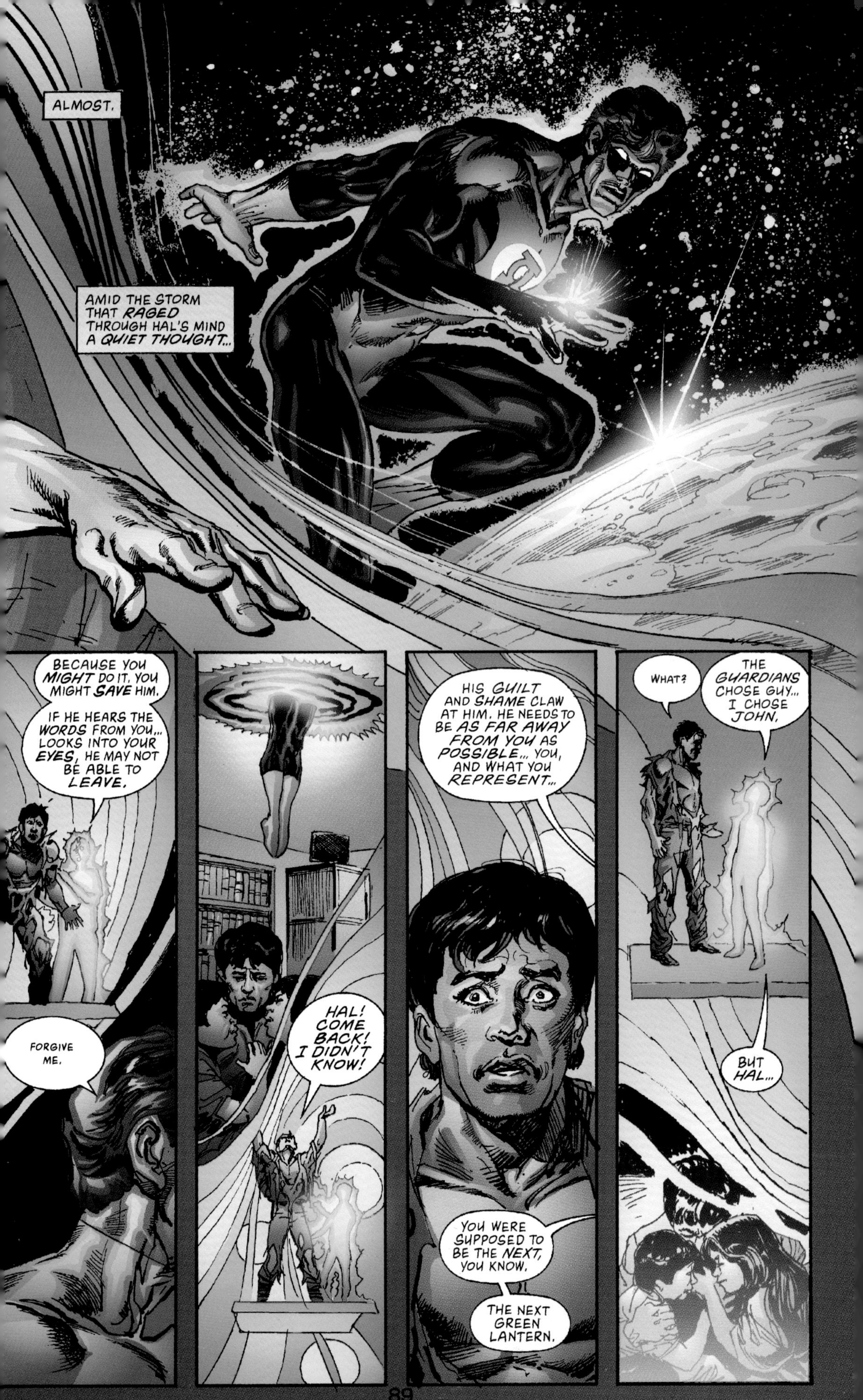
ALMOST.
AMID THE STORM THAT RAGED THROUGH HAL'S MIND A QUIET THOUGHT...
BECAUSE YOU MIGHT DO IT. YOU MIGHT SAVE HIM.
IF HE HEARS THE WORDS FROM YOU... LOOKS INTO YOUR EYES, HE MAY NOT BE ABLE TO LEAVE.
FORGIVE ME.
HAL! COME BACK! I DIDN'T KNOW!
HIS GUILT AND SHAME CLAW AT HIM. HE NEEDS TO BE AS FAR AWAY FROM YOU AS POSSIBLE... YOU, AND WHAT YOU REPRESENT...
YOU WERE SUPPOSED TO BE THE NEXT, YOU KNOW.
THE NEXT GREEN LANTERN.
WHAT?
THE GUARDIANS CHOSE GUY... I CHOSE JOHN.
BUT HAL...

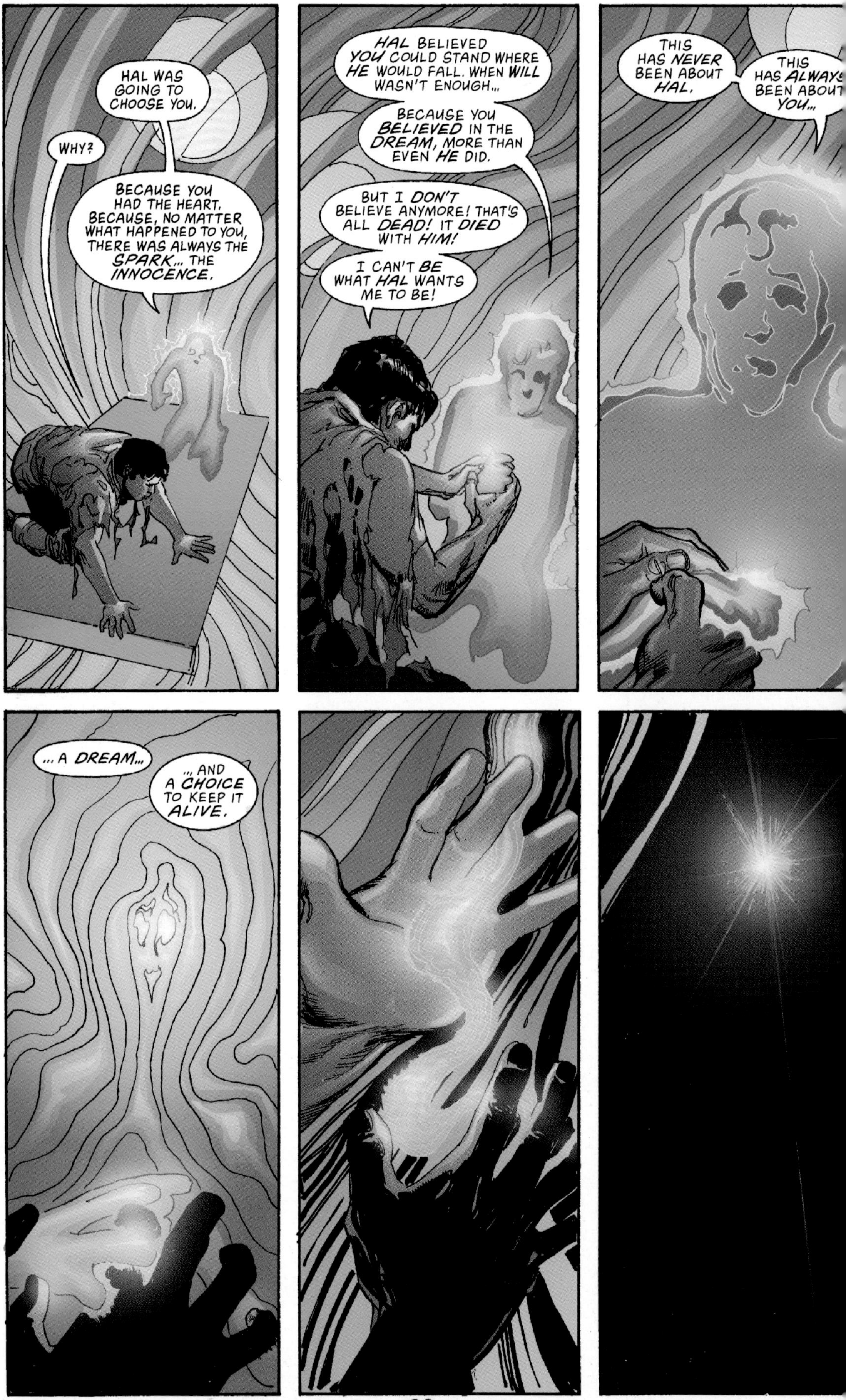
HAL WAS GOING TO CHOOSE YOU.
WHY?
BECAUSE YOU HAD THE HEART. BECAUSE, NO MATTER WHAT HAPPENED TO YOU, THERE WAS ALWAYS THE SPARK... THE INNOCENCE.
HAL BELIEVED YOU COULD STAND WHERE HE WOULD FALL. WHEN WILL WASN'T ENOUGH...
BECAUSE YOU BELIEVED IN THE DREAM, MORE THAN EVEN HE DID.
BUT I DON'T BELIEVE ANYMORE! THAT'S ALL DEAD! IT DIED WITH HIM!
I CAN'T BE WHAT HAL WANTS ME TO BE!
THIS HAS NEVER BEEN ABOUT HAL.
THIS HAS ALWAYS BEEN ABOUT YOU...
...A DREAM...
..., AND A CHOICE TO KEEP IT ALIVE.

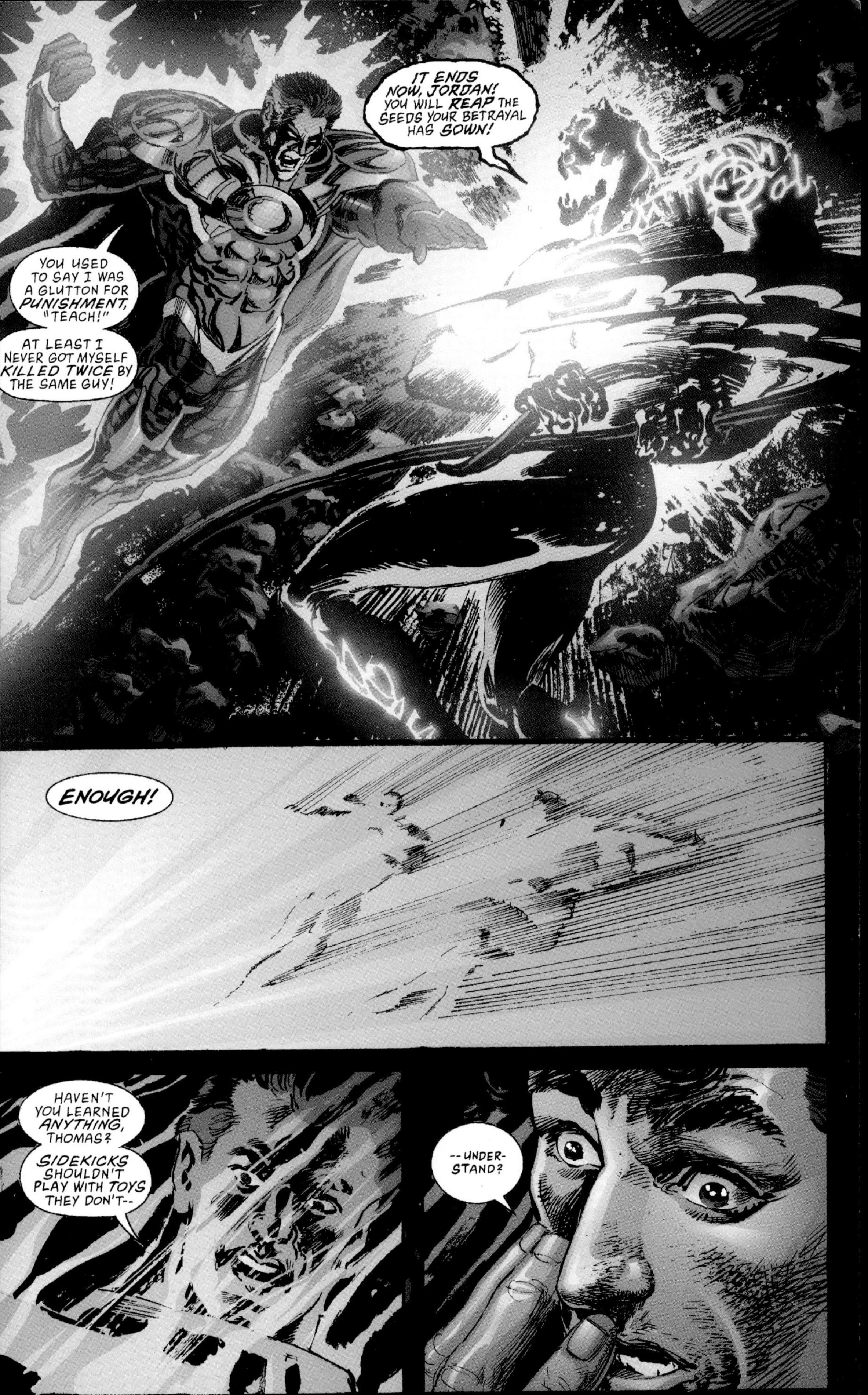
IT ENDS NOW, JORDAN! YOU WILL REAP THE SEEDS YOUR BETRAYAL HAS SOWN!
YOU USED TO SAY I WAS A GLUTTON FOR PUNISHMENT, "TEACH!"
AT LEAST I NEVER GOT MYSELF KILLED TWICE BY THE SAME GUY!
ENOUGH!
HAVEN'T YOU LEARNED ANYTHING, THOMAS?
SIDEKICKS SHOULDN'T PLAY WITH TOYS THEY DON'T--
--UNDER-STAND?

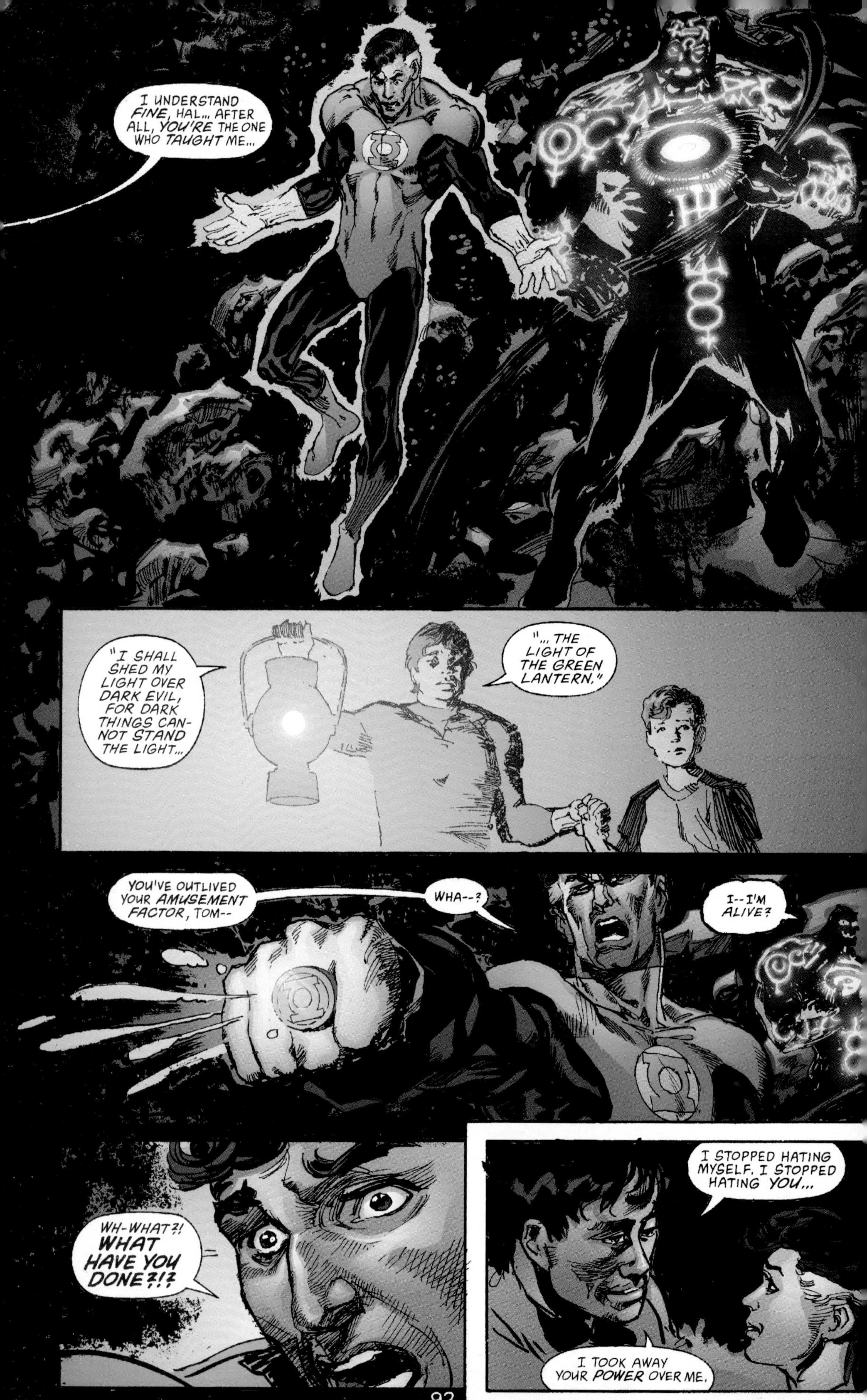
I UNDERSTAND FINE, HAL... AFTER ALL, YOU'RE THE ONE WHO TAUGHT ME...
"I SHALL SHED MY LIGHT OVER DARK EVIL, FOR DARK THINGS CANNOT STAND THE LIGHT...
"... THE LIGHT OF THE GREEN LANTERN."
YOU'VE OUTLIVED YOUR AMUSEMENT FACTOR, TOM--
WHA--?
I--I'M ALIVE?
WH-WHAT?! WHAT HAVE YOU DONE?!?
I STOPPED HATING MYSELF. I STOPPED HATING YOU...
I TOOK AWAY YOUR POWER OVER ME.

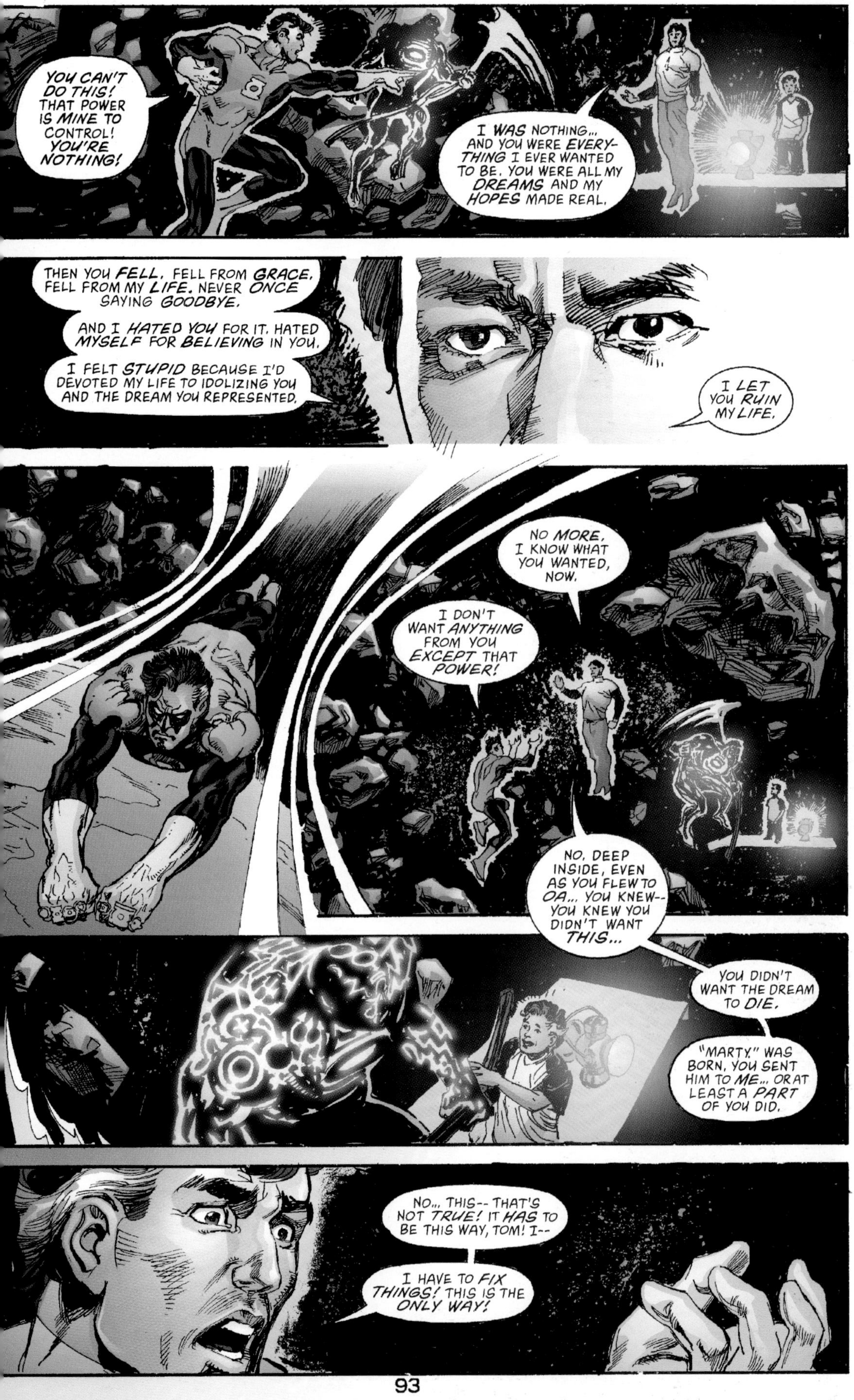
YOU CAN'T DO THIS! THAT POWER IS MINE TO CONTROL! YOU'RE NOTHING!
I WAS NOTHING... AND YOU WERE EVERYTHING I EVER WANTED TO BE. YOU WERE ALL MY DREAMS AND MY HOPES MADE REAL.
THEN YOU FELL. FELL FROM GRACE. FELL FROM MY LIFE. NEVER ONCE SAYING GOODBYE.
AND I HATED YOU FOR IT. HATED MYSELF FOR BELIEVING IN YOU.
I FELT STUPID BECAUSE I'D DEVOTED MY LIFE TO IDOLIZING YOU AND THE DREAM YOU REPRESENTED.
I LET YOU RUIN MY LIFE.
NO MORE. I KNOW WHAT YOU WANTED, NOW.
I DON'T WANT ANYTHING FROM YOU EXCEPT THAT POWER!
NO, DEEP INSIDE, EVEN AS YOU FLEW TO OA... YOU KNEW--YOU KNEW YOU DIDN'T WANT THIS...
YOU DIDN'T WANT THE DREAM TO DIE.
"MARTY" WAS BORN. YOU SENT HIM TO ME... OR AT LEAST A PART OF YOU DID.
NO... THIS-- THAT'S NOT TRUE! IT HAS TO BE THIS WAY, TOM! I--
I HAVE TO FIX THINGS! THIS IS THE ONLY WAY!

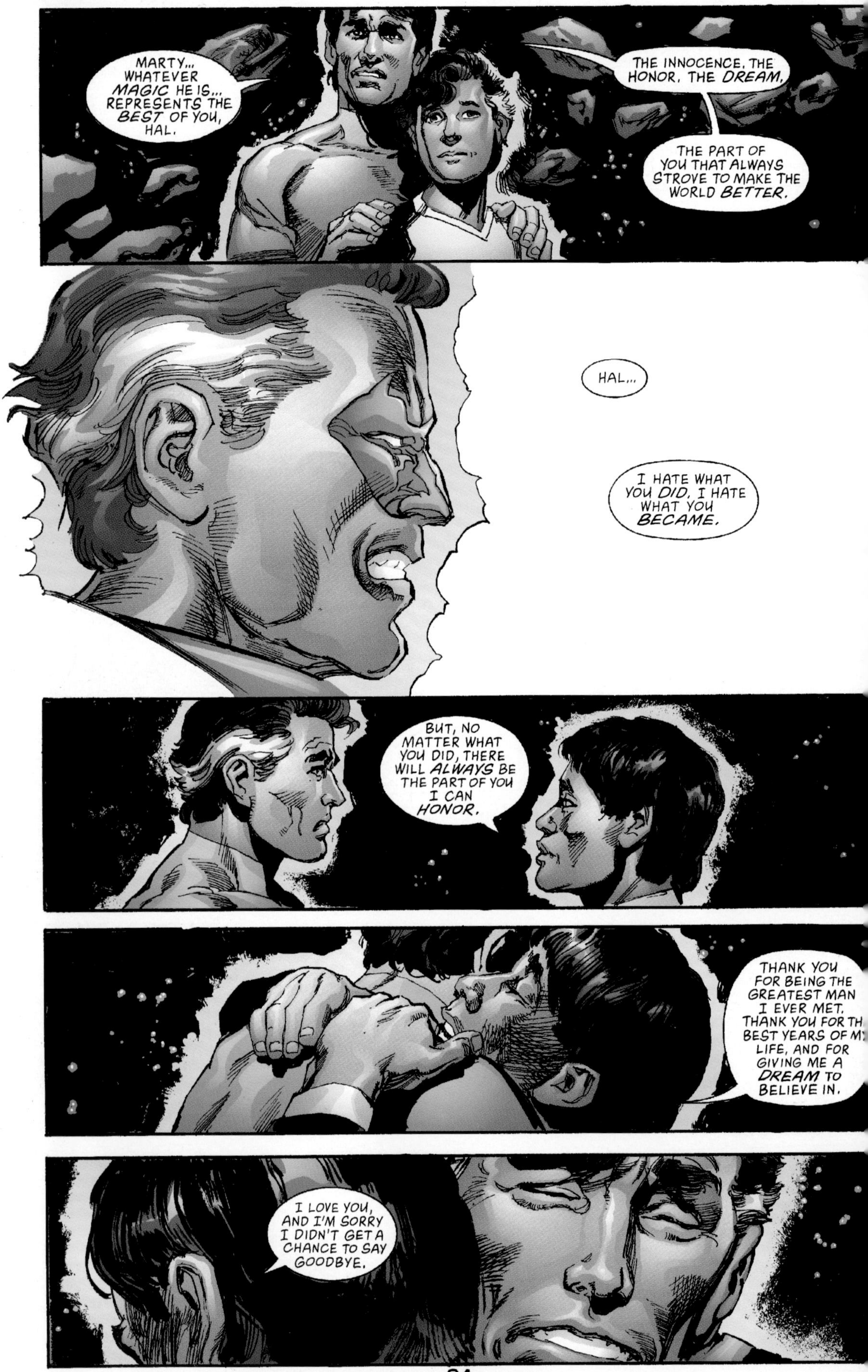
MARTY... WHATEVER MAGIC HE IS... REPRESENTS THE BEST OF YOU, HAL.
THE INNOCENCE, THE HONOR, THE DREAM,
THE PART OF YOU THAT ALWAYS STROVE TO MAKE THE WORLD BETTER.
HAL...
I HATE WHAT YOU DID, I HATE WHAT YOU BECAME.
BUT, NO MATTER WHAT YOU DID, THERE WILL ALWAYS BE THE PART OF YOU I CAN HONOR.
THANK YOU FOR BEING THE GREATEST MAN I EVER MET. THANK YOU FOR TH BEST YEARS OF MY LIFE, AND FOR GIVING ME A DREAM TO BELIEVE IN.
I LOVE YOU, AND I'M SORRY I DIDN'T GET A CHANCE TO SAY GOODBYE.

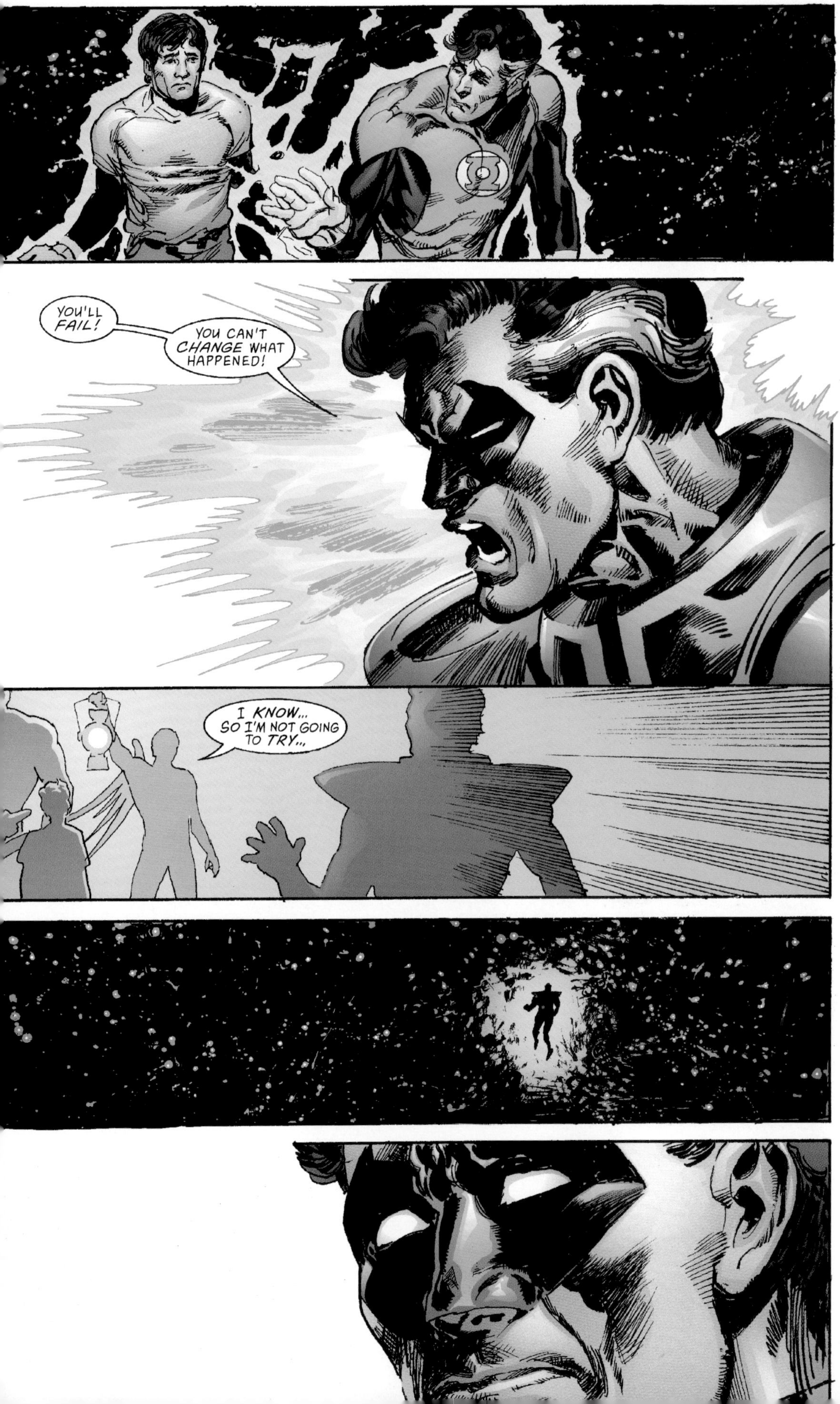
YOU'LL FAIL!
YOU CAN'T CHANGE WHAT HAPPENED!
I KNOW... SO I'M NOT GOING TO TRY...

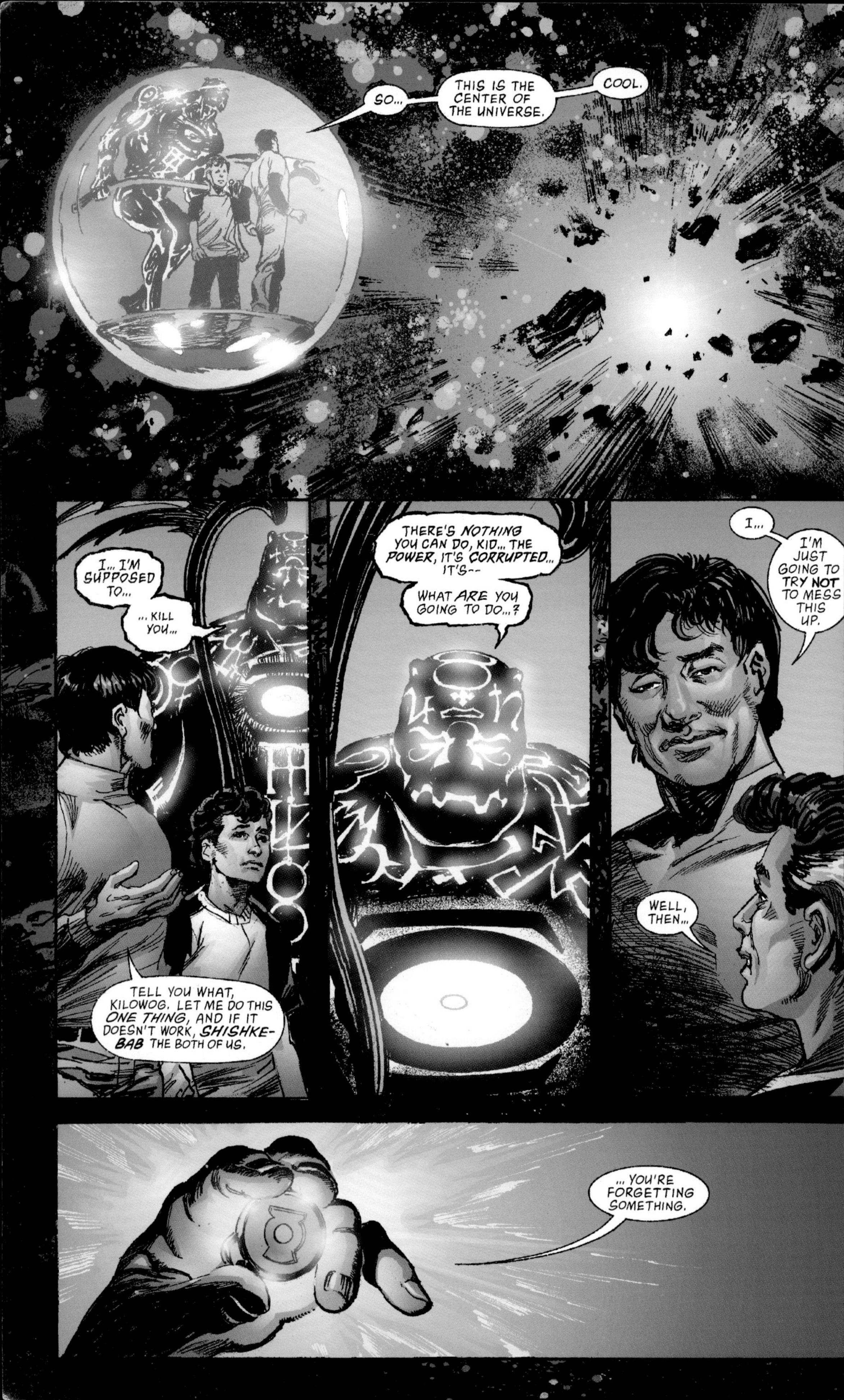
SO...
THIS IS THE CENTER OF THE UNIVERSE.
COOL.
I... I'M SUPPOSED TO...
... KILL YOU...
TELL YOU WHAT, KILOWOG. LET ME DO THIS ONE THING, AND IF IT DOESN'T WORK, SHISHKE-BAB THE BOTH OF US.
THERE'S NOTHING YOU CAN DO, KID... THE POWER, IT'S CORRUPTED... IT'S--
WHAT ARE YOU GOING TO DO...?
I...
I'M JUST GOING TO TRY NOT TO MESS THIS UP.
WELL, THEN...
... YOU'RE FORGETTING SOMETHING.

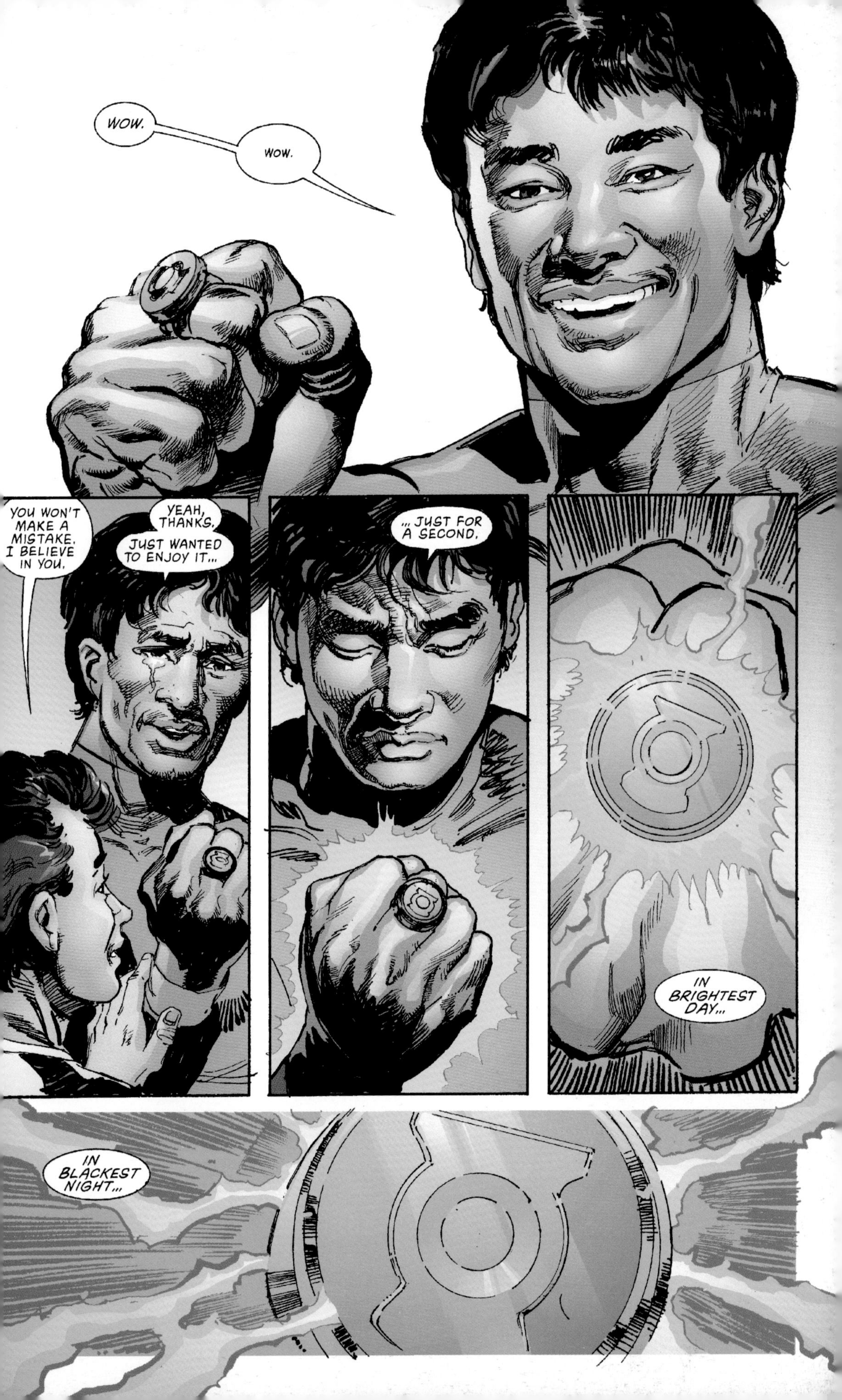
WOW.
WOW.
YOU WON'T MAKE A MISTAKE. I BELIEVE IN YOU.
YEAH, THANKS.
JUST WANTED TO ENJOY IT...
...JUST FOR A SECOND.
IN BRIGHTEST DAY...
IN BLACKEST NIGHT...

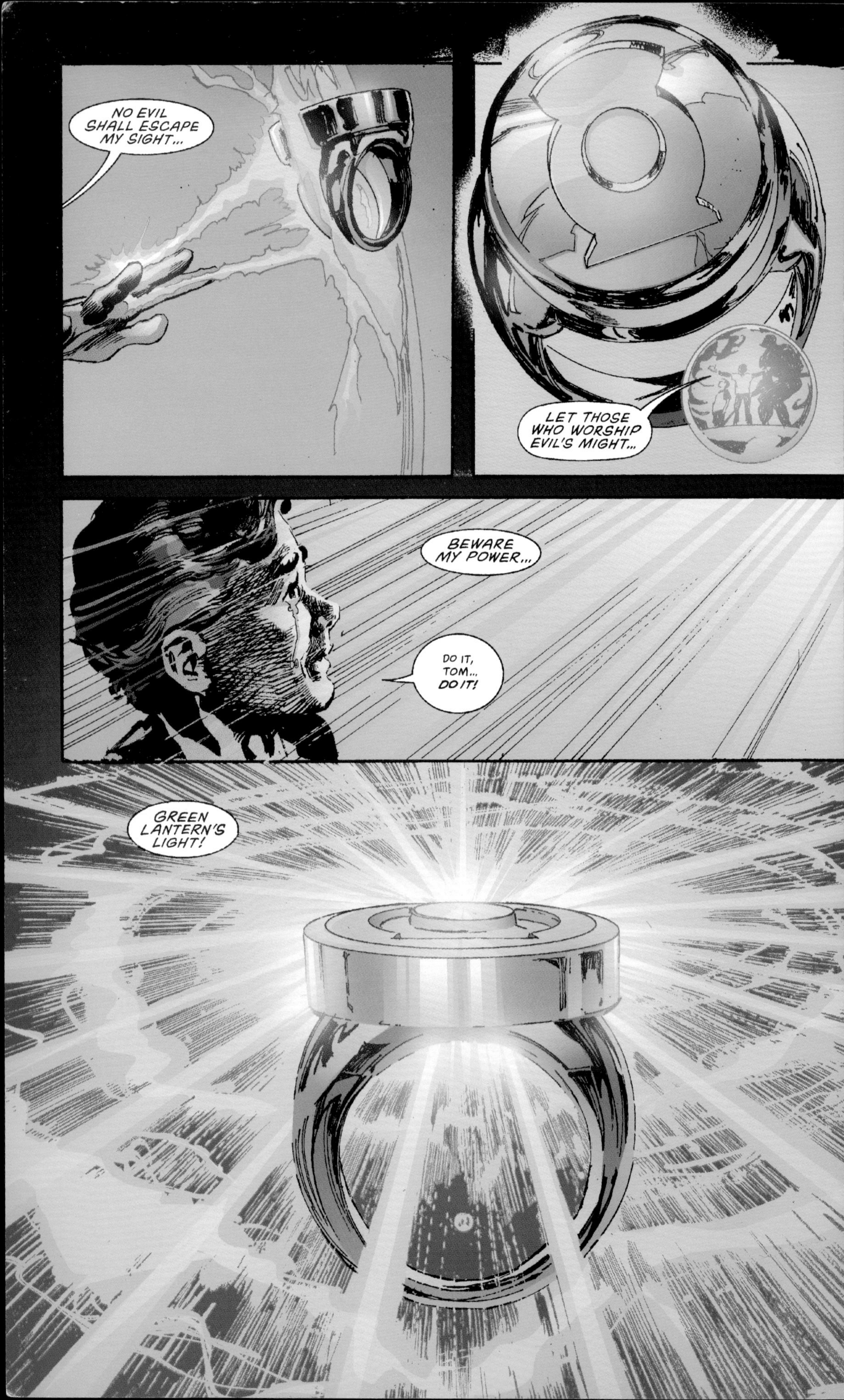
NO EVIL SHALL ESCAPE MY SIGHT...
LET THOSE WHO WORSHIP EVIL'S MIGHT...
BEWARE MY POWER...
DO IT, TOM... DO IT!
GREEN LANTERN'S LIGHT!

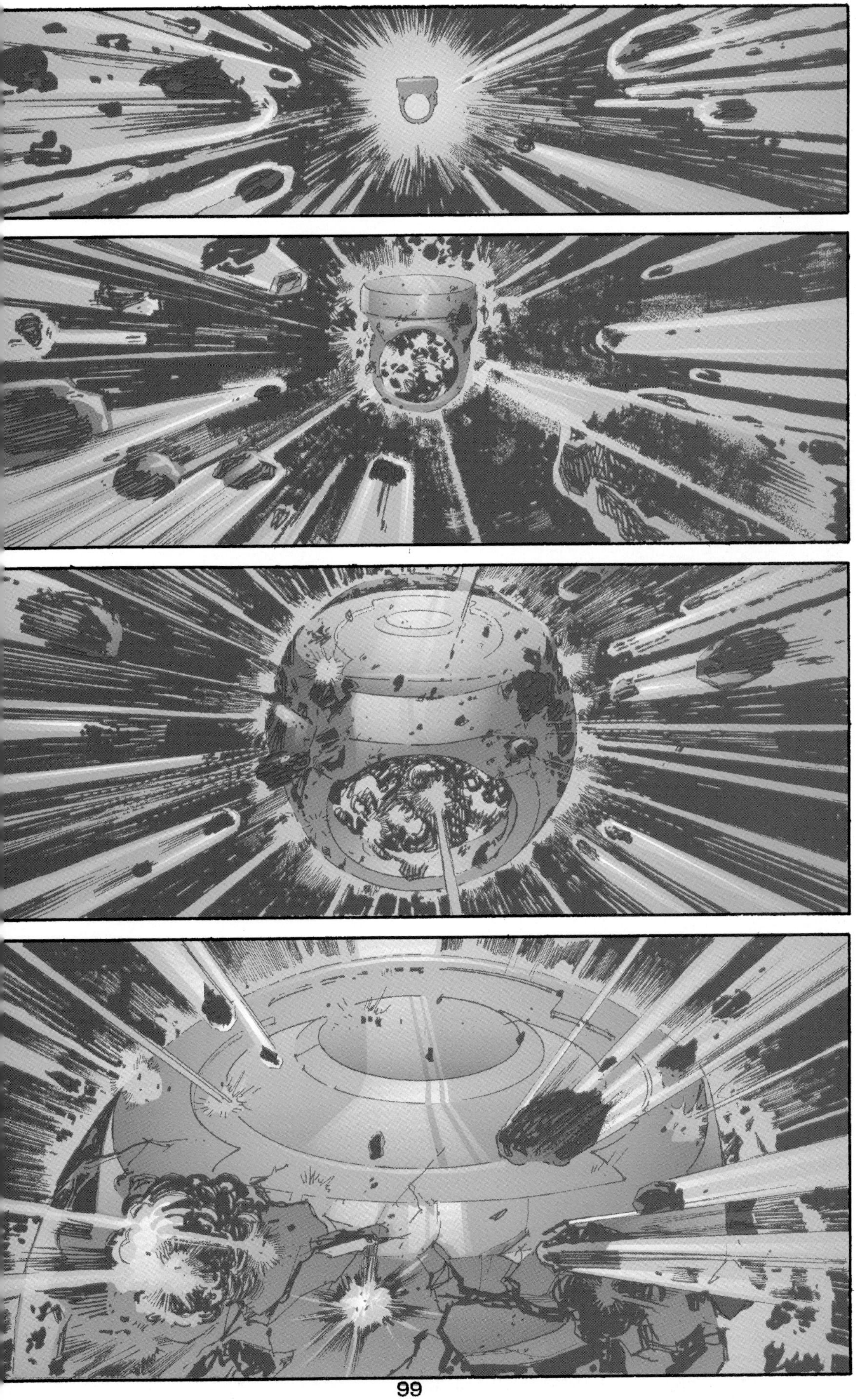

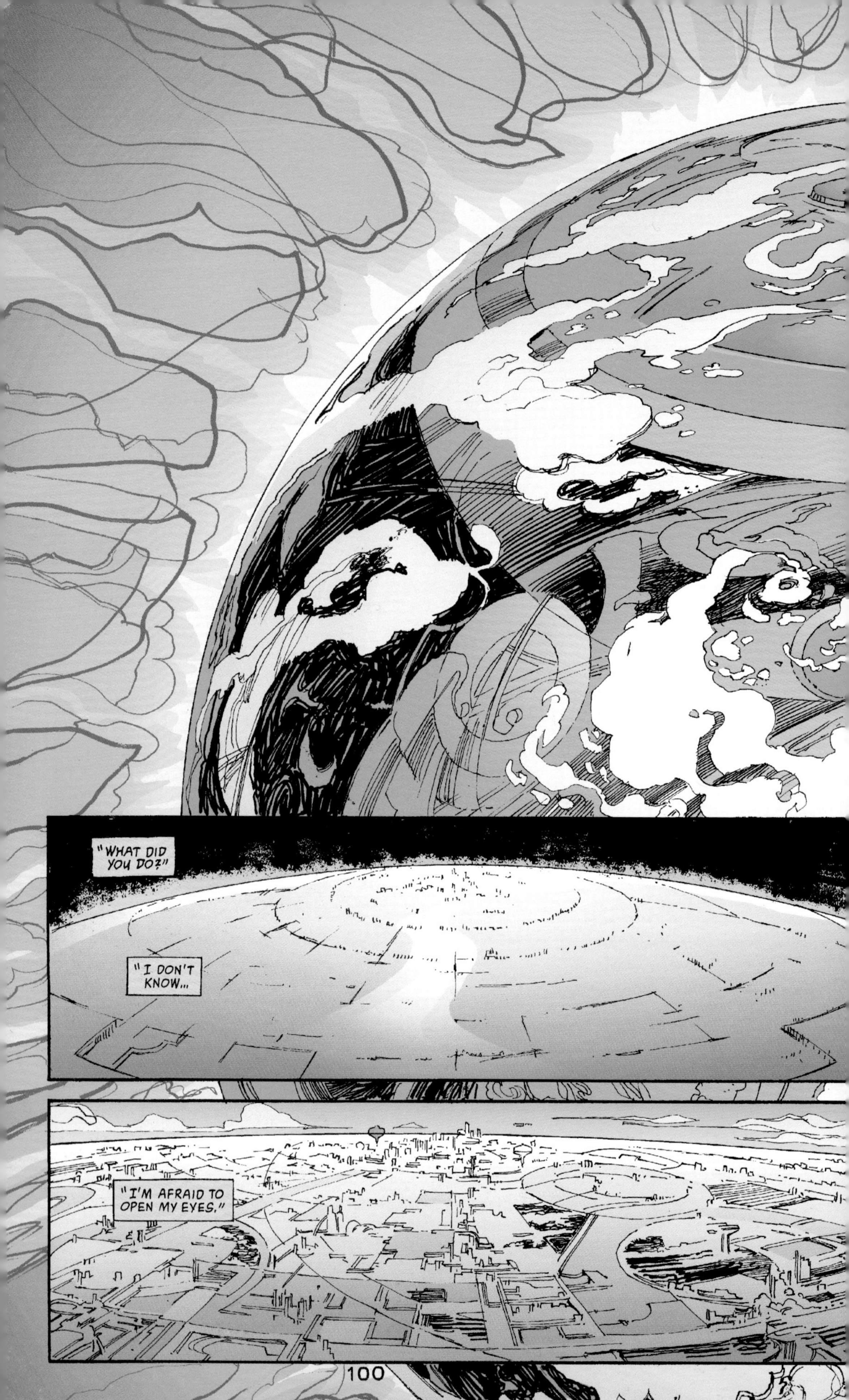
"WHAT DID YOU DO?"
"I DON'T KNOW...
"I'M AFRAID TO OPEN MY EYES."

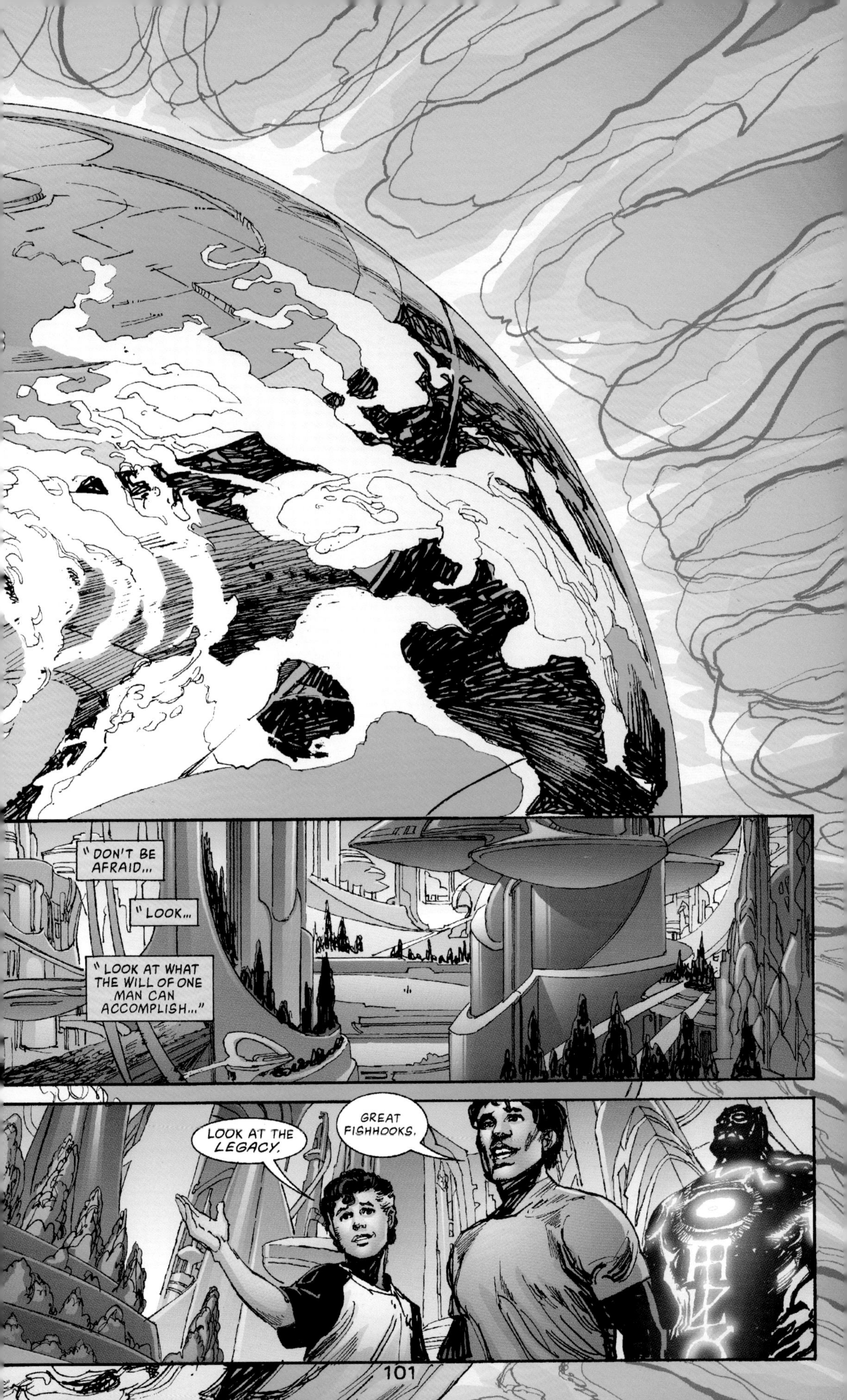
"DON'T BE AFRAID...
"LOOK...
"LOOK AT WHAT THE WILL OF ONE MAN CAN ACCOMPLISH..."
LOOK AT THE LEGACY.
GREAT FISHHOOKS.

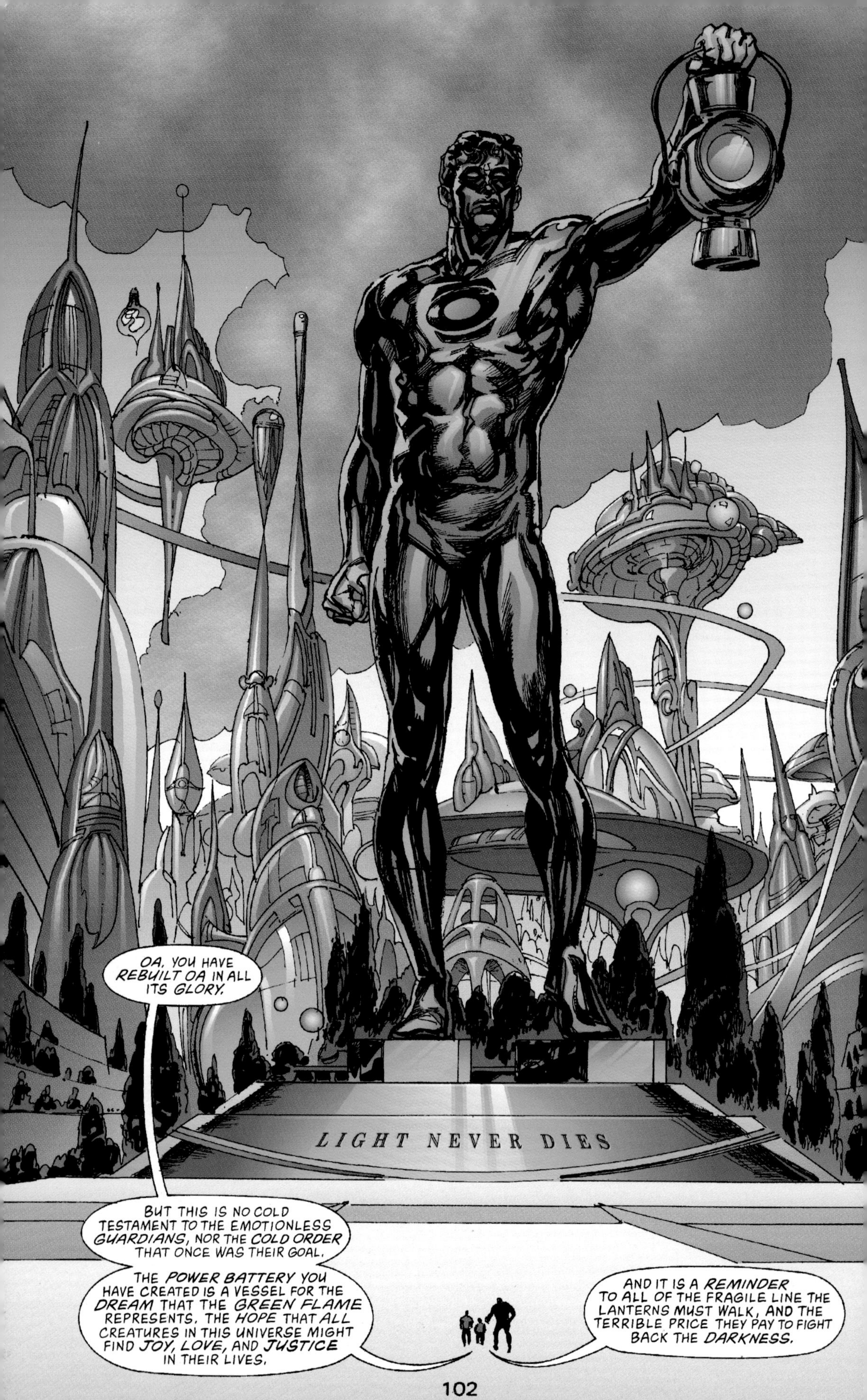
OA, YOU HAVE REBUILT OA IN ALL ITS GLORY.
LIGHT NEVER DIES
BUT THIS IS NO COLD TESTAMENT TO THE EMOTIONLESS GUARDIANS, NOR THE COLD ORDER THAT ONCE WAS THEIR GOAL.
THE POWER BATTERY YOU HAVE CREATED IS A VESSEL FOR THE DREAM THAT THE GREEN FLAME REPRESENTS. THE HOPE THAT ALL CREATURES IN THIS UNIVERSE MIGHT FIND JOY, LOVE, AND JUSTICE IN THEIR LIVES.
AND IT IS A REMINDER TO ALL OF THE FRAGILE LINE THE LANTERNS MUST WALK, AND THE TERRIBLE PRICE THEY PAY TO FIGHT BACK THE DARKNESS.

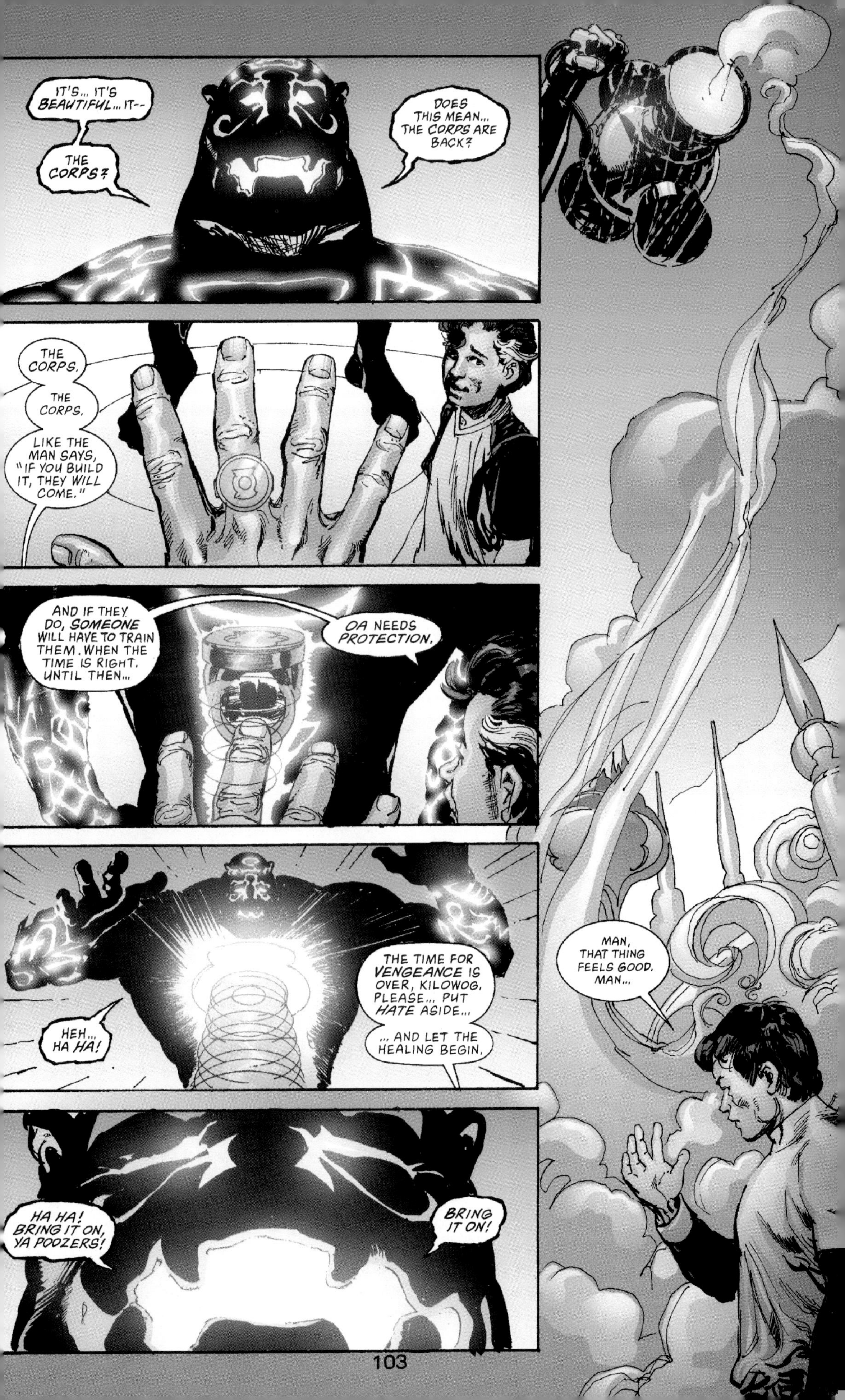
IT'S... IT'S BEAUTIFUL... IT--
THE CORPS?
DOES THIS MEAN... THE CORPS ARE BACK?
THE CORPS.
THE CORPS.
LIKE THE MAN SAYS, "IF YOU BUILD IT, THEY WILL COME."
AND IF THEY DO, SOMEONE WILL HAVE TO TRAIN THEM. WHEN THE TIME IS RIGHT. UNTIL THEN...
OA NEEDS PROTECTION.
HEH... HA HA!
THE TIME FOR VENGEANCE IS OVER, KILOWOG. PLEASE... PUT HATE ASIDE...
...AND LET THE HEALING BEGIN.
HA HA! BRING IT ON, YA POOZERS!
BRING IT ON!
MAN, THAT THING FEELS GOOD, MAN...

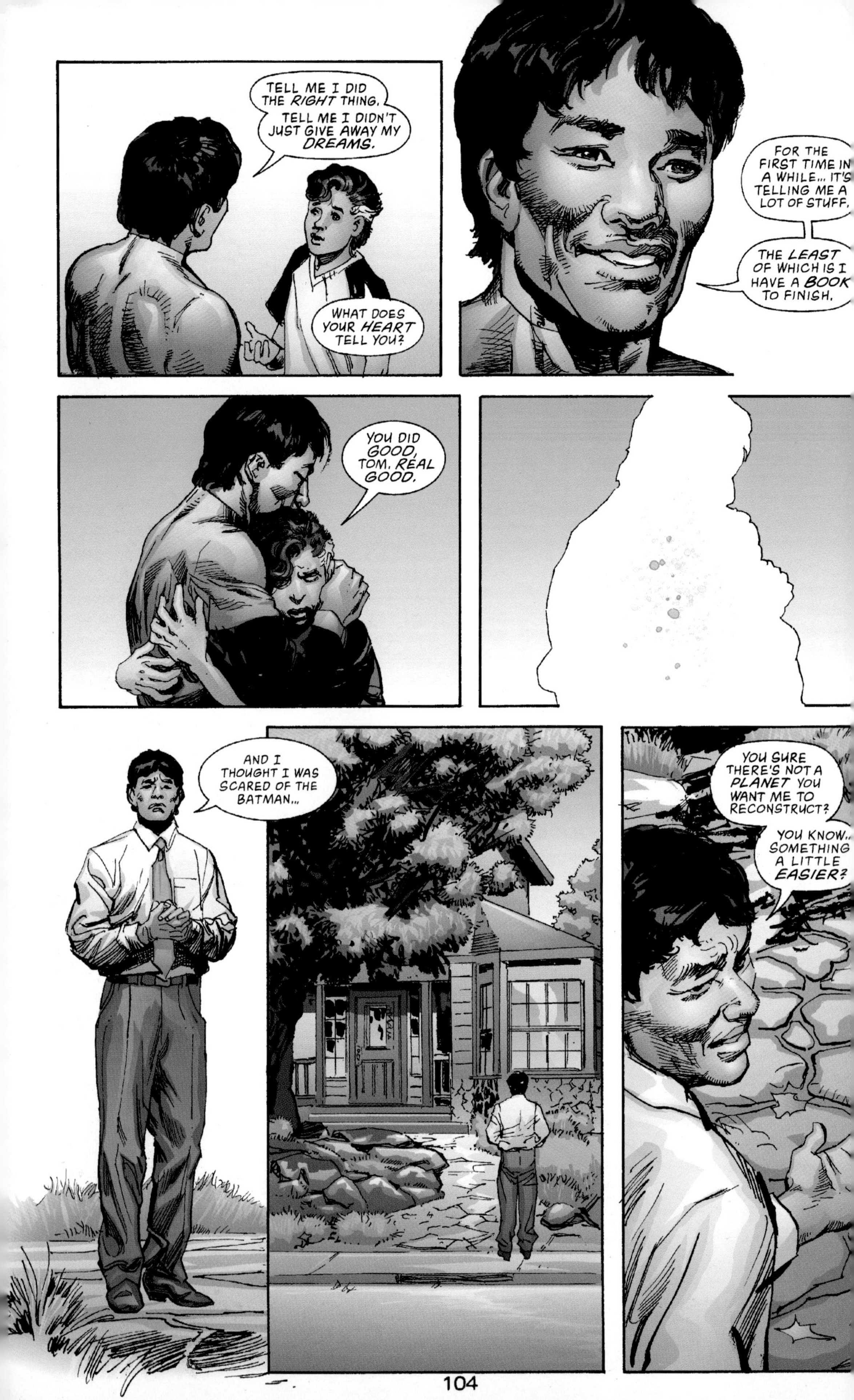
TELL ME I DID THE RIGHT THING.
TELL ME I DIDN'T JUST GIVE AWAY MY DREAMS.
WHAT DOES YOUR HEART TELL YOU?
FOR THE FIRST TIME IN A WHILE... IT'S TELLING ME A LOT OF STUFF.
THE LEAST OF WHICH IS I HAVE A BOOK TO FINISH.
YOU DID GOOD, TOM. REAL GOOD.
AND I THOUGHT I WAS SCARED OF THE BATMAN...
YOU SURE THERE'S NOT A PLANET YOU WANT ME TO RECONSTRUCT?
YOU KNOW... SOMETHING A LITTLE EASIER?

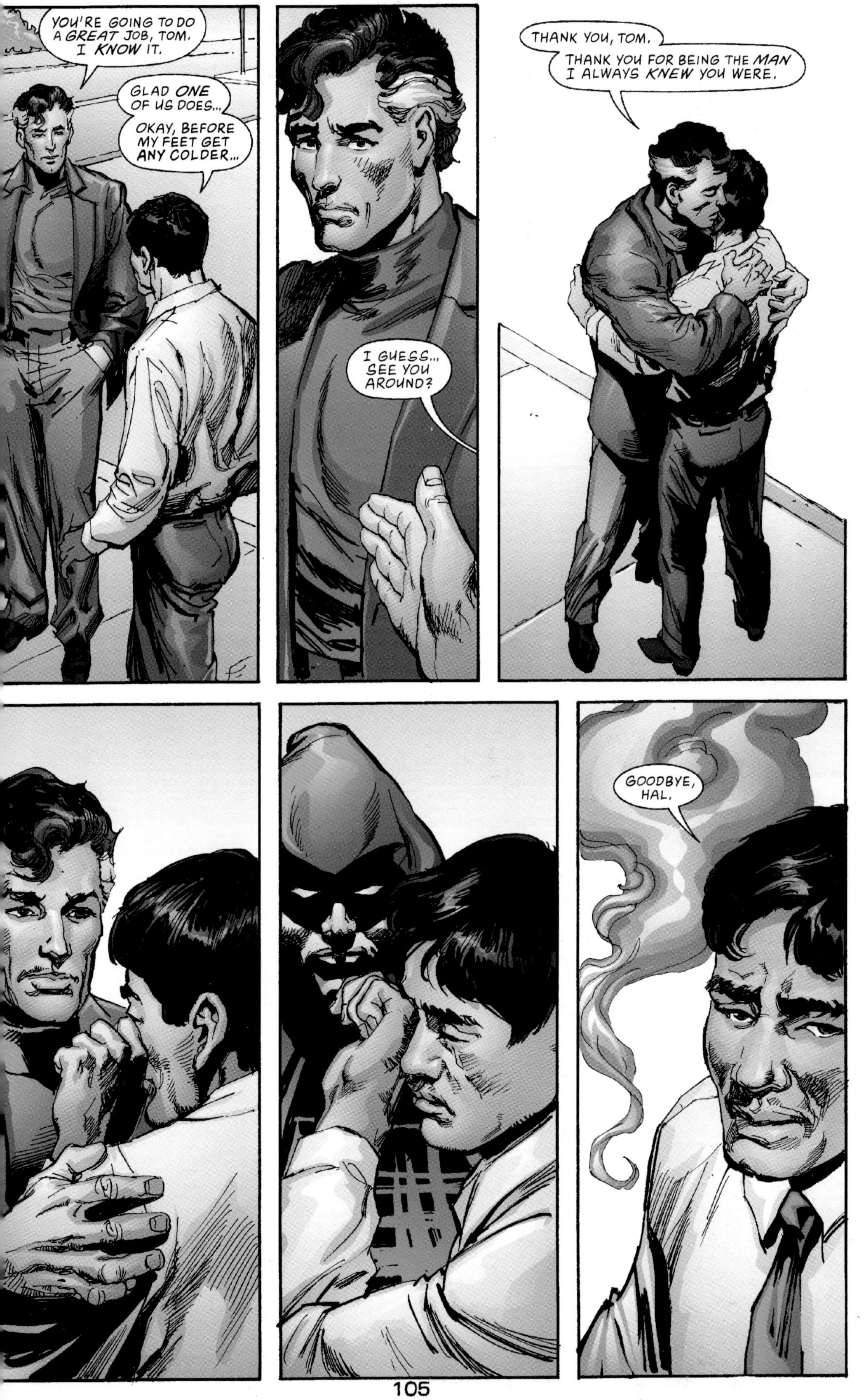
YOU'RE GOING TO DO A GREAT JOB, TOM. I KNOW IT.
GLAD ONE OF US DOES...
OKAY, BEFORE MY FEET GET ANY COLDER...
I GUESS... SEE YOU AROUND?
THANK YOU, TOM.
THANK YOU FOR BEING THE MAN I ALWAYS KNEW YOU WERE.
GOODBYE, HAL.

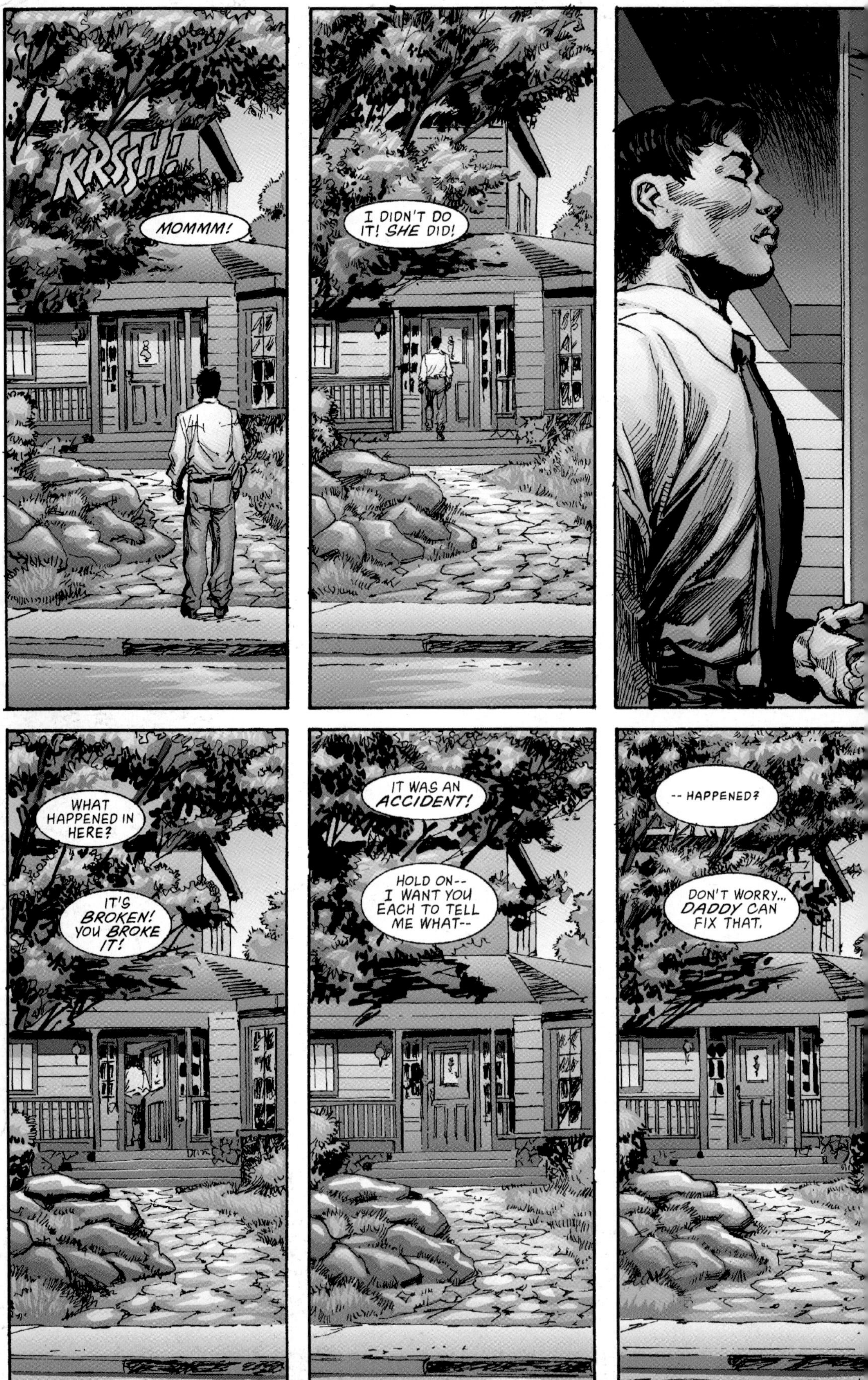
KRSSH!
MOMMM!
I DIDN'T DO IT! SHE DID!
WHAT HAPPENED IN HERE?
IT'S BROKEN! YOU BROKE IT!
IT WAS AN ACCIDENT!
HOLD ON-- I WANT YOU EACH TO TELL ME WHAT--
-- HAPPENED?
DON'T WORRY... DADDY CAN FIX THAT.

DEDICATIONS

JOE KELLY

To all the Keepers of the Green Flame, especially Jack Grimes, Michael Bond, and Eddie B., the Li'lest Green Lantern.

BRENT ANDERSON

To the true-life heroes of the World Trade Center disaster: the New York City Police Department, the Emergency Medical Technicians of New York, the New York City Firefighters and all the people who extended their hearts and hands to help. This book is for you, my heroes.

BILL SIENKIEWICZ

would like to dedicate his efforts on this book to all of those whose lives were affected by the events of September 11, 2001. Most important, to Jeremy Glick and the other brave passengers of Flight #93 who valiantly saved our country from even more unimaginable pain and human suffering.

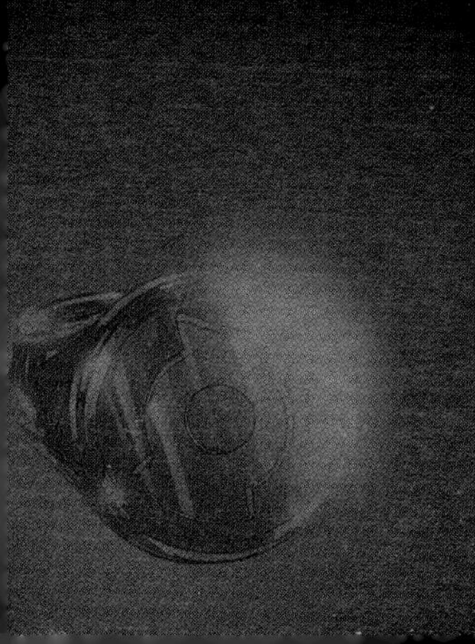

JOE KELLY broke into the comics industry in 1995 when he began writing regularly for Marvel, and gained industry recognition for his work on *Deadpool*. Less than a year later, Joe took on both fan favorite *Deadpool* and Marvel's premier franchise, The *X-Men*. In early 1999, Joe was offered the prestigious opportunity to write SUPERMAN IN ACTION COMICS for DC Comics, and soon after, SUPERBOY. His most recent work writing JLA debuted in December 2001. Joe has also launched two frenetic creator-owned projects, M.REX and *Steampunk*, and has developed two more set for release in 2002. Joe lives on Long Island, New York with his radiant wife and their two children.

BRENT ANDERSON, a California native, began his comics career at Marvel Comics in 1976 in *Doc Savage Magazine*. Since then he has worn many creative hats, as penciller, inker, writer, series co-creator, colorist, painter, illustrator, computer games animator and teacher over the past twenty-five years. During his prolific and multi-Eisner and Harvey Award-winning career Brent has worked on just about every major comic book icon, including Superman, Batman, X-Men, Wonder Woman, Judge Dredd, Doctor Strange, and Punisher. He has also been blazing new trails with books like *Kurt Busiek's Astro City*, and *Rising Stars* for Joe's Comics at Top Cow Productions,

BILL SIENKIEWICZ has had major impact on the field of comic books and graphic novels with his innovative use of collage, illustration and storytelling techniques. He has been honored with many major awards in the United States and abroad, and has exhibited his art worldwide. Among his works are the series *Elektra: Assassin*, for which he received the prestigious Yellow Kid award, and the critically acclaimed *Stray Toasters*. His other work includes the animated television series "Where in the World is Carmen Sandiego?" for which he received an Emmy nomination.